perfectly
invisible

Books by Kristin Billerbeck

Perfectly Dateless
Perfectly Invisible

perfectly invisible

A Universally Misunderstood Novel

kristin billerbeck

Revell

a division of Baker Publishing Group
Grand Rapids, Michigan

Published by Revell
a division of Baker Publishing Group
P.O. Box 6287, Grand Rapids, MI 49516-6287
www.revellbooks.com

Printed in the United States of America

Library of Congress Cataloging-in-Publication Data
Billerbeck, Kristin.
    Perfectly invisible : a Universally misunderstood novel / Kristin Billerbeck.
       p.   cm.
    Summary: During her final trimester at St. James Christian Academy, Daisy
  is determined not to graduate as a high school nobody, but plans go awry when
  she tries to leave her mark.
    ISBN 978-0-8007-1973-9 (pbk.)
    [1. Self-acceptance—Fiction. 2. Dating (Social customs)—Fiction. 3. High
  schools—Fiction. 4. Schools—Fiction. 5. Christian life—Fiction.] I. Title.
  PZ7.B4945Pg 2011
  [Fic]—dc22   2011004245

Published in association with the literary agency of Alive Communications, Inc., 7680 Goddard Street, Suite 200, Colorado Springs, CO 80920, www.alivecommunications .com.

11 12 13 14 15 16 17   7 6 5 4 3 2 1

To my wonderful kids, Trey, Jonah, Seth, and Elle, who keep me young at heart and in desperate need of hair color. I love you guys. You make the world go round for your mom.

❧ 1 ❧

It's not easy going to Silicon Valley's most elite private school as a poor girl. In fact, I might even say it stinks, but then I remember I'm in the home stretch. Only three more months of high school, and then I will take my fabulous self to Pepperdine University. That's right, *the* Pepperdine in Malibu, California. No more being a dating pariah, no more being known for setting my best friend's house on fire (it was totally an accident, but we tried to be popular and we did end up being known, but not in a good way). Finally and most importantly, no more homemade clothes by stylist-for-the-Denny's-hostess: my mother. It's the end of an era—not one I'm particularly fond of, especially working like a dog for my player-but-oh-so-gorgeous boss, Gil. Note my distinct lack of tears.

Pepperdine offered me a partial scholarship, and that's an offer even my frugal parents can't pass up. I mean, *the* business school . . . and me. Just a few more equations to make it all work out financially, but I'm not worried. I've done more with less to work with—my prom date, for example. If there's anything that proves my math skills, it's the ability to overcome statistics.

For the last seven months, I've been immersed in—one could say obsessed with—getting a prom date. My parents, who find it acceptable to dress me like I'm four and put on a rap/play about abstinence for my entire school—those parents do not find it acceptable for their daughter to date. So it's been an uphill battle.

In the end, I got to go to prom, but only because it was my punishment after our party gone bad. Claire (my BFF) and I had to work the Breathalyzers to make certain everyone was sober. Not exactly the night I was dreaming of, but it did end with me doing the tango with Argentine hottie Max Diaz. So it wasn't a total loss.

It was, however, a lot of effort for one measly dance, so I intend to work smarter now. Prioritize. Three months left, and I do not intend to be remembered as the girl who checked everyone's breath on prom night. By grad night, everyone at St. James Academy will be asking themselves, "How did we miss *her* all these years?"

"I'm here," I announce to the steps. Like the rest of the school, the stairs take no notice of me.

The campus of St. James Academy is as stark as ever with its bright, blinding concrete and aqua-blue painted trim. With that color, I think they're trying to give the impression that this place is fun, like Disneyland. But it's not.

Claire brings about the only color and drama to St. James's otherwise barren existence. She sees it as her ministry. Today she sports a purple stripe in her dark bangs and is wearing a matching ruffle scarf flopped carelessly around her neck. If I had to label her, I would say Claire is the Katy Perry of our school. Without the revealing clothes. Without the scary-skinny husband. One never knows which era Claire

8

will represent or what colorful adaptation she'll bring with her on any given day. It's like she can reinvent herself at will. I'm still waiting to invent myself once.

Claire is standing with our two other best friends, Sarika and Angie, whose shyness usually seems to serve as a spotlight for Claire, but she's not her normal self.

Stepping up to Claire, I yank at the scarf to get her full attention. "Hey, what's the matter? You look sort of green. That's not a new makeup, is it?"

"I . . . I have a brother," she says with no emotion.

I tug at the scarf again like it's a horse's bit. "You're not practicing for a soap opera, are you? This is not an audition gone bad, right? Are you supposed to have amnesia? How am I supposed to play this?"

Claire shakes her head. Claire is, by nature, an actress. I can never tell if she's rehearsing lines or if she's embroiled in real drama—as her life is much more turbulent than my own. Not more pathetic, just more turbulent.

Claire's expression is hard, which tells me this is no joke, and I allow the information to sink in. "A brother?" I asked. "Your mom's pregnant?"

She shakes her head. "A half brother. Older than me. Not younger. Apparently, my dad went on a cruise before he married my mom, and do I really need to say more? My flesh is crawling as it is."

"Eww! 'Nough said." I'd been hoping to be supportive, but my gag reflex took over. I must recover and search for ways to make it sound better than it is. "I mean, that could be good, right? Doesn't everyone want a big brother to look out for them?"

Claire raises one corner of her lip. "It's so common. Trashy.

9

Like the middle-aged man who runs off with his secretary. A cruise?"

"I'd like to go on a cruise," I say brightly. "Well, not one of those that people get sick on, but a cruise would be fun. I hear the buffets are great."

Claire lifts a single brow. "Daisy, my father acted like he was in a bad teenage movie. How do I face him now? It's bad enough he's a lawyer."

"Well, at least it's not splashed across YouTube, right? It was a long time ago. We all make mistakes."

"No, it's worse than YouTube. It's a reality show on MTV." She drops her face in her hands. "I don't know who my father is anymore."

I love my best friend, but to say she's a drama queen is to say *Twilight* is a romance. It doesn't quite go far enough, you know?

"We don't have MTV, so I wouldn't know," I remind her, as my mother doesn't allow "that kind of television" into our home. She says it's to protect me, but Claire's mother thinks it's because my mom saw *Poltergeist* as a teenager and believes evil comes into the house through the television. (Claire's mother has that kind of reasoning for a lot of things—for example, seeing *Jaws* makes the beach a nondestination. Personally, I think she ought to change her viewing habits, or at least keep her theories to herself, but whatever.) Anyway, the cruise story is new to me, not as common as Claire might think.

"Look, maybe it won't be so bad. Maybe your brother will be really nice. You always said you wanted a sibling. How's your mom doing with all this?"

Claire rolls her eyes in a way only she can, with nearly cartoonish-bulging eyes. "Enough with the optimism, okay?

My parents almost got a divorce this year. They're staying together for the money and supposedly me, but it's a shaky foundation, and now we have this long-lost kid? No doubt he's here to get my inheritance."

"At least you have an inheritance. What am I going to get, macramé supplies?" I ask her.

"Could you be supportive here? Didn't I stand by you when your parents wouldn't let you go to prom?"

I sigh. "Not really, no. You made fun of me and told me I had to stand up for myself."

"That's how I supported you!" Claire says with a frustrated exhale.

Angie and Sarika are standing beside us quietly, as they normally do, trying to stay out of the fray. Maybe we have too much drama, but their lives seem simpler. They have to go to school and get good grades, and their parents seem to go about their lives without the daily dose of entitlement.

"Real friends tell you the hard things that you don't want to hear. Would you rather I just sucked it up and played it mute?" Claire asks.

"Sometimes, yes," I say. "Sarika, Angie, wouldn't you sometimes wish that Claire played it quietly?"

Sarika has tears in her eyes. "Daisy, she's hurting. I'm so sorry, Claire. We'll pray for you and your family."

We all look at her, annoyed that the simple idea never came into our own fluffy heads. Sarika is from India. Her parents are Indian missionaries, and she seems about sixty years older than us in maturity. She's one of those girls your parents love you to hang out with because she's a good influence. And Sarika is a good influence, but sometimes that only serves to remind us of our own failures.

"Do you want me to pray right now?" Sarika asks.

"Praying is good. Maybe later, okay, Sarika? I have an idea that I want to discuss with you girls," Claire says. "Well, it's more than an idea."

Uh-oh. "This can't be good," I say. The last time Claire had an idea, we burned her parents' house down.

"I have to take care of myself, right?"

"Not really," Angie tells her.

"Look, I made this ring." Claire holds up her hand, which is manipulated into a Spock, live-long-and-prosper way. She's wearing a silver ring fashioned around two fingers, her pinky and ring finger. As far as Claire goes, it doesn't seem like that big of a fashion stretch, so we're all a little confused.

Angie's the first to speak. She has stellar taste. Granted, her parents don't allow her to use it much, but that doesn't mean it isn't there. "It's not very practical."

"Angie, you don't get it. This is my way out."

"Your way out of what?" I ask her. "Your mansion at the top of the hill? What exactly are you looking to escape?"

She brings the ring to my nose. It reads *Class of 2011.* "Control."

"It's a class ring?" I look up, trying to mask my confusion and strike a balance between optimistic and realistic.

Claire rolls her eyes again, annoyed with my slow mental processing. "It's a modern take on an old thing. People love that sentimental junk. No one buys class rings anymore, but if they were cool . . ."

"Yeah, if they were cool."

"Like this is." Claire lowers her brow, as if to will me to think her way.

"I just don't know how you're going to finish your senior

year with a ring that removes some of the benefits of opposable thumbs."

"It doesn't do that. It's nowhere near your thumbs!" she snaps, missing my point entirely. "You're so negative."

"You just accused me of being too optimistic."

"You don't have to wear it on your writing hand. Wear it on your left hand." She hands me a ring. "It makes a total statement."

"Me? I'm not sure I want to make that statement."

"Yes, you. How can I market the tring if my best friend isn't wearing one? Don't you think that will be weird?"

"Not as weird as—" I stop myself. "The tring?"

"Twin as in two fingers, and ring. Get it?"

"There's only three months left of school, so how many of those do you expect to sell—I mean, market?"

"I've already sold two hundred of them on the internet to graduates across the country."

My mouth drops. I don't know why this brings me down. Naturally, I want to be supportive, but I slave every day of my life in a check-printing joint that seems to take pride in typos, and Claire, living her charmed life, sells two hundred of a completely impractical item without even trying. I know we're not supposed to compare and all, but what am I supposed to take home from that lesson? Other than I will always have to work harder than everyone else.

Angie's dad has set her up with her own stock-trading account, and she's probably made more this morning than I'll make all summer. I confess, I want a Chinese father who knows stock and pushes me for excellence. And then there's Sarika. With her parents in the ministry, you'd think she might understand my plight, but no, her dad also owns some high-tech business and employs more people than I probably know on Facebook. Even though Sarika is as Americanized as me, her parents brought with them the Indian culture of buying gold for Sarika for her wedding, which they've done since she was a baby. Sarika is probably worth more than King Tut by now. I don't really mind being poorer than everyone else, I just mind how easy it is for everyone around me to be rich.

"Who did you sell them to?" I ask.

"Like I said, just people around the country. I started a blog on setting fashion and not being a victim of it."

I won't mention the irony here. "How'd you make them?"

"I had them made. It was cheaper to get them done in China, but I decided that was wrong. Do you know human rights—"

I hold up my palm. "Spare me the political speech. What does any of this have to do with your new brother?"

"Listen, if he comes looking for money, mine is protected from him. He may be able to go after my dad and mom's, but mine is home free, and my dad always said—"

"Did your dad make sure this is really his son?"

"You know how he did legal work for that company that's doing the home DNA testing?"

"It's a sad world when we need home DNA kits. How about if you just know who the baby daddy is, is that too much to ask?"

"It's his," she says shortly.

I slide my fingers into the contraption Claire's calling jewelry. I have to admit, it's better than a line of nose rings. But at least my mother wouldn't allow me to wear that, and I'd have an excuse. Only last month Claire was sporting a spider on her nostril, so I suppose as far as fads, this is a good compromise.

"So you know how Lance Armstrong has his yellow bracelets that say 'Live Strong'?" Claire asks.

"Yeah."

"These are made from recycled cans. One-tenth of the profit goes to the arbor foundation to plant trees. Trees. Tring. Perfect combination. I'm trying to find a supplier to do them in glass. You know how when glass washes up on the beach and it's all roughed up by the sand and waves? That would make a cool ring."

I'm sputtering. "How much are you charging for these?"

"Ten dollars with shipping. Only two dollars here at school—a bargain, wouldn't you say? They cost me eighty-eight cents to manufacture, though it would be cheaper if I did it in China, like I said, and I give away a dollar. So I make eight dollars and twelve cents on each ring."

"You sold two hundred of these? Claire, that's—that's sixteen hundred dollars. You made sixteen hundred dollars selling these?" I hold up my hand, which feels like it's stuck in one of those straw Chinese finger traps.

"Well, of course, there's my time and the marketing costs. I'm going to have a fund-raiser at the club this weekend, and I'm designing a webpage and tying it into the local arbor foundation. I have to pay taxes if I make over a certain amount, but my dad says I can just give more to the charity to keep my profits in line with not paying."

"I'm depressed." Just a few months ago, when Claire and I set her house on fire, her parents were about to split up and couldn't afford to. So it's like she's rewarded for being a complete screwup. "I bet your new brother turns out to be Robert Pattinson, because that is just the kind of life you lead."

15

"So I need you to take over handling the sales and mailing while I do the play. I told you they changed it from *Our Town* to *West Side Story*, right? I love *West Side Story*, it's so tragic! Unrequited love, emotion, dance skills. It's everything you want in an audition tape, and it will be perfect for my YouTube audition tapes."

"Let me guess, Zac Efron is starring in it opposite you?"

Her face crinkles up. "No, that's your fantasy, not mine." She pauses for a minute, like she's afraid to say something. Have I explained that Claire is afraid of nothing? "Didn't Max tell you?" she asks.

"Max, my boyfriend Max?"

"Well, I don't know if I'd call him your boyfriend." And of course, no one would call him that, but my best friend should call him my boyfriend if that's what I want him to be. What's a dream if I can't share it and pretend it's real with my best friend?

Claire goes on. "You went to prom together—after he got kicked out of school." She shrugs. "Not exactly boyfriend material, but supposedly his father got him back in—that's what he said on Facebook. So who knows, we'll have to see what he thinks, I guess."

"You talked to him on Facebook?" There's no way to hide my jealousy. It's out there, all green and ugly, for everyone to see. Angie and Sarika have the common sense to look away and leave me with some sense of dignity. Not Claire.

"Max is starring opposite me in the play. He joined the drama team when he got back in. I'm sure he meant to tell you. He needed to make up extra credits between public high school and St. James's requirements. From before this year, you know?"

16

"Max acts? I guess that makes sense . . . I mean, he dances, right?" I mumble this last part.

"He's Latin." She shrugs.

"All Latin people can act?" I ask her, trying to point out the ridiculousness of her statement, but the real issue here is that Claire totally doesn't get it. She is breaking the girl code. Max is mine, and even if I were done with him, and I'm not, you're not supposed to date your best friend's ex. It's against the girl code. I'm sure that applies to acting across from him in the school play without friend approval. Absolutely sure of it.

"I think," Angie offers, "maybe what Daisy is trying to say is that . . . you know . . . Max is sort of hers, so it seems weird that you know more about him than her. That makes her feel bad."

"Thank you, Angie. Yes, that's what I mean," I say.

"No kidding," Sarika says.

"Especially when he never called her after the dance," Angie continues.

"He needed more credits, so he tried out for the drama club at the last minute," Claire says. "There's only three months of school left, so what else is he supposed to do? Mr. Carroll let him in without hesitation because he was planning for *West Side Story* and he thought Max would be perfect in the role. I can't believe he didn't tell you."

This is not good. Not only because I had no idea that my crush is starring in our high school musical opposite my best friend, but because now I suppose I know I've been dumped, and he didn't even have the decency to text me with the information. Worse yet, I'm going to be wearing Trekkie hand gear while I figure it all out.

I play it cool, though. I don't want any Claire lectures about how I'm creating drama where there is none.

"I haven't really talked to Max." And I'm not even going to let my mind wander to all the far-off paranoid places it could go. I've grown. If Max doesn't want me, I'm mature enough to face facts. Right after I find out why the heck not.

"I thought he might have texted you over the weekend. It's a really big deal. He beat out so many guys for the part. You're not uncomfortable with it, are you? With me kissing him onstage? It's only acting."

"Isn't that what Brad Pitt said when kissing Angelina Jolie in that movie?" Angie asks.

"Y-you're going to kiss him?" I slip off the two-finger trash-as-jewelry ring and hand it to her. "I'm probably not going to have time to do this with finals coming up. My boss is trying to ramp up production for checks too. You know, all the bank closures have businesses wanting new checks." My boss, Gil, requires entirely too much of me, but he gave me a BlackBerry and I can work odd hours, so I'm basically his slave.

Claire pushes the ring back at me. "You have to at least wear it. Advertising, Daisy. Duh. Don't you want to save the earth and settle my future? Or do you want to be a common consumer?"

I guess I don't want to save the earth that much. Not if I have to wear aluminum cans. "As someone who has worn homemade clothes for most of my academic life, the answer to that question is yes, I want to be a common consumer. At least before I start wearing trash."

"Recyclables are not trash."

"Old tires would work too. Maybe give you the use of your fingers back."

"I checked into that," Claire says. "Too much petroleum process involved to make it healthy for manufacture and wear. The look of the year in jewelry is recycled materials, but we want to be smart about it."

"Of course we do," I say, as if I were serious about wearing old tires.

"So when do you meet your new family member?" Sarika asks Claire.

"Does it really matter?" Claire asks.

We all stare at her. "It does," Sarika says. "Your family is going to look different now."

"Sure they will," Claire says. "They will all be wearing the trendy item of the season: the tring!"

More blank stares. "That's your method? You're going to ignore the facts?" Angie asks her.

"Works for me," Claire says. "Besides, I have to be thinking about my future. This play is important. It's the last one of the season and I need top billing to get into the program at ACT. They don't accept just average people in their summer internship program, and I didn't get in this year. So I have to settle for next year."

Everyone's famous for something. Claire's like a shape-shifter. She easily slips in and out of personas to become all things to all people. And it works for her. She can fit in at her parents' country club (not that she tries) or at school, but she simply doesn't want to be bothered and she finds something new to try. Hence the tring. She is who she is, and she makes no excuses. I guess I admire that about her, even if I do want to wring her neck sometimes.

Me? I'm uncomfortable in my own skin. I'm good at math, which at this school isn't all that unique. It's sort of expected.

You're in Silicon Valley, you inherited the math brain. Big deal. It doesn't exactly make you special.

This calls for another journal. Because clearly I'm doing something wrong. Though Claire would call it anal, journaling helps me focus on things that don't come naturally to me, like social skills and fashion. All the things that are supposed to be important to a teenage girl. I thought I wanted a date to prom, but that wasn't quite the whole deal. I wanted to be remembered as more than invisible Daisy Crispin, the girl no one remembered in four years of high school. Now that I'm known for hosting the party that involved a police visit and an arson inquiry, I have to work harder than ever to get an image.

I tick off things in my head:

I'm smart.

I survived a private high school in homemade clothes. Without cable television (i.e., something to connect about).

I am a survivor, and I find it perfectly acceptable to want to rework my image from failed party planner to the girl who overcame . . . the last one left on the island . . . the poor girl who made it work.

I'm socially acceptable now. Not awkward any longer. I danced a hot tango at the prom. I will not be told it was all in my imagination and accept that Claire will dance off into the sunset with my tango partner. Do they change partners on *Dancing with the Stars*? They do not. I will not be remembered as a failure. And if Claire has her way, kissing my crush onstage (i.e., publicly) and having me sell recycled garbage, is there any way to salvage my reputation at this point?

"Daisy?"

"Huh?" Apparently, Claire's been talking at me.

"Are you coming over for dinner tomorrow night to meet my brother or not?"

"You're meeting your brother? I thought you just said—don't you want to meet him by yourself first?" Why doesn't Claire just take my firstborn? What more does she want from me?

Claire gives me an upturned lip. "No. I don't want to meet him at all. What could we possibly have in common?"

"DNA?"

"Right. So if I don't like him, where does that leave me? With bad DNA? What if he's a loser with no job? Is that my fate?"

I'm still on my last thought. "You don't think Max was anything special to me? I mean, I get that he's not my boyfriend, but does that matter if I liked him?" I ask her.

"You'll get over Max. You got over Chase."

"After having a crush on him since kindergarten. And only because he turned out to be a complete dog at your party that night. I'm nothing if not loyal."

"Maybe too loyal," Claire says. "Did you ever think of that?"

"I'm thinking that right now," I tell her, but she doesn't get my point. It's lost on her that she's asking me to meet her illegitimate brother, wanting me to sell bad jewelry, and kissing my crush, but I'm supposed to be loyal to her.

"What do you want from me? Do you want me to drop out of the play so you feel better about a relationship that doesn't really exist anywhere outside your own head?" Claire asks.

Sarika and Angie gasp.

"I think if you asked most people who were there that night, or at the party, they would tell you that Max clearly had a thing for me. It was more than a dance. Don't you think, Angie? Sarika?"

"Daisy." Sarika pats my arm. "We've got three months left in high school. Then it's on to college, what we've been preparing for all along. So what does it matter if some boy you will never see again remembers a dance?"

"Only three months to go!" Angie interjects. "We'll look back on this and laugh, Daisy. You're going to Pepperdine University and you'll come home rich with all that finance knowledge. Max is moving back to Argentina and he'll be nothing but a memory. Maybe a Facebook friend, right?"

Angie's only trying to help, and I know most likely she's totally right, but there's this romantic in me that's not willing to concede defeat just yet. "I thought Max and I had something special. You know, a connection."

"Have you been reading vampire novels again?" Sarika asks.

"I haven't!" I say honestly. "My mom doesn't allow those."

"This is not your lifelong soul mate." Claire shakes her plastic box of trings. "I don't get why you're making such a big deal about this. Do you want to marry out of high school like your parents did?"

"No, but—"

"Or worse yet, end up the secret child of a lawyer on the verge of a divorce? Like a bad Latin soap opera?" Claire presses.

"I just—I guess I just wish I knew why he wasn't interested. Maybe if he told me? You know, closure. Was I a bad dancer? Was my breath bad? What happened between prom and today?"

"Who cares?" Claire's tone tells me she certainly doesn't. "We have trings to sell. Do you know what this could do for your academic career at Pepperdine?"

Make me a laughingstock?

Sarika speaks up again in her quiet tone. "Max is such a nice guy, Daisy. I'm sure he doesn't want to hurt you. Maybe he didn't know what to say after the dance. It was awkward, since you weren't really allowed to go. He might be in love with you and doesn't want to hurt you when he leaves the country."

"Or he could just be over it," Claire adds. "Besides, he's going to be the perfect Tony in *West Side Story*. Between that and his classes, he doesn't have time for a girlfriend. You should be happy for him, Daisy. If you really liked him, you'd want what's best for him."

"Tony was from Puerto Rico. Max is from Argentina."

"That's why they call it acting, Daisy."

"Is that supposed to comfort me?" I ask.

"Will it really bother you to have me kiss Max in a play? Where we're both acting?"

"In my country, that would not happen," Sarika says. "There is no kissing in Bollywood movies. Only dancing and smiling."

"Can we get back to me here?" Claire interrupts.

Sarika and Angie back away, as they normally do when Claire and I are going to do battle. It's not for the weak of heart, and our friends can't handle the stress we create. They turn and jog off to their respective classes, leaving Claire and me locked in ineffective communication. She will never change my mind. I will never change hers, but the fun lies in trying.

"I only got a partial scholarship, you know," I tell her. My parents have promised things before and backed out when the finances got dicey. Until I am sitting on my dorm bunk, I am not counting my college credits. Explaining this to my friends, whose parents have been saving their college tuition

23

since their birth, is not worth my trouble. "Besides, I don't think my mom would like me spending schooltime selling trings."

"Angie and Sarika just left," Claire says. "Did you see that? They didn't take any trings. Sometimes, I swear, those two live in their own world."

"You can't expect your friends to do all your work. This is your business, right?"

"You're not getting out of this, Daisy. You're totally selling my trings. Or I won't ever lend you any makeup when you have a big zit."

"That is blackmail."

"Which I'm not above. Have we met?"

"You are so lucky we go way back and that I'm loyal, because right now . . . What are you doing this for anyway? You don't need the money, and aren't you busy enough with the play coming up? Why do you always add so much to your plate that you're overwhelmed? Do you need the extra drama? Because I don't. I have two acting parents for that."

"I'm trying to show my dad my business sense, in case this so-called brother of mine is trying to be executor of the will."

"Your parents are in their early forties, so I don't think you need to worry about that just yet. Besides, what did money ever do for your parents?"

"It's not the money. It's the principle."

"The principle of kissing your best friend's crush isn't all that nice."

"It's for the stage, I told you! You should be flattered I'd be willing to kiss him. Even for the stage."

"I'm not."

"No," Claire says, "I see that, but you know Max isn't

into me and I'm not into him, if you're honest. Don't blame me for Max's silence. The business just gives me something to do, all right? The trings take my mind off of everything that's bad, so will you help me or not?"

I exhale. "You know I will."

Claire smiles and visibly relaxes a little. "So are you coming to dinner or not? Don't make me do this alone, Daisy."

"I'll come." I groan. "But I might be late depending on how long Gil keeps me at work."

"Ooh, have Gil drop you off at my house. In his Porsche. Maybe I can say hello," she purrs.

"That's just what you need, my dirt-ball boss in your life. I'll bring my dad's Pontiac and you'll like it."

"Your dirt-ball boss is hot, though."

"No one knows that more than him. But if the current chaos is causing me to sell trings for you, I am not ready for that kind of escape."

The first bell rings and Claire looks behind her, gauging by the number of kids in the hallway how much time she actually has before the second bell. "What's this about Pepperdine? I thought you were all set."

"My mother says she knows that's my first choice, but she acted hastily, which I take to mean it's not a given at this point. But it is in my mind. I'm just preparing in case I have to make alternative arrangements. Apparently, it's more expensive than Stanford, and that little factoid left them with ample fears about finishing all four years, especially with my dad's health. She even copied an article about how expensive educations weren't great investments right now in this economy."

"So what does that mean?" Claire asks.

"Heck if I know. It's my parents. When I can make sense of them, shoot me."

My dad never subscribed to the Silicon Valley workaholics' pledge. He's a self-employed actor who wears my mother's homemade costumes and performs chastity talks at schools (unfortunately, mine being one of them) and gives wedding proposals dressed like ducks and other fowl.

My mom runs a successful business making high-end aprons and oven mitts for wealthy women who never touch a stove. But without good health insurance, my parents are never far from worry.

"What about your scholarship? And the money your grandparents put aside for you?" Claire asks, and these are perfectly relevant questions in a normal family.

"They can afford it, but you know my mom. She worries about that rainy day like we live in typhoon country." I scratch the back of my head. "So I want to be on my best behavior, and selling trings during schooltime doesn't line up with my priorities." I say this with complete authority. If I were Claire, I wouldn't question this very straightforward approach. But of course, I'm not Claire.

"Your mom always thinks the sky is falling. She'll see how serious you are about business when you start selling trings. She's just holding it over your head like she always does. Like when we'd want to go to the club swimming on Saturday. Remember? She'd say all week that unless you finished all your homework or helped in her garden, you couldn't go. Then she'd always let you go."

"After I finished my homework and the gardening."

"Right, but what I'm saying is your mom doesn't know how to function without something to hold over your head, and right now it's college. You got financial aid! And the scholarship! Plus all that money you've been socking away with your after-school job. You just have to have faith!"

"Faith and a few hundred thou. Like I said, my parents haven't said anything about it, but I have to be prepared."

"So I'm helping you prepare and you're throwing it back in my face. Sell the trings for me and I'll give you half the profits. Then you'll get a job when you're down there and you just do what you've been doing. One day at a time."

"Somehow I have trouble comparing my educational future to an alcoholic's mantra."

I look down at the rings. I'm sorry, but if they're fashionable, it's another sign that I am socially inept, because I think they're hideous, and I will feel worse about selling them at school than overpriced wrapping paper that no one wants. "I really don't think—"

"Look, if you don't like them, it's good practice," Claire says. "Marketing is all about trust in your product. Trust in the product, Daisy. You don't have to trust in it for you, but for other people, it gives them an affordable way to commemorate their high school years without the high price of a class ring."

"What if I can't do that?"

"Pretend."

I spy Max across the school courtyard, and my insides light with adrenaline. "Max, hey!" I shout and wave my hand. "Over here! Max!"

Claire pulls my hand down. "Could you try and not act completely desperate?"

"He's my boyf—" I stop when she gives me that "chill" look. "We're friends at the very least."

Max takes my breath away. As he walks across campus in

his cool plaid shorts and stretched T-shirt, I can almost smell the masculine scent he sports. He bears a striking resemblance to Enrique Iglesias, without that blonde tennis chick hanging off him—Enrique, not Max. I can't hang all over him. My dad had kittens over the tango at prom. I mean, he likes Max and all, he just worried that maybe I'd seen too much *iCarly*. Whatever that's supposed to mean.

Max notices me standing beside Claire, his eyes grow wide for a split second, and he ducks into the halls of St. James Academy.

"Didn't he see me?"

"The entire quad saw you." Claire hands me a plastic box with a handle. "The order forms are inside and we can add anything they like to the ring for an extra fee. Maybe they want to remember their boyfriend or a best friend, or even their clubs."

"I don't understand," I say. "I didn't smother him or call him my boyfriend. What happened?"

"He's a guy. Don't read anything into it."

My best friend thinks I'm her multilevel marketing chain, and I have no money for college. So unless something changes, this is not only my present, this is my future.

"So dinner's at seven tomorrow," Claire says. "I'm setting a sales goal of twenty trings for you today. No need to start too high. We'll ease you into it. Don't be late for dinner, my parents will freak out enough as it is. I won't be at lunch, I have a meeting with my manufacturer. He's coming here. Isn't that cool? I may even get business credits for this."

Why can't my life be normal? Why can't *I* be normal? Last week I had a boyfriend and a future at Pepperdine. Today I have tacky costume jewelry, a date with dysfunction for

28

tomorrow night's dinner, and yet another guy's rejection to add to my sorry history.

"I've got to get to class. You have your assignment." Claire skips off and makes me wish I possessed one-tenth of her confidence.

I take out my new journal, which was meant to be a Chemistry notebook, but emergencies call for drastic actions.

Social Ineptitude Journal; or, Daisy's Search for Significance
March 9

Random fact: 12 percent of teens have a boyfriend/girlfriend. So I am TOTALLY normal. Totally. It just feels like 88 percent of the high school world has a boyfriend/girlfriend when you don't.

> *Max dumped me. I think. Granted, he was never actually my boyfriend to require dumping me, but like that makes me feel any better. He's going to be singing, dancing, and—let's not forget—macking onstage with my best friend, so maybe it's for the best. When Zac Efron sings and dances, it works. I'm going to say it's not going to with Max. Is that rude to predict his defeat? His stone-cold, laugh-a-minute performance onstage?*
>
> *I'm not sure Max onstage will translate—all I'm sayin'. Probably because I've seen him in his primary-colored Hot Dog on a Stick uniform that he wears at the mall. Yeah, I'm totally over him. The important thing*

now is that I find out what makes me special so that I know why he went to prom with me, and why he now acts as if I'm a walking disease. What about Daisy Crispin is utterly and fantastically unique? And how do I focus on that? There has got to be a way to get noticed at this school and be remembered.

Math + ? = Daisy

In my last journal, I focused on a prom date, but this time I'm going deeper. I'm delving to the core of my issues. Since I'm a perfectionist, I think I try too hard. And the messy thing is, the harder I try, the more my life goes wrong.

So in this journal, I am devoting myself to prayer and waiting on the Lord. I will not run ahead of him and topple over yet another cliff. I'm going to be a patient perfectionist, and then maybe I'll be closer to perfect. It's brilliant! From now until the end of school, I will devote myself (by waiting and being patient, of course) to the following:

1. I will be content with my work. Even when Gil wastes my time with his serial dating stories, I will not be rude. I will listen patiently because listening to Gil is an important part of my job. Maybe God has me there to be a witness, and that's the real work, not getting the spreadsheets done—even though I'm totally behind and

Gil's stories scare me . . . No, it's about being in the moment. Appreciating the work God has given my hands—and my ears—even if they're bleeding at five o'clock.

2. I will be more accepting of people and not tell them a better way to do everything. I will love my best friend Claire where she is—it's clear she was sent to this earth to teach me more tolerance for those who are different from me. Thanks for her presence, Lord. Help her to chill out on all her drama—for her own sake, not mine.

3. I will not let my parents' lack of social awareness embarrass me. They have been able to support our family while working in the arts. Okay, God, I will even allow myself to consider that puppet shows and singing telegrams have their place in culture—who am I to judge? (Gosh, I totally feel myself growing even as I write this.)

4. I will not obsess about finding the perfect guy. I mean, sure, I have a boyfriend now (unless I really don't), so that's really easy to say. We're just working out how we're going to play it at school. Are we cool? Do we hold hands? Do we see each other only at church? I'm sure that's all it is. See, I'm already working out being more accepting.

But the fact is, I've grown in this area already. I won't torture myself looking for text messages that aren't

31

there because I know that if he texts me all the time, there won't be any mountaintop experiences. So yes, I'm going to find the contentment in my relationship with Max. If there is one.

Daisy Crispin, perfectionist no more. Patient, tolerant, accepting, self-confident woman of God—totally. But I will allow myself some mistakes. I will offer myself some grace. If it seems reasonable.

I sidle up to Max in Chemistry, which is only fitting, right? Advanced Chemistry . . . Max. They go together like peanut butter and jelly.

Max is staring into a beaker, swirling a liquid, and honestly, I'm not sure I've ever seen anything so fantastic as Max in protective eye gear. His dark hair and perfect olive skin tone against the clear plastic—well, it's magic. He looks like a Calvin Klein model with a PhD. I should tell you, I have a thing for smart guys. Always have. Right now I want to snap his picture and slap it on Facebook with a caption that reads, "My senior prom date: Max Diaz. Eat that, Amber Richardson."

But that wouldn't be tolerant nor accepting and thus against my goals for the remainder of my senior year. Naturally, that would also be neither Christian nor nice, so I wouldn't do it, just saying I'd like to. I wish that sinful nature would hide itself farther down in my psyche, but it pops up at the most inopportune times. I do wonder what it's like for naturally nice people. Do they wrestle with these catty thoughts? Or is it just me? My mom is one of those nice people, and I'd ask her, but I can't dare admit the ugly truth to her or she'd feel as though she'd gone so very wrong with me.

Max swirls the liquid faster in the beaker when he notices my presence, but he doesn't look at me. He clears his throat as if to dismiss me without wasting time, but I can't bear to pick up on his clue. Maybe he just has something stuck in his throat.

"Max," I whisper. "Are you angry with me?"

He finally stares at me over his plastic glasses, using his forefinger to flick them down his straight nose. His deep brown eyes linger on my face, and there's so much depth in the way he stares. I refuse to believe he doesn't feel what I do. Am I that pathetic? Do I want this so bad that the truth is not in me?

He keeps staring, silently. Right now I want to reach over his beaker and kiss him. Right here in Chemistry. I want to remind him of our prom night, of our tango at Claire's party . . . of our *connection*. But as he stares at me with a faraway look, I suddenly wonder if I imagined all of these things. If I wanted them to be true and Max felt none of what I did. Currently he makes me feel as if I'm something he stepped in and couldn't avoid.

Our teacher, Mr. Kelly, saunters around the raised tables in the stark, gray room with only a yellowed poster of the table of the elements as a decoration. Max nudges his chin toward the teacher but keeps his disdainful look. "You'd better get back in your seat. This project takes the whole period. Or didn't you notice?"

"Max!" I say too loudly. A sea of faces turns toward me, but I'm on a mission, and after four years of dreadful social missteps, I have nothing to lose here. I lean in with my elbows on the table. "Answer my question," I plead. My command sounds much more desperate than I'd hoped. I was going for strong and confident, but I've led with pathetic and weak-willed.

"I—I can't," Max answers.

"Miss Crispin, is there a problem?" Mr. Kelly strides over with his arms crossed in front of his chest in that passive-aggressive, judgmental way of his. He's one of those men who waits with joy for someone to screw up, and then with eager relish he hands out behavior reports like they were candy on Halloween.

I look to Max, but he's following his finger on the assignment sheet and makes no move to acknowledge my presence or help me out with Mr. Kelly. My eyes are swimming behind tears and Mr. Kelly appears waterlogged and wavy, but his harsh glance over his glasses is enough to send me back to my stool like a bad dog with its tail between its legs.

"No, sir," I say as I turn back to my lab partner, who shakes his head with a small laugh.

"Are you planning on doing any of this project? You know, *partner*? It means I'm only supposed to do half the work." Curt, a water polo star and serious student, asked for me as his partner, and until now I haven't let him down. I've been an excellent partner, diligent in my studies, without fear in compounds, but then Max and prom changed all that. This invisible guy in my Chemistry class became . . . Max. Being girly somehow became more important than Graham's law of diffusion.

"I'm here now." I sit down on the stool and park my elbows on the table. "Where are we?" I look at the paper, but it's all one fuzzy paragraph.

Curt leans in. "Daisy, we're on part C." He's annoyed with me. Curt has never been one to take mercy on the less fortunate, but when that ill luck steps into his path, he's downright rude.

"Okay." I hiccup and try to focus. I glance over at Max, but he hasn't looked up and his lab partner works by herself.

"Miss Crispin," Mr. Kelly says in his stern voice. "Am I disturbing you today?"

"No, sir."

"He's a player, Daisy," Curt says without looking up from his beaker.

"Who's a what?"

"Your Latin lover. He's a player."

"He's not."

Curt shrugs. "Listen, I don't care. I'm just telling you what I think. Can we get back to this? Or do you want to make a bigger fool out of yourself with Romeo over there?"

"Why do you say that?"

Curt keeps looking at the beaker, his eyes buggy from the protective glasses. I'd think he'd look cooler in them with all the time he spends in goggles, but he's a serious mess.

"Look, everyone saw you two at prom, dancing that stupid dance. Like you were on *Dancing with the Stars* or something. Now he acts like he doesn't know you at all. Swats you away like a mosquito. Do the math, Daisy. You're a smart girl." He stops swiveling the beaker, puts the flask back in its wire holder, and stares at me with his baby-fat face and the distinct message that I'm the village idiot. Someone he must painfully endure until the end of the year.

I find my gaze drifting over to Max's table, and I wonder what the truth is. Is he a player? Did he realize I was a hopeless cause sexually, with my dad staring on and my purity ring glaring at him? Did he decide to quit wasting time?

But he said he'd wait. At the dance, he said I was worth it. Maybe I looked like an easy target to begin with—a naive country bumpkin to his international prowess. Or he was simply looking to make himself known among the kids—being here fresh as a senior. Maybe I served my purpose.

"So are you done here?" Curt asks.

"I'll mix up the last part." I read the elements necessary, but my heart isn't in it. I go through the rest of the period in automatic.

As the bell rings, I clamber to get my backpack ready and talk to Max again when he's not sidetracked, but he's gone before I can zip it up. I stand there and allow my mind to do the math, as Curt so eloquently put it. Max hasn't called me. He's barely acknowledged my presence in the hallway. He's signed up for the school musical with Claire and I didn't even know he was interested in the theater. With horror, I realize maybe that's not what he's interested in.

I look down at the tring and rip it off my finger, and as I do, the plastic sales box Claire made me tumbles to the ground. "I'm an idiot," I mutter as I pick it up, counting the twenty bucks I've already taken in within the last hour. People want this garbage. Go figure.

Chase, the guy I had a crush on since kindergarten— emphasis on the *had*—stands in front of me. "Are you talking to me yet? You've tried me without a fair trial, you know." Chase, the guy who broke my heart when he turned out to be a boorish brute wrapped in a genetically gifted package, towers above me and waits while I get myself together.

My eyes thin toward him as I remember the facts of

December's party. He left the girl he slept with at our party, and he didn't ensure she was out of the room before the fire department came. He ran like a mama's boy and claims to know none of it. He'll enter the Air Force Academy in the fall as though the whole event were nothing more than a figment of my imagination. Worst of all, the girl he left there, Amber Richardson, is the daughter of a congressman—the congressman who will write Chase's letter of recommendation to get into the Air Force Academy.

"Chase, I convicted you of nothing. It's your own telltale heart pounding away." Inwardly, I congratulate myself on this very smart literary reference.

"I can't believe with all we've been through that you would just believe me guilty of this, Daisy. It's not like you. That cabana boy has done something to your head."

"What?" Suddenly I'm not feeling smart at all. It bothers me immensely that Chase still has the power to make me question myself. "What do you mean by that? Max had nothing to do with this. You left the party that night when the sirens started. I saw you running away with my own eyes."

"You didn't see what you think you saw." Chase looks away and rolls his eyes as if to say he's exasperated with me, but he slows down so I can keep up. He lowers his voice, and he sounds as sincere as I've ever heard him. "I had no idea where Amber was that night, or I would have gone back into the house and gotten her. Daisy, that night— nothing happened between Amber and me. Were you jealous?" His expression softens. "Is that why you thought I was involved?"

The way he's gazing at me, with all the sincerity in his gorgeous eyes . . . seriously, if he told me right now that I was blue? I'd have to stare at the back of my hand to make certain I was still a pasty-peach color.

"I have to get to class." I turn on my heel and head toward the concrete building's ice-blue doors. For a brief moment I am the picture of calm, cool, and collected, but at the last minute I glance over my shoulder to see if Chase is watching me. He is.

His expression is pinched, and I just don't know . . . I'll never really know the truth because I simply can't believe he's capable of what my eyes saw. Or think they saw. When someone looks like Chase, it's hard to believe anything but the best of the guy. I imagine that's why Angelina Jolie gets mixed up with Mother Teresa in this world. The church isn't immune—it's easier to believe what you want to about good-looking people. We're blinded by the visuals. And clearly I'm not immune either.

❧ 3 ❧

After another long and unsuccessful day at school and work, the last thing I want to do is go to Claire's family (dys)function, but seeing as how I was partly responsible for the house burning down (by association, mostly)—AND that I didn't sell one tring by my own efforts today, I can hardly refuse. Claire needs me. Her warped family needs me, and since I can't do anything about my own warped family, I might as well offer my services to my best friend.

Besides, I'm anxious to see what this brother looks like, see if he has Mr. Webber's looks or the man's standoffish nature. I'm always curious how genetics work. How else can I explain my own parents? I need to see more apples falling farther from their trees. What can I say? A girl needs hope.

If I'm honest, I can't wait to see if Mrs. Webber can keep it together. Claire's mom has one of those cool, beautiful exteriors that always seems like it's about to blow, and when it does—look out! Her true feelings simmer beneath the surface, and maybe I've watched one too many bad nighttime soap operas, but I can't say I'm without interest in the matter. For her sake, I want her to be able to hold it together and welcome this guy—as much as she's able. I can't help hoping this may be a new beginning for Claire's family.

As I approach Claire's magnificent house—with the plant my mother made me bring as a hostess gift—this visit feels significant. Not like the many times I've brought my jammies in a pillowcase, but a grown-up dinner party—like I'm a real guest. The fact that her parents are letting me come to such a family event speaks volumes.

I park my dad's beater car off to the side on the driveway, where I've seen the gardener park. Smoothing out my floral dress, I climb the brick steps and peer into the beveled window to the side of the double doors.

Mr. Webber is incredibly handsome, so I guess it's hard to believe he didn't have a past. Then again, I cannot imagine my dad having a past either . . . ick, I'm shuddering. The idea is more than a little disturbing. Let's face it. We don't get this kind of excitement out of the Christian parents from St. James Academy.

I ring the doorbell and hear it echo through the great house, which from the outside is marred by scaffolding around its edges—a visual reminder that all is not well in the house. They're rebuilding what burned at the party Claire and I threw. The smoke and water damage caused more trouble than any fire.

I pace the porch as I hear Claire clomp down the marble stairs, and she whisks open the door. "You are totally late." She pulls me in by the arm.

"I think you meant to say, 'Thank you for coming,' and you're totally welcome. I came as soon as I got off work, and my dad had to lend me the car."

Claire rolls her eyes at the sight of my dad's clunker. "Is he ever going to trade that thing in?"

We both repeat my dad's mantra. "A car is only about getting you from point A to point B." We giggle. *As if.*

"Is he here yet?" I whisper.

She shakes her head. "Not yet. My parents have been fighting since I got home and I think my dad tuned out my mom's voice hours ago. My mom is freaking, and when he was listening, my dad was hollering about her not ever making a mistake and thinking she's perfect." Claire rolls her eyes. "Be extra nice to her, and don't mention the prodigal until he gets here, then act surprised."

"You didn't tell her I was coming?"

"You're always here. Why would she be surprised?" Claire is dressed like her mother tonight. She's got a cashmere sweater set in aqua-blue and a black-and-white houndstooth skirt. "Where's your tring?" She lifts up my hand and then tosses it down in disgust.

"I couldn't type with it. My boss made me ditch it. Besides, you might be able to get away with it, but somehow it doesn't cut it on me. I'm not cool enough for it." My excuse goes unheard.

"Just make sure to wear it at school for sales. Listen, I hope you don't mind, but I invited Max over for dinner and to do some homework. He's been having trouble in Chemistry."

My mouth is agape. "And? Claire, has it occurred to you that your family is in crisis, and maybe inviting the school over may not be the best idea?"

"So I offered to help."

"With what?" I ask her.

"Duh. Chemistry."

"Claire, aren't you forgetting an important fact here?"

"Such as?"

"You shouldn't be tutoring anyone in anything, except maybe power-shopping?"

She flicks her wrist to wave my concerns off. "No, it's not a big deal. I'm sure Max is just having trouble with his English in there. I can read!"

"Forgive me for asking the obvious, but why on earth would you care if Max passed Chemistry?"

"We have to keep his grades up or he won't get to be in the play, and rehearsals have already started."

My breath is shallow. "*We?* Are you completely clueless?"

"What? I don't want some loser who can't dance and who looks like Quasimodo starring opposite me. I have to do everything I can to ensure Max is in that play."

"Then you should hire him a tutor," I say, failing to state the obvious—like maybe she should find someone other than my boyfriend, even if our status is currently unspoken and his Facebook status does say *single*. "Why wouldn't you ask me to tutor him?"

"What do you mean?" She blinks her wide, cowlike eyes at me.

"I mean, you're not exactly a star student, Claire, or do you need a report card reminder? What makes you think you can tutor Max? And let's not forget he's, you know, he's mine." *There, I said it. He's mine and it felt good.* "Friends don't go after friends' boyfriends. Did you miss that memo?"

"Go after . . . what? Yours? Daisy, I'm not trying to take Max away from you, but let's be clear, is he worth having if I could take him away? I haven't even seen you two have a conversation since the dance. I mean, first you're like all romantic in front of the whole school and now it's like you never met. Are you trying to say there's something still going on?"

Her question catches me off guard. First, because it's so totally rude, even for Claire, and second, because I don't have a clue what happened between Max and me. One minute he was sashaying me across the dance floor, implying that I'd make an excellent pastor's wife and I'd be worth waiting for, and the next, he's ignoring me in Chemistry. I don't know what kind of effect it is I have on the male population, but it rhymes with revulsion. Oh wait, no, it is, in fact, revulsion.

"There have been a lot of projects this week. We haven't gotten a chance—"

"Well, if a guy doesn't want to stay around, you can't force him."

"Are you saying I'm forcing him?" I ask her, and suddenly I have a terrifying thought. What if I'm a bad kisser? What if, on the dance floor—in front of my father, no less—I let Max kiss me, and what if he was disgusted? "You haven't had a boyfriend since Greg—"

She tosses her hand again. "I'm not crushing on anyone, but you have nothing to worry about with Max and me." She shudders.

Is that supposed to make me feel better?

"What time is dinner? I have a lot of homework," I tell her.

She checks the button on her sweater. "You don't think I'd take your crush from you. That's so *Gossip Girl*. Even if he isn't interested anymore, you're getting paranoid, Daisy." Claire walks away from me, and I close my eyes in prayer to remind myself her world is falling apart. She doesn't mean any of that. It's just that I'm the target, and that's okay for a short amount of time. But it had better be extremely short because my patience is wearing thin.

"I would rather not attend grad night alone."

Claire shrugs. "So you won't. It doesn't have to be with Max, does it? I mean, prom was all about Chase, and you changed your mind on that quick enough."

"Because I thought he drugged another girl and didn't bring her downstairs when the house was on fire. Look, I may not be exceptionally particular about my dates, but I draw the line at attempted rape and murder."

"Come on, you don't really think Chase did any of that."

I sigh. "No, I suppose I don't."

"Great, so let him make it up to you by taking you to grad night."

"What's that supposed to mean?" I follow Claire as she walks into her cavernous kitchen with its cherry cabinets and pristine stainless steel appliances, most of which have never been used.

Claire's mother stares at me as though I've just stepped off an alien planet. Claire turns back toward me and ignores her mother's pained stare. "I wouldn't have invited Max over if I knew you were going to be here—if I had interest in him, I mean. Right?"

Now seriously, Claire would never do anything to intentionally hurt me, but that doesn't mean she doesn't have serious gaps in her social skills. She has my back, but she also has this natural inclination to flirt with anyone and everyone, and while I have no doubt she has no genuine interest in Max— okay, very little doubt—that won't stop her from violently batting her eyelashes and giggling at everything he says.

She's smart about whom to flirt with too. She knows her limits—who is in her league and that type of thing—and if Max is in my league, he's definitely in hers because we both bat for the same AAA league.

"Claire," Mrs. Webber says with her full lips pressed together tightly, "what is Daisy doing here?" Mrs. Webber's Botox-enhanced forehead is crinkled, and it's somewhat upsetting to see her face move—I'd gotten so used to its stationary stance, like a doll on a shelf. "No offense, Daisy, you're always welcome, but we have some family business tonight and I'm not sure if it's appropriate that you be here." Mrs. Webber looks at Claire and frowns. "Which I'm sure Claire has made you fully aware of, so go wash up and put the glasses on the table, you two. The green goblets."

"You got two extra lobsters. I just assumed one of them was for Daisy." Claire mumbles the rest. "And if Max comes early, he can have the other one."

"What was that?"

This is code for Claire is so in trouble, and Mrs. Webber wouldn't think of yelling in front of me—which I imagine is why Claire invited me in the first place. Mrs. Webber always shuts the door and wails like a stuck pig as if the door is soundproof, but I've yet to see her do it in front of me.

I do as I'm told and walk to the guest bathroom, wash my hands to the elbows like a surgeon, and then hightail it to the dining room, where I open the cabinet and start dusting the goblets and placing them on the table. One time I put them on without dusting them, and that was a half-hour lecture by Mrs. Webber on proper hospitality and cleanliness. In her defense, Mrs. Webber always tells me that one day I will be mistress of a home like this, so I need to know how to properly care for what I've been entrusted with in life. You can't argue with that kind of encouragement, even if it is garbage. For one thing, I am adamant that my house will not look like my mother's. It will be clean. And I don't

46

ever want to be responsible for cleaning a monstrosity like the Webber house.

The doorbell rings, and the hushed lecture is still happening in the kitchen, so I go to the door. Behind the glass I can see a young man, and he's holding a bouquet of flowers as he paces in a small circle on the porch. I turn on the light in the foyer so he can see me, and he stops moving instantly. I glance over my shoulder, but there's no sign of anyone coming, so I open the door.

"Claire, I assume?" He holds out his hand. "I'm Jeremy." He does have his father's good looks. His hair is a nondescript brown and his eyes are warm, and in the yellow porch light, they appear dark blue and perhaps fearful. He's like a lost puppy, and my heart goes out to him. Maybe his eyes are just large for his face, I can't tell. His nose is big and he has full, girlish lips. But somehow it all works together and he's amazingly good-looking—so much so that I realize I haven't said anything.

"Not Claire . . ."

"You're not Claire?"

I shake my head and can't stop staring at him. I'm looking for signs of Claire in him, but he seems nothing like her. He's not pushy, for one thing. Jeremy has a strong jawline like his father, but he's clean-shaven and wearing a cheap suit. I'd never know a cheap suit if my boss didn't wear expensive suits and show me the difference. It's amazing how much this skill has helped me discern poseurs among the really wealthy—though I only use this skill at Claire's country club, and they're all wealthier than the likes of me. Jeremy's suit fits him like a flour sack, and the shiny material screams acetate, which I know well from all the costumes I've made with my mother. I half expect him to break into a dance of some sort.

47

Mr. and Mrs. Webber will notice the suit is cheap, but hopefully that will not taint their view of him—that he's after their money. He doesn't seem the type, actually. He wears the cheap suit with style—like he'd look uncomfortable in a good one.

"I'm not Claire." I finally mumble a full sentence. "I'm Daisy Crispin, Claire's best friend. You must be—"

He nods. "Jeremy Winters." He reaches out his hand and clumsily takes my own. We shake in a perfunctory fashion. I think he's one of those guys who is incredibly gorgeous and has no idea. Or maybe he does and he's good at the bumbling act. I can't tell until I see more of him in action.

"Nice to meet you, Jeremy. You're younger than I imagined."

"Twenty-four," he says, allowing me to avoid the guestimate.

"Come on in." I spread out my arm and open the door wider. Claire's family is all behind me suddenly, and they're staring at the long-lost family member as though he's just broken in with a gun. "This is Jeremy," I say with too much enthusiasm, like he's a game show prize.

Mrs. Webber has that look on her face, the one where she's noticed someone in a prettier dress at the country club. Mr. Webber has tears in his eyes and Claire is simply a deer in the headlights.

"Jeremy." Mr. Webber finally reaches out his arm and greets his son properly. He pulls him into a hug by his handshake and roughly pats him on the back three times. "I can't believe it." Mr. Webber pulls away but keeps his hands on Jeremy's upper arms. "Let me look at you, boy!" He shakes his head. "You are a sight for sore eyes. So much lost time to make up for. Tell me how all this happened." Suddenly remembering his family alongside him, Mr. Webber tones

48

it down. "This is my family. This is my beautiful wife, and my lovely daughter, Claire. Claire's graduating from high school this year."

Jeremy smiles awkwardly and reaches out a hand. Mrs. Webber has a hard time holding it together, and I can see her bottom lip quivering. Claire remains stoic, as if she's still unsure if the trings will cover her future if this thing with her half brother and father works out. No one else would notice by the casual smile on Claire's face, but I've known her too long. I know exactly what she's thinking. She's not that good of an actress.

"Nice to meet you," Claire says with all the enthusiasm of a child told to kiss an old relative.

"You too," Jeremy answers eagerly. "A little sister. That's something."

"Half sister," Claire says.

Mrs. Webber never greets their guest, and it's clear the resemblance to her husband is too much for her. She must have been hoping this had all been a mistake, and the reality in front of her makes me feel sorry for her for the first time in my whole life. I always thought Mrs. Webber had it all.

"Dinner's ready," Mrs. Webber says as she stalks off toward the kitchen. Her clicking heels echo throughout the cavernous room—like several stabbing exclamation points.

"This is quite a place you've got here." Jeremy searches the high ceilings and then nods slowly, as though he's run out of small talk. "I think my whole apartment could fit into this entryway."

"Is that so?" Claire asks. "Are you looking to get a bigger place?"

"I'm a legal clerk. It's not possible," he answers.

"You're going into law?" Mr. Webber, a lawyer, perks up. "It's in the blood, I suppose."

"Is it? Do we have DNA proof?" Claire asks, and I shoot her a dirty look.

Something about the way Jeremy's treated, as the underdog, immediately makes me want to protect him and tell him how much of his father I can see in his eyes. I don't do any of this, naturally—Mrs. Webber would have my head—but I could. Jeremy's well out of high school, and that means I can talk to him. Heaven forbid I ever have a jury of my peers.

Mr. Webber leads us to the dining room, which now has six candles of all different lengths glowing around a centerpiece of brightly colored gerbera daisies. Everyone is silently staring at Jeremy, and I'm a traitor for having put the goblets on the table. Mrs. Webber is wrong. Clean goblets don't offer hospitality. Sometimes they let a person know he's not welcome in their lives.

Jeremy is rubbing his palms back and forth as if it's frigid in the room, and I suppose it is, but it has nothing to do with the weather.

"Jeremy, can I take your jacket?" I ask him.

He shakes his head. "I'm used to wearing it in the law office."

I almost say, "Suit yourself," but now does not seem like the right time for a pun.

"So, Jeremy," Mr. Webber finally says in his baritone voice, "sit down and tell me what you've done with yourself for the last twenty-plus years. Is there a reason you"—he coughs— "and your mother chose to keep this to yourselves for so long?"

The screech of chairs echoes in the room and the smell of burned toast comes wafting out from the kitchen, but everyone's attention is centered on Jeremy. Claire's eyes are narrowed.

We're all seated around the table, and Mrs. Webber brings in a huge platter with six red lobsters lying on a bed of lettuce, with lemon wedges wrapped in cheesecloth and small personal-sized bowls filled with melted butter. "Daisy, I didn't know you'd be here, so you and Claire will have to share."

I want to point out that there are six lobsters and only five of us, but I guess that would be rude.

"Lobster? Mom, not exactly easy to eat. How are we supposed to share?"

Mrs. Webber's eyes flash. "I don't know, Claire. Why don't you eat the lettuce?" she snaps. She slams a small bowl beside everyone's plate and uses tongs to maneuver the crustaceans onto each plate. They land with a clatter.

"It looks wonderful, dear. Thank you." Mr. Webber visibly swallows. "So, Jeremy, why don't you tell us how this visit came to be? We were interrupted."

Mrs. Webber lets her husband know what she thinks of that comment.

Jeremy clears his throat and shakes out his linen napkin to place on his lap. "Well, my mother died." He pauses. "So we talked about you, Mr. Webber, before her death. She said she'd tell me someday about my father, but she waited until the last minute. She always said God was my father."

"Did she mention why she never said anything about your existence to me?" Mr. Webber asks, and I wish I could crawl away unnoticed. This hardly seems like appropriate dinner conversation for a guest. Even if I'm not considered a guest.

"She said we'd only complicate your life, and she was sure we'd be unwelcome."

51

Mr. Webber drops his lobster cracker with a clang that echoes through the house. He clears his throat. "Did you say your mother is gone? As for being a complication, I do wish I'd been given the opportunity to decide that for myself."

Jeremy nods. "She never got married, so she never really talked about, you know, my father . . . you . . . until the end. She wanted me to know you were a good man, and that you didn't know about me."

Mrs. Webber pipes up and stares at her husband. "I thought you met her on a cruise."

He swallows hard. "Actually, I knew Helen through school. The cruise was a high school trip, and . . . we—"

"Well, we know what happened. We see the result!" Mrs. Webber drops the tongs and throws her napkin on the table. "I'm sorry, Jeremy, but I'm afraid I have a bit of a headache, if you'll excuse me. Claire, clear the table when you're done." Mrs. Webber puts her hand to her forehead and breaks for the stairs.

"I'll just see that she's all right. I'll be right back." Mr. Webber places his napkin on the table and follows his wife. The three of us—Jeremy, Claire, and I—stare at the lobsters, wondering if we should wait or just start eating and get the awkward moment over.

The doorbell rings before any decisions are made. Claire screeches her chair back and runs for the front door like it's her salvation. Jeremy and I are both trying to decide where to look, and it's obvious we're wishing we had a reason to answer the door.

"This wasn't quite how I pictured things." Jeremy shrugs.

The lobsters slump on their plates, deserted, probably wondering why they had to be boiled alive for this. It's as if the crustaceans' beady black eyes question our irresponsibility as they balance on their huge, defenseless red claws. I know how they feel.

"It's not your fault," I tell Jeremy. I'd tell him Claire's parents always fight like this, but somehow that doesn't seem appropriate. "I'm sorry." I shrug too. "I guess it's just hard."

"I expected that. I should have said no to dinner. Coffee would have been better. We should have met for coffee first. Without his family." He seems to say this more for his own benefit than mine.

"Yeah, like a bad date," I joke. "The shorter the plan, the easier the escape route."

He smiles. "Something like that. It's only natural I'd want to know my only living parent."

"Sure."

I watch Jeremy try to smile and find the best in the situation as he nervously shifts in his seat, and I think, *At least my family drama is G-rated.* My mom won't let me watch *Desperate Housewives*, so I'm sure she wouldn't approve of me seeing it live.

I start to summon excuses in my head. I'm a terrible liar, and right now that's a bad thing. If I were Claire, how would I get out of this mess? Without eating the beady-eyed crustacean in front of me, which has apparently died for nothing.

My thoughts are interrupted by the entrance of Max Diaz in all his hot, Argentine glory, and suddenly my own love triangle trumps Mr. Webber's. Max is wearing a white-collared shirt open at the neck, and his dark, wavy hair licks the collar deliciously. Whatever he may think of me now, when I look at him with his gorgeous olive skin and searing eyes, I think (victoriously), *That was my prom date. You can't take that away from me, Amber Richardson, mean girl extraordinaire, nor can you, best friend Claire!*

Max is so out of my league, it's not even funny. I can see that clearly now. Maybe I took advantage of his St. James Academy status as a new student. Maybe he knows it now. Sometimes knowledge sucks. *Sigh.*

Max's wide, deep chocolate eyes intoxicate me, and he looks at me as though he's trapped. Then he looks back at Claire, apparently questioning his role here tonight. As if anyone knows the answer to that thought.

"Would you like some lobster, Max?" Claire asks him. "I think we have extra."

He looks at the table, not acknowledging my presence. "I thought we were going to work on chemistry." The strain in his voice is blatant. "Didn't you say seven o'clock?"

"I'd better get home." I put my napkin on the table, pick up the lobster with my fingers, and plop it on Claire's plate. "I'll talk to you tomorrow. Jeremy, it was nice to meet you."

Seeing Max sends a sick wave to my stomach. I thought he was different. I thought he meant what he said, that I meant something to him, that my purity ring meant something to him, but now I feel like an ignorant noob all over again. I want to crumble in Claire's grand entrance, but even that would make too much noise, so I summon my inner confident heroine and stand with my shoulders pressed back. Max was caught up in the moment. Just like my father said boys would be. *I'm nobody again, and certainly nothing to Max.*

"Daisy, are you okay?" Jeremy stands up and walks toward me as I open the front door. "Do you need something to drink? You look pale."

"No." I shake my head quickly, just wanting to escape. "But I should go home. You all have enough to think about tonight, and I have a lot of homework—"

"'K. See ya, Daisy." Claire waves me off without a pinch of guilt, when I want her to have a lifetime serving of the emotion.

"Hi, Daisy. Bye, Daisy!" Max raises a hand, waves, and then follows Claire to the kitchen.

"She has no shame. None at all. Right now I think the best idea Claire's ever had is that stupid tring!" I open the great wood door. "Bye, Jeremy." I step onto the porch and let the door slam behind me. With great satisfaction, I hear the motion echo off the cold marble floors.

We've had a good run since kindergarten, but maybe it's time I found a new best friend. But even if I wanted to be, I'm not like Claire. I can't cast people off when I'm done with them—even if I should.

❧ 4 ❧

I'm just about to get into my car when I hear the great door creep open, and Jeremy calls my name. He's followed me outside and now he's standing beside me. "You should come back inside and eat. Don't let me stop you from a good meal," he says.

"Trust me, it's not you."

"What's going on between you and that guy? The one who came late."

"Max, his name is, and nothing."

"His eyes lit up when he saw you. Did you notice?" he asks.

"It's probably guilt. You're not leaving, are you? Mr. Webber would be disappointed."

"I'm not leaving. I've waited a long time for this invitation. Can't let the fact that I'm not wanted here stop me."

"I guess that's the difference between males and females. I can take a hint."

Jeremy bursts into laughter. "You're saying I can't take a hint?"

I grab onto the frame of my car door and lean toward him. "I'm saying if you came here looking for a healthy father figure, you may be at the wrong house—and I don't care how big those lobsters are, they're getting skinnier by the second as more people come to eat."

"Pardon?"

"Never underestimate the beauty of chaos when running from emotions."

Jeremy thins his eyes. "You're in high school? You seem a lot older."

I know I'm probably imagining things, but the way he says this creeps me out and my body lets out a little shiver. Yet I maintain a strong stance. "They tell me I'm an old soul. Which is just a polite way of saying I don't fit in and I've got my nerd on, but yes, I'm in high school. But you have to remember, I've grown up here and your father is Claire's father—" I stop myself. "You need to make up your own mind, of course. I don't want to gossip."

"I wouldn't ask you to."

"Usually Mrs. Webber is so good about guests. I think she wasn't expecting you to look as much like your father as you do, and you can understand this is difficult for her." I lean against my father's purple Pontiac. "I should go." I start to get in the car and Jeremy stops me.

"That guy is into you. No matter what game he's playing. What's his name?"

"Max. He's not into me." I pull the door, but Jeremy hasn't let go of it. "I really have to go." I stare at Claire's new brother, who has a darkness behind his gaze I can't quite place. There's a wounded look to his eyes that seems like it's been there for a long time. I rest my chin on the car's door frame. "What do you want from him? Mr. Webber, I mean."

"I'm curious. Wouldn't you be?" Jeremy asks.

"He's suspicious, you know. I mean, it's sort of in his

nature. Maybe he's seen too much dishonesty being a lawyer and all, but you don't seem like the type who's here for money."

"Thank you. I'm not here for money. I want to know who he is, what he's about. Why he could be brilliant enough to earn this house and yet senseless enough to abandon my mother." Jeremy shrugs. "What do you think of him? Don't edit yourself this time."

I don't trust him, I'll say that much. "I don't know much about Mr. Webber." I mean, this could be true. Sure, I've practically grown up in his house, but Claire's father was never around much. Not that Claire didn't tell me her opinion many times, but I would never give up information like that to a stranger. "He's kind of reserved. I think of him as always working."

"You've known him since you were young. I thought by the way you're practically family, you might have some insight," he presses. "Is he a partner at his firm?"

"Mr. Webber is sort of hard to get to know. I barely know what he does." I'm lying and I'm not sure why, but it just feels like there's an ulterior motive to the question.

"I summed up that much, that he was hard to get to know. Given time, I'll prove myself to him."

I feel like I should throw Mr. Webber a bone. "Things are strained in there. It has nothing to do with you, Jeremy. Don't take it personally." *But maybe your mother could have been more honest with the people in her life.*

"Think you could put a good word in for me?"

"I accidentally burned their house down with Claire, so I'm probably not an ally you want." I keep staring back at the house, wondering what Claire and Max are up to. I'm torn between wanting to rush in between them and get the heck away from all the drama.

Jeremy rubs his hands together again as if it's cold, but it's a balmy night. Most likely he's just avoiding the house—and I can't blame him for that. Conflict, to dinner party guests, is like garlic to vampires.

"My mother loved him." He looks toward the front doors. "So I have to believe there's some good in him somewhere."

"That's true of everyone, right?" I ask hopefully, because right now I'm looking for some good in Claire herself, and I do not want to partake in more of this information about Mr. Webber's background. It needs to be saved for a soap opera that needs a plot. "And who knows? Maybe Mr. Webber was different back then." I regret the words as soon as they're out of my mouth. It gives him the opening he seems to be looking for.

"Mom said he was ambitious, that he wanted more in a wife than she had to offer."

"Then why didn't she dump him before the cruise?"

"Pardon?"

"Your mother and Mr. Webber. If your mother knew there was no future, why . . ." I let my voice trail off, realizing I've just accused his dead mother of being loose.

He drops his chin and his words come out stilted and angry. "They disintegrated on that cruise. My mother dated him all through high school. She'd hoped to marry him, but when he went off to college without looking back, she said she knew what she'd meant to him. If only they hadn't taken that cruise to celebrate graduation, life would have been a lot different."

I gasp and immediately regret it. I will definitely not play poker in this lifetime. "Oh . . . well—" I stammer. "If he'd known about you, maybe things would have been different."

"She didn't tell him she was pregnant on purpose. If he didn't want her for her, she wasn't going to manipulate him. She said she wasn't the kind of wife he would have wanted, or he would have kept their relationship going when he went off to college."

"He might have surprised her," I say, suddenly feeling very protective of Mr. Webber. "When Claire and I burned the house down, he was only worried for our safety." *And maybe a lawsuit, but he definitely worried about our safety first.*

"I just want to know what my mother saw in him—if there's a scrap of that man left."

"He was really more of a boy, don't you think? Younger than you."

"That's no excuse!" Jeremy's teeth are clenched, and he speaks through them with what I would call seething anger.

"People will always let you down. Maybe not in fantastical ways like your father did to your mother, but in small ways, so don't set him up for failure. Give him a chance. That's why you're here, isn't it?"

"There's that old soul again, huh?"

"I'm just saying sometimes people let you down. Usually it's their issue, not yours." I try to remember that at times when my crush shows up to study chemistry with my best friend, who wouldn't know a molecule from a beaker. "Like inviting someone else's boyfriend over to study chemistry when you, in fact, have no knowledge of chemistry whatsoever."

Jeremy grins. "The way Max looks at you, I suppose you're right, but I think we all have to take that sage advice from

60

today's Gandhi: 'If you liked it, then you should have put a ring on it.'"

"Or a tring, at least."

"What?"

"Never mind."

"So do you think he loves her? Mrs. Webber, I mean. Did he marry for love?"

"He must have, because she is one high-maintenance woman."

Jeremy looks hurt by my words, as though they're aimed at his mother.

"I shouldn't have said that. I need to go."

"I want some answers."

"I hope you get them," I tell him, but I'm not hopeful. I've been Claire's best friend forever, and I couldn't begin to explain her parents.

"I need to go," I say again. I raise my arms off the door frame. "Good luck in there."

Jeremy steps closer. "You think I'll need luck?" He has a coolness about him, an aloofness that keeps him slightly separated from the emotions at hand. I don't like it, but I do admire it. Just once in my life, I wish I could experience that: the ability to stay outside my feelings and not let the entire world know exactly what I'm feeling. What a gift.

Naturally, my thoughts come pouring out of my mouth. "I thought you'd communicate to him. That you'd have some secret Morse code that he'd understand. Maybe that will happen over dessert."

"I don't have any expectations. I'd just hoped to see something my mother saw in him. She was certainly devoted to him. I never heard a bad word out of her mouth about him, and it didn't sound like her love had waned any in the end. It's a trait I admired in her, the ability to be blind to people's faults and devoted to their better natures."

"Even when the devotion is unwarranted?" I ask. "I was devoted to someone for a long time, and he wasn't worthy of it."

"Max?"

"No. Someone else, but I think believing the best about someone doesn't always make it so." I look down at my feet, and my shoes look scuffed and ratty. I suppose they go with the car. "It was nice to meet you, Jeremy. I hope you get what you came for." I'm anxious to get away from the house. From Claire. From Max. From everyone.

He finally lets go of the door frame. "You too, Daisy. Thanks for being a friendly face tonight." He enters through the giant doors. I head home to tell my tale of woe to a journal. To tell the truth as I see it after these eighty years of living in this seventeen-year-old, shapeless body.

March 10

Search for Significance, or Impossible Mission and Holy Grail? Only time will tell where this path is leading.

Random fact: My SAT numbers put me in the realm of "highly gifted." If social skills were included, I would be in the special class.

So . . . what makes me special? I feel no closer to finding an answer since I started this journal, and really, I feel less special for asking a stupid question I can't find the answer to. I mean, Claire is a natural chameleon. She can be whomever she likes depending on the company.

Angie is on the fast track to being a chemical engineer, and Sarika is an Indian princess meant to spread the Good News in her beautiful saris and gold bangles that her father has collected since her birth. Chase knows he's meant for the Air Force Academy. Heck, even Amber knows she's meant to be a trophy wife.

They have purpose. I, on the other hand . . . my future is always questionable, because every time I think I have the answer to it, some ugly truth invades my dreams. Like thinking my future was wrapped up in finance when I don't know the first thing about money, which is obvious by the fact that I didn't recognize the dream of Pepperdine was just that—a dream. But I can't give up hope before at least discussing it with my parents. Even though I know how that will probably go.

Am I special because I have one of those faces that people tell their story to? I mean, Jeremy told me more than he said at the table. Maybe I should get out of finance and go into psychology. Maybe I have a gift for helping people, and I'm clearly comfortable around the troubled. Except I guess I didn't help anyone, I just acquired information. Useless information at that. I can acquire information in finance, and unlike human emotions, the numbers will add up.

If I were totally honest, I might say my social ignorance makes me special, but after hearing Jeremy's mother's story, I'm not sure I want that gift either. She believed the best about Claire's dad, and look what it got her: a lifetime of raising a child by herself. But I don't know, I'm inclined to believe there's more to that story. What kind of woman would supposedly be in love with a guy and not tell him he was a father? That's ignorant.

I too am incredibly naive and such a romantic, and that is not going to serve me in life. Romantics live in their heads and don't take reality into account. I can't be a finance major and a romantic at the same time. I have to squelch my romantic notions because they do not serve my purpose, and if I'm going to find a purpose, that's a good place to start.

I have to remember the lesson of Jeremy's mother. She died devoted to a man who didn't seem to know she existed, much less that he might have a son out there. That doesn't add up. And Max may look at me with combustible eyes, but that might be only in my romantic thoughts, not reality.

And what about Chase? His truth can seem like God's Word to me, and yet, what would any right-minded guy be doing with Amber Richardson in a bedroom at a party?

64

kristin billerbeck

No good can come of that. That's reality. I'm not a romantic. I'm not.

That's not me. I'm good at math. I have to train the logical side of my brain in the emotional aspects of life.

Realities I don't want to face:

1. My best friend may be stealing my boyfriend.

2. Claire won't call Max my boyfriend.

3. She'll kiss him onstage, and she invited him over to practice this in front of me. (Cruel and unusual punishment.)

4. My best friend doesn't know the girl code. Or she doesn't adhere to it anyway.

5. Max was pretty readily stolen away.

6. Chase may have turned off the gas that night of the fire, but he isn't the hero I thought he was. No matter how sparkly his eyes are.

I know there's more, but breaking the girl code is what stands out to me. Wouldn't Claire have learned the girl code same as me? This is wrong on so many levels. You don't take a friend's boyfriend. Even if he wants to go, am I right?

And it seems Max could stray a little farther to leave me. Does he have to go virtually next door when he dumps me? Seems crass. It's betrayal. That's what it is: betrayal. I think my best friend may be toxic.

65

It's time to wake up and smell the java. I cannot read guys any better than I can read Hebrew. And quite frankly, Hebrew would be much easier to learn. There's an actual code at least. Look at my track record. Chase—who is less than heroic. And I saw him as an Air Force hero, come to swoop me out of my mundane life into his *Top Gun* world. Shot down.

Then there was Max, who I felt connected with me on an innermost-soul level. He knew how to dance with me and lead me. Now I think he just knows how to move women in general. He's an Argentine Don Juan and he's gone to use his pretty words on someone else. What if Claire tells me? Ugh. I won't be able to stand it. College cannot come quick enough.

So what I've learned besides the need to squelch romantic fantasies is that I have a definite character flaw: my heart is easily influenced by the simple act of quality eye-candy gazing. My heart is so easily influenced and taken away from me and—dare I say it—shallow. A few whispered words and scalding glances and I have no discernment whatsoever. God says to be as gentle as a dove but as wise as a serpent. I am currently showing all the intellect of a potted plant. Must crush this tendency.

Face it, Daisy, if Max had told you he was the future king of Buenos Aires, you would have believed him. You are void of discernment, and this must be your goal: crush all romanticist views. Find out what Jeremy's mother saw in Mr. Webber, and then avoid it under all circumstances.

I was falling in love with Max. I thought he'd really been enraptured by me, that we had a connection that went beyond physical attraction. I thought we spoke to one another without words, and now . . .

These feelings are true in my heart, but then they evaporate as quickly as gasoline spilled on the asphalt. The truth may be that there isn't anything special about me.

All things work for the good of those who love the Lord, right? I love the Lord, so something good has to come out of this pain of Max not speaking to me and suddenly moving in on Claire. I just wish I knew why. Without the reasons, how is there any closure? Isn't it natural to want some closure so I can move on?

Lord, I really need some purpose here. It all feels so perfectly pointless right now.

❧ 5 ❧

I come home to find my parents "rehearsing" for an appearance at the Toy Train Society. My dad, who is not a small man, is dressed up as a conductor, or an engineer. Whatever part he's playing, he's got a red scarf tied around his neck and striped overalls on his round, pudgy body. He looks like a striped Teletubbie. And it's not pretty. I pull my key out of the lock.

"That's just wrong, Dad. Have you no shame?"

He stomps his heel with his toes up, tips his thumbs into his pockets, and starts singing, "I've been working on the railroad all the livelong day." Just when I think it can't get any more painful, he takes the whistle from around his neck and blows an ear-piercing wail throughout the living room.

"In answer to your question, none," my mom says. "He has no shame whatsoever, but isn't he cute in his outfit?" She winks at my father.

"Ewww! Dad, the neighborhood dogs are barking. Give 'em a break. The visual is enough."

"Woo-woo! Chugga-chugga, chugga-chugga, woo-woo!"

"Please, Dad." I cover my ears. "My day's been bad enough. Please don't regale me with Barney show tunes. Show some compassion. I still have homework to do." I left the R-rated version of family dysfunction for this, the Barney version? At least Claire's family doesn't pretend to be healthy.

"Daisy," my mother says over her sewing project as she stops her needle midair. "Your father only does these things to bother you. Quit reacting to him." She shakes her head. "You two are terrible to each other."

"Au contraire," my father says. "If I can make Daisy laugh, I know I've won over the crowd. She has no humor in regard to me because she no longer thinks it's cute that I get to play for a living. How many fathers would get up in front of their daughter's entire high school and do a rap for the love of keeping kids off drugs?"

"A better question is, why couldn't anyone else's father do that instead of mine? Maybe someone who has a connection to Jay-Z?"

"Jay who?" my dad asks. "Don't you love it when she plays my mommy?" he asks my mother.

"I'll love it when she appreciates the joy in her father making a living by setting his own hours and using his creativity."

I soften and kiss my father on the cheek. "I've always appreciated that. Except the part where you come to my school. It was cool in first grade, but now . . ."

My father chuckles. "She's at that age, Molly. We embarrass her."

"Oh, we've always embarrassed her, Pierce. Give us some credit."

"Someday, when you're in corporate America and your head is so full of numbers it's ready to explode, you might long to wear a train engineer's costume to the office."

"Somehow I doubt that, but I reserve the right to change my mind."

My mom stabs her needle into her clown pincushion and sets it on the sofa arm. "Before you hole up in your room for the night with homework, your father and I have something we need to discuss with you."

"'Your father and I'? That doesn't sound good." I stare at her wide-eyed.

My mother's gotten so thin over the last few months, I barely recognize her as my mother. She's still wearing upholstery for clothing, so there's that, but she now has cheekbones and more structure to her face. She's looking more like Claire's mom. If she has a cocktail party (considering she doesn't drink), then I'll start to worry.

"Sure, Mom." I drop my backpack on the floor and check the chair before I sit down. My house isn't exactly safe for easy relaxation. My mother, God love her, starts one project before she cleans up another one, so our house tends to have no clear, flat surfaces. Sitting down or walking barefoot without checking first is done at your own peril.

"We need to talk to you about college." She has that "someone died" look, and my dad has cleared his recliner and sat down, so I know this isn't going to be about how my scholarship has been raised. Nor that my dad has viable employment outside of the train engineer. This is the conversation I've been dreading. But I will not be deterred, because my mom has the essence of Eeyore and maybe there's a bright spot in what she's going to tell me—somewhere. Anywhere.

I cross my hands on top of my knees and wait, but she's stalling and keeps looking at my dad. I pipe up to break the silence. "Only five months to go! Five months and I am a coed. What are you going to do with my room, Mom? Will it be your craft headquarters?" As if the whole house isn't my mother's craft headquarters. We are merely patrons in the Michaels store that is our home.

70

She pulls her brows down as she looks to my dad for some help. Now he's got nothing to say. I get up and sit behind my mom on the sofa.

"Well, honey . . ." She pats my wrist. When she treats me like a sick puppy, that is never a good sign. I look at my dad, who is staring at the floor. Lack of eye contact = not good. I brace myself for what I fear is worse news than my dad readying himself for "Thomas the Tank Engine: A Night with Sir Topham Hatt."

"This isn't about a Christian college again, is it? Because my heart is really set on Pepperdine, Mom. Their school of business is amazing and the partial scholarship is—"

"It's not about that."

I can breathe again.

"Mom, what is it? Is Dad all right?" I look at my father. "He hasn't had another stroke." There's a lump in my throat.

She sighs. "No, nothing like that." She laughs nervously. "Oh, I'm sorry, honey, it's nothing like that. We've just been looking at ways to pay for your college. Suze Orman says to take care of yourselves first, but we're not sure we agree with that."

Yes, I heard about Suze Orman's advice. Suze Orman should mind her own business!

"Which is good. Right?" I say. "Listen, I know that Pepperdine's first payment is due pretty soon to secure my space, and the timing isn't great, but I can use my money if funds are low right now. Is that it? Because all that money I've been saving for a car—well, a car isn't going to do me any good if I don't have a school to go to, so I think I'll make the first payment. Would that help? You know, just to make sure it's there on time and everything is in order. That way I'll have the best shot at a good roommate too."

"Your father and I have been talking about Pepperdine further, and we just aren't comfortable with taking on that kind of debt in this economy."

"You said it wasn't about that! You let me breathe, and now I can't breathe again!" I grab a paper bag off the floor and start inhaling deeply.

"Daisy, let me finish," my mom says. "I know you have a scholarship there, but we don't think it will be enough and we don't want you to be pulled out before your degree is received. We thought maybe the first two years you might think of going to school here. It would give us time to save all the money necessary and we'd send you without worry. We've prayed about it, and wouldn't that be better for all of us?"

I straighten my back. *They've prayed about it.* Like I said, I'm good at math. I knew the issues here all along because of my mom's fears, but living in denial was so much prettier. The view from that hilltop on Malibu's campus kept me going in my delusional, happy world. I nod while trying to force back tears.

"Daisy, we're sorry. But the school—the school is more expensive than Stanford, sweetheart," my dad says.

I nod again. "No, I know. You're right. I know you're right, but I still have to take some time to mourn. Get used to the idea that I was so close. You know?"

My mom looks like she's going to cry. "We know, baby."

"I told all my friends. I shouldn't have done that."

"There's no shame in honesty," my dad says.

"There's a little bit." I grip my forehead, processing that the one thing I was certain about, my purpose as a student, is gone now. "So what now? Who am I if I'm not a student?"

"You'll still be a student, of course, just not at Pepperdine. Not yet. Lots of kids are making this choice right now."

I nod yet again. "So I should accept one of the universities of California?"

My mom shakes her head.

"State?"

"Your mother and I think community college for your basic courses. That allows all of us to save up tuition fees, and you won't have ample debt when you graduate. We don't want to saddle you with that, sweetheart."

"No, I understand, Dad. But community college? I just never saw myself there. Even Amber Richardson is probably going to a four-year school. That is, if her daddy can give a big enough donation to make up for her grades."

"Now, Daisy, there's no need to covet what other people have. You're going to a four-year school as well. Just not yet. Be thankful you don't have to be at school with Amber any longer. That's been going on since we can remember. She's jealous, of course. You always knew that."

"Yeah, she's jealous." Only parents could think something so ridiculous. Amber, with her perfect, swingy hair, model figure, and expensive designer clothes bought by her senator father with his gold card. She's jealous of me.

"I wish I was that mature to be happy about Amber's leaving. Right now I hope her hair dye fries what brain cells she has left."

My mom gasps.

"I don't mean it, Mom. This is just raw, that's all. She's going to taunt me and tell me I never belonged in that school and community college only proves it."

"Well then, she's hardly worth impressing, is she?"

I exhale deeply. "I guess not."

"Daisy, we did have to use allotted college finances after

your visit to the hospital for that burn, so we've tapped out our savings. Insurance only covers so much of an ER visit."

Ack. Guilt. "I'm good at math. Just tell me what I'm working with, and maybe—"

"We know you're good at math, Daisy, but zero minus zero is still zero," Mom says. "Your father and I went to write out that check, and it just felt irresponsible when you could get a perfectly good education right here at West Valley College."

"Mom, I worked my tail off to get into the best universities. All my friends are going to Stanford and schools like that. Four years and no social life and for what? West Valley College?"

"Don't say it like that. It's a perfectly good school and you can transfer when your two years of general education are done. People come from all over the world to get educated here. It's nothing to be ashamed of."

But it sort of is. At least at St. James Academy it is.

"I know. You're right," I say. "Can I go to my room now?"

"Well, I know you're disappointed now, but you'll see, it will be great having you here. Grandma and Grandpa were very excited about it when we told them."

"Grandma and Grandpa?"

"That's the other thing we had to tell you. Your grandparents are moving in, and they're going to be paying us rent that we can put toward your tuition."

"Moving in where?" I look around at the massive piles of fabric and laundry and my parents dwarfed between them.

"Here, of course. They're having their kitchen remodeled and some repair work done. They were going to move into some corporate housing, but your father said not when we've got a perfectly good room here. And you know Grandpa, he wouldn't hear of paying nothing for their stay, so we told them we'd take that money if we could put it toward your education."

"But we don't have a perfectly good room here. We have my Pepto-Bismol pink room, but I inhabit that. Are you going to clean out your craft room?"

"That would take forever!" my mother says. "No, I thought I'd fix up the garage, and then it could be like having your own apartment right here. It will give you more independence and be just what our collegiate girl needs: a little more space. Grandma and Grandpa will bring their car, so you'll have the use of that too. I think it's going to be a win-win situation for all of us."

Great. The 1985 Buick. I can hardly wait. If that doesn't build my self-esteem, I'm not sure what will.

"I'm tired. I'm going to lie down." I try to keep the pout out of my voice, lest I get another sermon on gratitude.

"Daisy, this is not the end of the school of business at Pepperdine," my father says. "It's only two more years. Nothing to be ashamed of."

Unless all your friends are leaving for incredible schools. Then it's a tad shameful. Just a tad.

I nod once more. I can't bring myself to say anything or I will burst into what my mom calls an unnecessary display of emotions.

I stop listening now. I don't mean to sound ungrateful, but finances have been tight since my parents inhabited the world. They have what I call a poverty mentality. It wouldn't matter if they won the lottery tomorrow—they'd have a reason why we couldn't go to McDonald's for dinner, as if God is waiting outside their door to take it all away for their selfish greed. Yet at the same time, I know they're right about this. I know it in my heart and it hurts.

I had my escape route all planned. I was going to go to Pepperdine University in Malibu. Rich people, school of business, the beach—everything my life is not. It's not that I think money is the answer. I've seen enough of Gil's life to know that isn't the truth, but I wanted the chance to see what else was out there. I don't want to blame God every time something in my life doesn't go right and call it God's will.

My own will dies a bit. The scenario does sound fishy. My maternal grandfather is not a big fan of my father, and my grandmother cannot stand to be in my mother's mess (my grandparents' house is spotless). This is a nightmare waiting to happen, and I for one don't want to be here. When it comes to my family dysfunction, I've found escapism to be a perfectly acceptable alternative.

"Your grandparents are arriving April 7," Mom says. "We'll have the garage cleaned up and put a space heater out there. It will be very nice for you. You can paint the walls any color you like."

"I hope no one hits the garage door button when I'm dressing. That could be bad."

"This is going to be wonderful. Think of all the other people around the world who live in multigenerational homes."

"They're used to it. I think it only causes more homicides in the States. Look it up."

"Daisy Crispin! Your sense of humor is getting dark! Check your attitude," Mom says. "Until you fix that, you will never be content. Never."

When I'm content with a Pepto-Bismol pink room and stolen wireless from next door, I'm done. Stab me with a fork.

6

It's like I'm naked walking into St. James Academy. Well, more naked than I've felt for the last four years in my home-made clothes and backfiring Pontiac. And by naked I mean not dressed in anything one could conveniently buy at the mall. I don't want to meet anyone's eyes, and I pass through my morning in a haze.

Angie has been avoiding me for fear I will pawn off trings on her to sell, but I run after her until I catch up. "I see you, Angie."

"Daisy, I do wish you'd stop carrying those. You're like a suit peddling religion on a Saturday morning. People are avoiding you!"

"You're avoiding me! People are actually buying these things. I haven't taken them of my own accord once."

"Well, there's that. My dad would kill me if he knew I was selling things on campus—if it wasn't for some ministry or something."

"I only have these two boxes left." I raise them and she presses them down to my hips.

"Are you ever going to stop carrying out Claire's hare-brained schemes?"

"I earned 440 dollars doing this. To me, the humiliation-to-cash ratio was low. Much lower than the time she had me play Ding-Dong Ditch at Curt's house and his mom answered the door before I rang the bell, for instance."

"You know what they're doing with these, don't you?"

"I've seen some girls smash them to hold their colored hair extensions."

Angie takes the trings from me. "Sometimes it's hard to believe you're our best and brightest." She points to a large oak tree in the center of the courtyard, where trings are nailed into the trunk to spell, um, *unsavory* words.

"Well, that explains the rush this morning."

"Miss Crispin, may I have a word with you?" Mrs. Clater, the vice principal, is walking toward me, and she does not look happy. I push the trings toward Angie, but she shoves them back at me. I don't hold out my hands, and the contents spill on the concrete, spraying Mrs. Clater's black Mary Janes and landing in a glittery pile.

"Want to buy a tring?"

She gives an exasperated sigh. "Miss Crispin, while I admire your entrepreneurial spirit, I believe we have a problem." She turns toward the tree littered with vulgar tring graffiti. "It seems the tree is wearing more of your creations than the students are."

"Maybe we should have an art contest! We could provide corkboard and make it a lunchtime rally activity."

"What I'd like is for you to get that cleaned up before you return to class. I'll have the janitor meet you with some pliers. In the meantime"—she looks at her feet—"it seems you have cleanup right here."

I consider begging for a reprieve so I could do it after the bell rings, but Mrs. Clater is not exactly the grace sort. I bend down and start to pick up the smattering of novelty rings at her feet and notice Angie is long gone. I'll say one thing for my friends: self-protection is clearly their focus.

I'm now aware of the pointing fingers and giggles around me. I focus on the plastic boxes in my hand as I saunter to the now-defaced tree.

I am forever branded with the luck of Job. Though thankfully no one has died. Yet.

"What is going on with Claire?" Sarika's singsong accent greets me. She shakes her head. "What are you doing?"

"Sarika, I'm busy. Just because I've known Claire since kindergarten doesn't mean I have any insight into that psyche of hers." I turn and stare at Sarika, who still looks like she's twelve but acts like she's forty. She doesn't wear any makeup and often wears her dark black hair up in a ponytail or back with a childish headband, but she's not interested in any of the guys at our school, so it works for her.

"I tried to give her back her weird rings," Sarika says. "She left a box of them in my locker. She's carrying a briefcase! What are you doing?"

"The same thing I was doing the last time you asked. I'm cleaning up tring graffiti, what does it look like I'm doing? And I'm trying to prove I'm a good friend, even when Claire doesn't deserve it."

"That doesn't explain the briefcase."

I roll my eyes. "Of course it does. Entrepreneur is her current role of the week."

"You've got to go and talk to Claire. She's going after Amber's part in the school play and they're making my life a living nightmare. This morning Amber told Mr. Green I let her cheat off my homework."

"He believed her?"

"Well, no, but that only made things worse. I'm sure we're all in for it later."

"I can't tell Claire anything, Sarika. She's trying to star in this play opposite my Max, remember? What do I have to do with Claire's choices?"

"You're good at, you know, at manipulating her into changing her mind on stuff."

I take the pliers and grip a tring and pull it out of the tree. There's a mark in the bark, and I instinctively try to brush it away.

"You have to tell her to leave that part alone," Sarika says. "We only have a few more months of school. Can't she wait for her acting career without making our high school careers miserable?"

I pull another tring out of the tree. "I think the answer to that question is no. I've barely even seen her today." I turn and face Sarika, who is stone-faced. "Was she with Max when you saw her?"

Sarika stares at me for a moment, apparently wondering how she should answer, her big brown eyes blinking.

"It's all right, your face tells me the answer anyway."

Sarika doesn't respond to that. "Where should I leave these?" She holds up her plastic box of trings. "I told Claire my father won't let me sell things at school. It's like begging to him, and he left that life behind in India."

"You can give them to me. I'm used to begging." I take the plastic box and set it next to mine at the base of the tree.

"Oddly enough, students were starting to get into them. I guess the investment was small enough."

"You cannot write papers in them. We are students first, and I do not understand why Claire did not respect my wishes that I should not be selling them."

I laugh. "Really? You don't understand why Claire didn't listen? Does Claire ever listen?"

"Not really, but she makes me so mad! On top of my books, I had to carry that box around all morning because I didn't have time to go to my locker." Sarika pouts. "All these years we have put up with Claire's ways, but I'm really getting tired of it, Daisy. Really tired!" Sarika stamps her red ballet flat. "Enough is enough. My father already forbade me from hanging out with her off campus. I tried to stand up for her, but I don't have any excuses left. It's time she got a dose of her own medicine." Sarika bats her long, dark eyelashes. When she's allowed to flirt, she'll be more than competent at the skill. "Would you talk to her for me?"

"Me? Sarika, I'm currently holding two boxes of trings and spending my lunch hour pruning a tree. All while Claire walks around the school with my crush." I hold up my hands to show the remnants of the burn marks I still sport from the party where we set Claire's house on fire. "Do you think I have any credence with her?"

Sarika shrugs. "I guess not. I thought Chase was your crush. Max was only a momentary diversion. You two confuse me the way you can't keep boyfriends straight." The way Sarika says this, it's like a roller coaster of words. Her accent really comes to life with more syllables. "I thought Max was only convenient for prom since Chase let you down."

Did he ever. "Changing crushes once since kindergarten doesn't seem that fickle to me, Sarika."

She shrugs. "To date these boys is pointless."

"Perfectly. But considering the extent of my social calendar, it gives me something to do other than homework."

"After college, maybe your father can arrange your marriage." She says this as a joke, but Sarika is perfectly willing to allow her father and mother that right. She's seen arranged marriages work, and she believes in them. Which is all well and good if your father doesn't dress like a duck for work.

"What if I'm meant to be single my whole life? What if that's what high school is preparing me for? Independence and solitude, not a school of business and a career."

"You're seventeen, Daisy. Even in India, that is not considered cause for alarm." Sarika gazes at two freshman boys wrestling like kindergartners on the grass. "Is it so hard to believe your Prince Charming may not be here in this small pond? When you get to Pepperdine, things will look different."

"I'm not going to Pepperdine." I give her the details, and Sarika's look says it all. She knows what it means to me.

"We'll worry about Claire later. I have to get into cooking and make phyllo dough again. I forgot to add the butter. I browned it but then left the pan on the stove." She shakes her head. "I'm praying for you, Daisy. Don't let this get you down. It isn't you. Claire's acting incredibly selfish. Even for Claire."

As I look across the quad, I see Claire. She's in a group of popular kids—athletes—laughing and standing beside Max. I try not to let it phase me. I guess I just imagined prom night. I made it more than it was, that's all. Who's to say where daydreams end and reality begins?

Claire ignored all the obvious sources of conversation this morning, only to say to me, "Yeah, you're below your quota on tring sales. You need to get busy today. I know you do fine at your job, but when it comes to being proactive at sales, you suck. I really think you need to work on your confidence level. I have a future to think about. Not all of us have been admitted to a stellar school of business."

"Did you apply to any stellar school of business?" I asked.

She huffed, turned her back on me, and took off. *Yeah, I'm the snotty one.*

Even though I was ready to fling those boxes of trings, I wandered around campus and straightened my shoulders to sell. I told myself I'd rise above Claire's actions. I wouldn't abandon her when she needed me most, even if she couldn't admit her behavior was nuts.

"Trings!" I said in a barely audible voice, as though I was testing to make sure my voice was there. "Trings for sale!" I said slightly louder, while the kids in the hallways acted as if I were offering them a virus.

And now I sit in the center of school, plucking garbage armor off a tree.

"Daisy."

I look up from the grass into the blinding sun. Chase's outline takes shape against the light, and I blink a few times until he comes into view. Whatever my opinion may be of Chase, God certainly wrapped him in a pretty package.

"How'd you get stuck doing this?"

"I guess it's the girl with the lowest tuition payments."

"Daisy, really, how'd you get stuck doing it?"

"The kids have taken to maiming this tree with trings. I was the one holding the trings when Mrs. Clater was called, and because end-of-the-year donations are approaching, calling on Claire might prove costly."

"You don't mean that."

I exhale. "No, I don't. I'm just bitter today. Forgive me." I open up my plastic box. "Want to buy a Class of 2011 tring?" I say without inflection. "I can only sell them to you if you promise not to deface property with them."

He looks at the boxes of goodies like it's an infestation. "Not really." He lifts his shoulders. "Will you talk to me if I buy one? You're avoiding me."

I shrug. "I could be persuaded."

His eyes meet mine, those enchanting, deep eyes that make me believe anything that comes out of Chase's mouth. "For you, I'll buy one. Though I think I'll just hang it from my rearview mirror if you don't mind. I'm not really a jewelry kind of guy. How much are they?"

"Two dollars." I take one of the male versions out of the box while he riffles through his Velcro wallet and comes up with two bucks. He reaches out with the bills in his hand.

"Does this mean a truce?" he asks. "I miss you."

I shrug again. "I guess." It's not like I have any more friends to lose. As long as I keep my distance and do not allow myself to become emotionally overcome by Chase and his deep-set, mesmerizing, falsely sincere eyes and strong jawline, we're good.

"If there was one thing I could always count on at St. James, it was a big, Daisy Crispin smile. You almost seem like someone else lately. Who let the air out of your tires?"

I yank another tring out of the tree, and Chase starts to help me.

"I need to find a way to fund my college education. Right

84

now I only have the first payment, and that only lasts until the first day of school. It was due fifteen days ago, and if we don't pay within the next ten days, there's a penalty."

"What about your scholarship?" he asks. In typical rich boy format, he has no clue that a scholarship is a drop in the bucket in most cases.

"That's *with* the scholarship. I suppose I could make the second payment, but I have to buy books, pay rent. You know the drill." Actually, he doesn't. Chase, like most of the kids from St. James Academy, is rich and will never have to worry about paying a thing. He just smiles at Daddy and the credit card comes through. "It's probably going to be community college for me."

"That's rough. Financial aid?"

"I'll figure it out."

"I know you will. If there's anything I love about you, it's your tenacity. No one stands in your way when you want something. I wouldn't mess with you."

"We'll see about that."

"Daisy." He slides the tring onto his left ring finger and pinky, then his face contorts. "This is really uncomfortable." He looks at me and we both burst into laughter.

"No returns or exchanges." I grin.

He hands me a ten-dollar bill. "I'll take five more. I'll make my friends wear them. You're not the salesman type, and anything I can do to get you to Pepperdine I consider a privilege."

"I hate talking people into something they don't want. Will you really take five more?" I put my fingers on the bill and he lets go. I take out five more trings, which he takes and stuffs in his backpack.

He looks down at his feet and finally back up at me. I break my resolve and get pulled into his eyes. "Daisy, it kills me that you don't look at me like that anymore. I didn't do what you think I did, and it drives me nuts that you don't believe me. The cops believed me, but it was worse looking in your eyes and seeing you didn't believe me."

I remember myself and look down at the concrete. "It looked pretty bad, Chase. I saw you with a pill. I heard that you asked Max about roofies, and I saw you take Amber up to Claire's bedroom at the party that night. What would you think if you were me?"

I stand there waiting for his answer, which I almost can't bear to hear because I want him to lie to me. No, that's not true. I want my original version of Chase Doogle to be the truth, not some created fantasy in my head. It hurts me to think evil of him, even if it's true. I don't want to believe people I care about are capable of such things, which I suppose is why I put up with Claire. I'm a doormat. Maybe Dr. Phil will have me on his show, heal my deep woundedness, and fund my education. Weirder things have happened.

"I don't know what I'd think," Chase says.

"I want to live in my special, rose-colored world, where no one wants to control other people and we all share the planet equally." I giggle. "Yeah, I know. I sound like a Miss America speech."

Chase shakes his head while he stares at the ground. "I shouldn't have let you down. That's the worst of it. You always believed in me, and I broke that trust."

It's as though the school campus has gone quiet. I hear nothing but his breathing, because I'm waiting for him to convince me.

"I did have that pill with me. I did go up to the bedroom with Amber." He swipes his shoe against the ground. "I guess I would think the same thing as you, except it would be *you*. I'd like to think that I know you, Daisy Crispin, better than that. That you know *me* . . . my character, better than that, and you'd let a momentary lapse of judgment slip. I'd been listening to the guys and full of myself, but I couldn't have ever done such a thing. I shouldn't have gone up to the room at all, except the guys were ribbing me that I was too chicken. It clouded my judgment, but if I'm going to be a pilot, I can't let that happen again."

"Let's just move on, all right?"

"Maybe I was about to make a mistake —"

"You can stop convincing me now. That would be good."

"I didn't make the mistake. I got up there and I saw your face in the back of my head. The way you looked at me, for as long as I could remember, and that image of the way you looked at me. I wanted to be *that* guy. Amber was looking at me like she expected the very worst in me. I don't know. I'm not explaining it well."

Chase puts his hands on my shoulders and steps forward. I feel awkward and like I'm all limbs, while he seems the picture of assurance. He takes the tring boxes from me and sets them down on the ground beside his backpack.

"Daisy, I blew it."

"Let's forget it, all right?"

"I want to see that look in your eyes. For as long as I can remember when you looked at me, I felt like I was a hero, like I belonged at the Air Force Academy. I don't think you know what it's done to me to have you stop believing in me. Just look at me."

"Uh-huh," I say absently while silently counting the trings in the boxes at my feet.

Chase steps closer, and I hear myself swallow. With the tip of his thumb, he gently guides my head up toward his. It makes me feel so completely inadequate when I look into his gorgeous eyes and believe anything he tells me. My head is saying, *You know better, you know better*, but I sort of want to experience this—I've been waiting forever for Chase's attentions. Since kindergarten to be exact. Do I really care if he's pretending? Okay, I do, but if I pretend, then aren't we both just doing what Claire plans to do onstage with Max? Just playacting?

"I mean, look at Samson, what an idiot he was," I hear myself say. "Every time Delilah would tell him what he wanted to hear, he'd just say, 'Duh, okay, Delilah,' and he'd get taken in again."

"What?" Chase whispers, still in his romantic efforts. With all his good looks and winning charm, he is my Delilah. I wouldn't know the truth if it knocked me in the teeth, and what is any relationship that's based on a lie? Oh my gosh, I'm thinking like my mother now. *Just kiss me, Chase, before I overthink this.*

My eyes are closed as I repeat this mantra: *He's not that into you. He's not that into you.* My eyes snap open as I feel Chase's lips on my own. I blink wildly as I look at Chase.

"You kissed me," I say.

"I did."

I can't help but look around and see if anyone's noticed. I mean, where is everyone with the camera phones when Chase Doogle is kissing me? If I'm flat on my back in the gym, they're going to catch that for YouTube, but no, not this.

"Say something," he says. All those times I dreamed of this happening. I dreamed of Chase Doogle kissing me for

88

all to see, and right now I feel . . . nothing. It all happened too fast. I missed it!

"I'm not sure what to say," I stutter. "It wasn't all I expected it to be."

He kisses me again, pressing harder this time. I look around—still no witnesses. What the heck?

"I'm sincere. You know that, right?" He says this with all the sincerity of a politician, and this time I'm not fooled.

I'm about to nod when I see Max and Claire staring at the two of us. My stomach drops out from underneath me, and I feel my face flush hot. I want to explain. I've been waiting for that since kindergarten. I had to find out . . . It wasn't all that great, really. It was built on a fantasy I'd created. He's not even a good kisser! (Not that I'd know, but still.)

I straighten my shoulders. I owe them no explanation, but this moment feels like one more nail in the coffin. With no pallbearers. Max has a wounded-animal look on his face, and I steel myself against it—I will not feel guilty for his emotions when he never thought of mine.

"I need to get to college. High school is clearly not my cup of tea."

"Daisy?"

"I've got to go, Chase. We'll talk later." I drop the trings I've collected into the box and leave them for Claire to pick up—or not—but I'm done.

I walk past Claire and Max, and they both watch me like they're at a slow-motion tennis match.

March 11

Random fact: A kiss can contain up to 278 different colonies of bacteria, 95 percent of which aren't dangerous. But you know what that means—5 percent are, and what are the chances Chase brushed his teeth after lunch?

Chase Doogle kissed me today. How long have I dreamed of writing those words—Chase Doogle kissed me. Yet they fall flat, and I can't explain why. Maybe I'm just a discontented person. Fickle, perhaps? When I get what I want, I reject it?

It was out of left field. Never did I think a box of trings would bring us together. That I'd be straddling the boxes when the man of my kindergarten dreams kissed me. Heck, I didn't even know there was such a thing as a tring, so how could I have foretold this?

I thought there would be butterflies in my stomach and tingling in my toes, but all I can remember is wondering about being filmed and possibly going viral on YouTube. I think I missed the moment. I can't remember the actual kiss. I'm sure it was fantastic. Too bad it wasn't with Max.

Max. I wonder if he cared when he saw us. Was it only a sick fascination, or did his stomach turn with guilt over his great and terrible loss? I'm so hoping it's the latter.

❧ 7 ❧

TEXT MESSAGE FROM: Claire Webber

TO: Daisy Crispin

Purity ring off for burns and now kissing Chase
in quad? Tsk tsk. What would my mother say
about her perfect Daisy? Tryouts today, pray!

Pray? Is Claire really so clueless as to ask me to pray for her shot at kissing *my* Max onstage? It's not enough that she didn't care to pull out, though Amber made our lives disastrous in the hallways this week, calling attention to every detail of our sordid fashion faux pas.

When life goes terribly wrong, as it often does when your name sounds like a nutritious part of any breakfast, at least I can count on the sanctity of my job. The Bible says to be happy in your work. It is a gift from God, and I am happy at my work, if only because it gives me a place to go after school and I don't have to buy four-dollar coffees to be there. Not to mention I don't face more rejection from my fellow schoolmates—who leisurely suck on frappuccinos like they aren't liquid gold. Claire's text is making my fingers itch, and before I exit the city bus, I pull out my BlackBerry and punch out a text.

TEXT MESSAGE FROM: Daisy Crispin

TO: Claire Webber

Purity ring intact, as is purity. Conscience is good too. Haven't stolen anyone's boyfriend lately.

Entering numbers mindlessly into a computer, answering phone calls from angry bank tellers, listening to my boss's latest dating conquests—these are things I can count on, and today I need that. It's a foundation, a place to begin. Maybe it isn't my life's purpose, but for now it's good enough. At least it takes my mind off a singing and dancing Claire in Max's arms.

TEXT MESSAGE FROM: Claire Webber

TO: Daisy Crispin

Nice. He was never your boyfriend!

I take two buses to get to my job, which I got as part of a work-study program at school. It started out as the sort of brain-dead job that the world thinks high schoolers are capable of doing: simple filing, typing in orders they gave me to copy verbatim, and then, of course, getting my boss's coffee off the roach coach. It grew into a lot more responsibility as they saw I wasn't nearly as inept as they thought high school students were.

In those early days, the hardest part of my job was transferring buses to get there. I'd start reading my homework and forget about my stop. Now, however, I have blossomed into this office staple who helped the check printers get automated and computerized. I have some killer résumé keywords, and if I could convert a systematic success story into high school popularity, I'd be unstoppable. As if on cue, I get another text.

TEXT MESSAGE FROM: Claire Webber

TO: Daisy Crispin

Not that u care, but I'm a finalist. So is Amber. Would u rather she kiss Max? Jus sayin.

TEXT MESSAGE FROM: Daisy Crispin

TO: Claire Webber

Yes! It would serve you both right. Maybe he deserves Amber!

As I was saying, I even created an online program to centralize customers' orders and make their misprints as easy to fix as the press of a button. Work rocks. I'm ready to leave these immature acquaintances behind.

TEXT MESSAGE FROM: Claire Webber

TO: Daisy Crispin

So what flavor lip gloss does Max prefer?

"How was I ever friends with you?" I yell at my phone. "You are evil, Claire Webber!" I pull the trings out of my backpack and toss them under the seat before I exit the bus. "Claire should have claws like those lobsters. The way she deals with people, honestly!"

Some homeless guy gives me a strange look for talking to myself, but sometimes you have to vent, am I right? Although you really have to question your own sanity when homeless people look at you strangely.

I heave my backpack over my shoulder, still mumbling to myself, and stride into my office. "You are not going to believe this day!" I shout from the foyer. It's always fun to make an entrance, and since Lindy and Kat have been cooped up in the office all day, my pathetic world is even more interesting than their own.

No one answers me, and the Blend doesn't emanate from the speakers. In fact, it's elevator music. I pause in the hallway for a second and then peer around the foyer wall. I take a whiff of strong, old-lady perfume. The skin on the back of my neck prickles. I'm not big on change. Change that involves bad music is never good.

I peek around the false wall and find an old lady at Lindy's desk. She sounds like a New Yorker, and she has the phone up to her ear rather than one of the headsets we normally wear to answer the phones. She's speaking at a decibel level that drowns out the bad music for the moment.

"That's right, honey. You just send that to me here, and I'll have the plant make all the corrections. I'm so sorry about that. No, no, we don't have email, but we'll get that fixed up ASAP," she says in a way that takes an eternity to spit it out.

ASAP means fast, right?

I round the wall. "We do have email." I lift one of Lindy's cards from the desk and point to the email address. "Right here. Tell her—"

The older stranger bats her hand to shush me and rips the card from my hand. "Make all the corrections by pen, that's right. You have our address? That's right. Thank you for calling. Goodbye now." She slams down the phone and glares up at me. "Young lady, didn't your mother teach you not to interrupt a person when they're speaking on the telephone?" The way she says this, it makes me wonder if she was around for its invention.

"But we do have email, and it's much faster for the corrections. People don't like to wait for their checks, especially when they can go online and purchase them now."

The phone rings again, and she speaks as if she has all the time in the world. "These are bank customers." She shakes her head.

Have I mentioned that I hate to be treated like a dumb kid? Because it really annoys me.

While the phone continues to ring, my hand hovers over the handset and she presses the phone to let me know it's hers. "You're giving false information. We do have email. Is Lindy sick?" I look around the office. "This is a check-printing business. We don't have time to waste for snail mail. The banks want their customers' checks." I pause for a second, hoping we just have a bad temp service for the day. Maybe Kat and Lindy both have the flu. "Who are you?"

The woman, who looks like she belongs behind the DMV counter, smiles without baring her teeth. The lipstick-filled wrinkles around her mouth separate like the parched earth when it receives water. The phone stops ringing. "You must be Daisy. Your last check is here." She hands me an envelope and then begins filing papers in an old-fashioned, alphabetized collator.

"My last check? I don't understand. Am I going somewhere?"

"New management. They've cleaned house. You were in school, so this is the first we're able to talk to you. The new manager isn't here right now, but I doubted you want to wait for your check. So I took the liberty of passing on the envelope."

"It's not payday."

"There have been some changes."

"I see that. For one thing, it sounds like I'm in an elevator."

"They told me you were such a nice girl."

"I am a nice girl, but I'm confused."

"This is your last check."

I let this sink in a minute. "This check is to tell me I'm fired?"

"Oh, honey, you're too young to be fired. You're laid off. Fired makes you eligible for unemployment, and with your hours and the company's situation, that won't be an issue."

I start to panic. "Are Kat and Lindy gone too? They have families."

"I'm just the messenger, darling. You don't need to be angry with me. I'm sure there are lots of jobs out there for a talented girl such as yourself. You've got a healthy week of severance and a new path to forge."

"Why are the computers in the corner? The entire office has been computerized. You can correct checks without having any sort of hard copy. You just take down the information, look up the record in the computer, and generate a new order."

Again with the placating smile. She glances at the computers in a heap. "Apparently, the new management doesn't want to do business that way. They have their own system."

"Which is what, the new and daring Pony Express? Letting the entire staff go without warning? Where is Gil?" I press my palm on her desk.

"Gone too."

"What do you mean, gone? He owns the company."

"His father owns the company. Or he used to, before he sold it," she says. "Young lady, I really have business to attend to. Would you kindly be on your way and take your check with you. If you have further questions, call the number."

"Well." I try not to sound annoyed, as something tells me this would only excite my nemesis. "Where is Gil's father?" I say through clenched teeth.

She flattens her mouth and shakes the envelope at me. "Take this, young lady, and be on your way. It's none of your business where anyone is. You've been relieved of your duties, that's all I am legally required to tell you. Employment at Checks R Us is at will. You can be terminated at any time, for any reason."

I stand there, refusing to take the envelope while maintaining my patience. "I want to talk to Gil's father. I've worked here for nearly two years, and I don't even know you. He needs to understand how much more streamlined the company is, why it was succeeding!"

"Sweetheart, there are other jobs out there. Be on your way."

"How do I know you don't have the entire office locked up in the plant and this is a ploy of some sort?" I let my backpack slide to the floor and raise my eyes to the ceiling. *Listen, woman, I've been selling trings all day. Your threats have nothing on me—nothing, do you hear me?*

"Young lady, do you know who I am?"

Gassy old windbag with an attitude? I do wish I was more like my mother. "No, I don't know who you are! You can certainly understand my frustration when I come into work on a typical day, and nothing is as I left it on my previous workday. Surely you can identify."

She releases another one of her sighs, like a balloon let loose to fly across the room. "Young lady, I have work to do. Take your check and be on your way. There have been some changes made, and you'll learn how to accept failure. That's part of doing business."

"But I haven't failed at anything. I work here to make money for college. Do you know how much grief I've taken from bank tellers to eke out some savings? Lots of overtime, lots of extra projects, and I'm not your average high school worker. I've taken everything online. I've automated the accounting." My voice is rising, so I take a deep breath before I continue. "I'm sure that Gil would be very upset to hear I've been let go without warning. I'm very cost effective, and I just want to give the new owners a chance to evaluate my work before they unwittingly let me go."

I glance at the empty desks, where people like Lindy and Kat who support their families usually sit, and feel my teeth clench. Gil wouldn't have done this. He may use women like tissues, but in business, he's fair-minded and concerned about his staff. He gave Roberto, a plant worker, a week off with pay when his baby came early and there were complications.

The phone rings again, and with a voice as smooth as silk, the woman picks it up. "Checks R Us, this is Mrs. Packard speaking. How may I help you today?"

I tap my foot while she gives yet another customer the runaround and doesn't fix a single thing. She wraps up with a smooth tongue.

"You can fix their problems, you know. Is there a reason you're not fixing their issues?" I ask her. "That's your job as a customer service rep. Customer service. There's a record of every check printed on the computer. Type in the branch name and the customer number and you can see what we've printed. That way you'll know if it's our fault or theirs. I'm happy to show you—"

The woman pats her gray curl, which appears as though she hair-sprayed it with the curling iron barrel in place. "Daisy, I'm capable of handling this. I think you should be on your way. If I needed your help, obviously you'd still be employed. Must I call security?"

"We don't have any security," I tell her. I can't help the roll of my eyes. Like I said, I wish I were more like my mother. Nice by nature.

"Miss Crispin, it's really not my job to inform you of the company's current status. You've been let go, and the sooner you start to look for new opportunities, the better off you'll be. This is your last check. Please take it before I change my mind." She shakes the envelope again.

I cross my arms in front of me. "You're planning to take the place of three full-time people and me?" I tap my foot. "Without a computerized system?"

"Young lady, there is a letter of recommendation in that envelope, but if you keep up this obnoxious chatter, I will have to revoke the contents of that letter. And in this job market . . ." She purses her lips together and the red cracks of the Sahara reappear. "Now please leave."

I take the envelope, feeling like a traitor. I wrangle into my backpack and skulk out of the office, looking back at the glass doors in disbelief. I take the envelope and tear into it.

It is a check. I'm *so* fired.

❧ 8 ❧

"Daisy?" I hear my name called and use the back of my hand to wipe my cheek.

"I knew you'd be upset." Gil is standing in front of me, and he envelops me in a tight hug, which forces me to emit the sob I was holding inside my throat. Still, it feels good to be held—even by a player who just fired me, which tells you how low my standards are at the moment.

"I'm a jinx! You lost the company!" I say into his chest.

"No, no," he says while he pats my hair.

I look up at his striking face. "You've been eating In-N-Out again. You got into a fight with your dad?"

Gil's family has money, and his mother provides a family meal every night, even though he's twenty-four. Gil either goes out on a date or eats at home. When he smells like onions, I know he's doing neither. It's a sign of life gone wrong for him.

"It's just a small disagreement."

"No one's taking care of you. You smell like onions."

"It was just lunch. I'm fine. I waited for you to get here because I knew you'd be upset and worried about Kat and Lindy."

"And?"

100

"They're fine. They both have a month's severance, and if I get my new business up and running quickly, they'll both have jobs with me." Gil looks back at the office. The windbag is staring at us through the window. "Come on, I'll take you home."

"You don't have to have a date to treat yourself to a decent meal, Gil. You're worthy of a decent meal."

"Thank you, Dr. Crispin. I'll keep that in mind. Today I was just in a hurry to get here before you left."

"What's going on?"

He looks at me with his Josh Lucas gaze. Gil is a consummate womanizer, but to me he's like a big brother. It's like I'm immune to his charms. He wouldn't let anyone remotely like him come near me. He's been such a great sounding board when it comes to guys and my pathetic attempts at a social life.

"Get in the car, I can't discuss it here." He motions toward his Porsche, a college graduation gift from his father and, in my opinion, one more link that binds him to the chain of his father's control. He opens the passenger door for me, and I lower myself into the black leather bucket seat. He rounds the car and gets into the driver's seat.

"That woman in there is awful," I tell him. "Who is she?"

"My father's executive assistant." He grins. "I knew you'd hate her. That's why I love you, Daisy. You are an excellent judge of character."

"I don't hate her. I'm a Christian. We just have a difference in the way we see the world, that's all. Is she aware that phones have buttons now? And they don't need cords either!"

"I doubt it." Gil ducks his head. He's too tall for the Porsche, but that doesn't stop him from driving an impractical sports car. I suppose it wouldn't stop me either if I could afford it. He stares at the office forlornly. "Checks R Us was making money. Apparently, that wasn't the main objective. It was one of my father's tax write-off businesses, and he wanted me to start here and see what I could do. I passed, but my success meant his financial failure in this case. He sold the business before it looked too good on paper. He can still take a loss this year."

My cell beeps.

"You've got a text," Gil says.

"I know, but it's probably Claire. We're fighting."

"You're always fighting, but Claire's there for you."

"Not right now. She's competing with me. I think to make herself feel better. She feels abandoned since everyone is going off to college. Or so she thinks."

"What's that mean?"

"Never mind. Just more drama from my parents and money."

Gil's jaw is set. "Daisy, I told you. Go away no matter what. You can work when you're in school and just take longer to graduate."

"I can't, Gil. I can't afford Pepperdine. It's over. So let's talk about something else, can we?"

"So go somewhere else," he says casually.

"I am going somewhere else: West Valley."

"Community college? Daisy, no. If it were anyone else, I'd say fine, but you beat all those brilliant kids at that private school. You even played soccer part of the time. If anyone should go to a university, it's you. You're the one who will get the most out of it. You know where you're going."

"It's done, Gil." I can't help but feel like I've let him down. Gil saw me as his different future. A future that didn't answer to parents when their vision for the future was different. "I'm not different than you, Gil. My parents are convinced that I need more time at home to mature, and they've tightened the purse strings."

"What about Bible college? They wanted you to go there. Didn't you apply to any?"

"I did. I got into one, but there's no money for that either. I need to stay at home. It's a long, drawn-out tale."

"I think that's a worse idea than going away anywhere, Daisy. I know you love your parents, but I can't imagine you not going to college. Even waiting to go to college seems like a waste. But if you're going to be here, help me start my business and go back to college in a few years. I have a rock-solid idea. No one says you have to go to college in the fall. Get some experience in the business world with me, and start in a few years."

My mouth is wide open. "I—I—"

"Don't decide now, but think about it. Put away some money and you'll get to go wherever you want. Pepperdine can wait. Let me do some numbers, and I'll let you know what I can offer for a starting salary."

I feel like such an adult when I'm with Gil. He never talks down to me or thinks he needs to explain something like reinvestment of capital. I love that about him. He's one of the few people who trusts me implicitly and understands I'm worthy of that confidence.

"Gil." I shake my head. "It's over. I'm not going, but look, I'm not you." I shake the envelope. "This is just the tip of the iceberg. My parents don't have the money to own me the rest of their lives. I'm safe from that. Maybe I'll only be able to go to junior college, but I won't be under their roof forever."

He takes a deep breath. "Promise?"

I pat his dashboard. "It's hard to believe you think your life is so miserable, Gil."

He looks at the instrument panel and then back at me. "Freedom is everything, Daisy. When faced with being owned and rich or freedom, choose freedom. Right now"—he pats the dashboard too—"this is my freedom."

I laugh. "I doubt I'll have that choice, but if I ever do, duly noted."

He looks me in the eye. Another thing most adults don't do, but I can see he doesn't believe my life will turn out differently from his own.

"God's in charge, Gil. I'll be fine. Even at community college." But I don't mean it. Maybe I'll get there with prayer and petition, but right now I just want to go to college and have these last four years mean something.

Gil's deep-set eyes don't waver. "It's not community college, Daisy. It's giving up your dreams for someone else's." He rakes his hand through his coiffed hair. "Look, it's personal for me. Like watching myself all those years ago and wanting to scream, 'No, turn back!' I see so much potential in you, Daisy. I see you forgetting about all that to make other people happy. If you forget about yourself now, you'll think, 'Well, later it will be my turn,' but that's not the way it is."

"I'm a Christian. The Bible says to honor your parents, and I'll do that." But even as I say the words, I know in my heart I'll be crushed if I can't find the money for Pepperdine. Claire can squander her chances for college when her parents can send her anywhere she wants to go, but there aren't enough scholarships in the world for kids like me.

"Honor your parents, fine. Just don't ignore yourself. That's what I'm saying. You understand money. That's a gift."

"Money just emphasizes what you already are, so before I go racing in my own direction, I have to stop and listen for God's voice."

"Daisy!" he snaps at me. "You're giving up!"

"I'm not. I promise you. I'm selling trings to get the money for college. I'll have to find another job, of course, and it probably won't be Pepperdine, but that just means that dream wasn't meant to be. God will give me another one."

"Trings?"

"Don't ask." My phone rings, and I stare into my backpack guiltily. "Your BlackBerry." My heart sinks at the realization that I have to give it up. "Now I will officially be out of place at St. James. It was the one way I fit in to the elite world of my high school." The one thing I owned (borrowed) that didn't make me a complete freak or separate me out like the one cow with a different brand. Only an iPhone would have brought more prestige.

Gil stares at the phone. "It's paid for the next six months. You'll be off to college before you need to get your own plan. Take it. I would pay more to cancel the contract now."

"No, I can't do that." I pluck the pink BlackBerry from the side pocket of my backpack and feel my fingers clench tighter as I hold it out toward Gil.

"I'm not taking it, Daisy. It really is cheaper for me to finish out the contract. Look it up if you don't believe me."

"It's charity."

"So what? Know when to take charity. It will serve you well in this life if you can put your pride aside and take a gift when it's offered."

105

I grab the door handle and kiss Gil's cheek. "Thank you, Gil. You made a huge difference in my future, even if I don't get to the school of business."

"Thirty thousand dollars," he says.

"What?"

"Thirty thousand a year to start to help me with this business."

"Gil, I'm seventeen. Trust me, I'm not worth that kind of money and I can't get sidetracked. I have a plan."

I stare at my phone as it keeps buzzing. There's another text from Claire.

TEXT MESSAGE FROM: Claire Webber

TO: Daisy Crispin

Amber just missed her high note. Not going to be Maria. Principal banned West Side Story, but I'm the lead in whatever it is. WOOT!

"I hope it's *The Taming of the Shrew*!" I say to my phone. Gil roars his car to life and I push open the door.

"Daisy, don't be ridiculous. I'll drive you home."

I clutch the envelope. "I can stop by the bank—it's light now for a while."

"Do you have to argue about everything people try to do for you? What did I just tell you about knowing when to take a gift?"

"Gil, you're hard for me to say no to. And I don't want to just work. I want to go to college. You know how my parents don't see enough in me? I think maybe you see too much in me. I'm not nearly as bright as you give me credit for, and I'm not going to be responsible for you screwing

106

up this next venture." I step out of the car and he lowers the window.

"So don't say no. Say maybe. If we went public, you wouldn't ever have to go to college."

"No."

"Just get in, a ride at least. I hate putting you on that bus. I feel like it's child abuse."

"Is your ride worth the cost of my father nagging me about the old man in the Porsche who pays for my BlackBerry? I think not. He already finds you very shady."

"I'm shady all right, but not where you're concerned. Does he know that?"

"He does, but my dad thinks Brad Pitt would abandon Angelina if only he laid eyes on me. Well, my dad *would* think that if he had any idea who Brangelina was. Why can't I talk to anyone my own age like I can to you? Or Kat? Or Lindy? Or even Claire's brother. People over twenty don't make me nervous. I need to transfer that skill."

Gil laughs and pushes opens the door. His eyes are dead serious and laser-stuck on me. "I'll tell you again. You're an old soul, Daisy. That's what it is. I look at you and I forget that you're seventeen. It's easy to believe you're twice that age."

I nod. "It's being raised around all adults. I missed out on the fun gene. Or it could be that you're a toddler soul."

"The fun gene is overrated. I got your share and, I'm sure, more than double your share of trouble for it."

I get back into the car and sink into the black leather seat. I wonder if the fun gene is overrated or if I've been sold a bill of goods and I'm missing out on what matters in life.

"So, Daisy, how's that prom date of yours?"

"Practicing his singing and kissing skills on my best friend. Strike that—former best friend. At least that's what her text implies." I hold my BlackBerry up to him.

"It's her way of saying she won't miss you when you go to college. My high school girlfriend pulled that same crap on me when I left for college."

"So what did you do about it?"

"I said, 'See ya!'"

I groan.

Gil called me an old soul, and he's not the first person to do so. I'm like Benjamin Button—I'm going backward, only I'm going nowhere. I'm never leaving the nursing home.

"Gil?"

"Yes?"

"You've always said I'm an old soul, but answer me this— what does an old soul do in life?"

"They live to get out of high school and get on with life. You're going to do so much with your life, Daisy. Just bide your time. Only a few months left."

"Sure, if I had a chance to make myself known in high school. If I have a chance, what would I do?"

"You matter, Daisy. That's the problem in life. You never understand how much you matter until you're missing. My dad's about to learn that lesson." Gil pauses and stares at me, then he presses the gas pedal and I feel the g-force about to come. "You're not saying anything."

"What should I say?"

"Usually when I have anything remotely vengeful to say, you start talking quietly and preach at me like a Sunday school teacher."

I grin at Gil. "You never know how much you matter until

you're gone. Someday when you least expect it, my preaching will come back to you. May Jesus convict you."

He laughs and pulls out of the industrial parkway and onto the road toward my home. I'm glad my pain is so entertaining. Apparently, it serves a purpose.

"You want to matter?" Gil nods. "I've got you covered."

"Why does that scare me?"

He grins and keeps his eyes on the road.

My phone buzzes with another text, but I ignore it with ease. It's not until I get home that I see it's from Chase.

```
TEXT MESSAGE FROM: Chase Doogle
TO: Daisy Crispin
Re: Kiss. No regrets. You? Skype tonite?
Chase
```

No regrets, but I don't remember it either. My head was too full. I take the Scarlett approach—I'll think about that tomorrow. No way am I Skyping with red eyes and a bulbous nose anyway. Skyping is for girlfriends only. To tell you if your butt looks fat in something.

❧ 9 ❧

March 14
Two months of school left!

Random fact: The unemployment rate for my age is 19.9 percent. The odds are against me.

Without work, my life is incredibly empty. I'm seventeen. Work shouldn't even be a part of my vocabulary. I know, right? I've been doing homework on the bus for so long, I've almost forgotten how to make it work at a desk.

On a happy note, kissing onstage is a no-no for the political hotbed of emotion that is St. James, so regardless of what lead Claire has, chances are it won't include the opportunity to kiss Max publicly. Ugh. I never thought about her doing it privately! Even Claire would know better than that. Right?

Since I feel so empty without my job, I'm wondering if maybe Gil's offer was a hint to my true calling. Maybe

I've been too focused on the wrong thing again. So I'm giving it prayer.

I'm avoiding Chase since I don't know how to answer his kissing question and Max averts his eyes every time I come near him. Maybe my calling is to be a pariah.

All these years I would have jumped at the chance to have Chase text me. Now I act like an answer is an everlasting commitment to his heart. Maybe I only want what I can't have. I must test this theory, as it could lead me to many bad choices in my future. Including homemade clothes when I can afford to purchase my own.

As I exit my dad's car, I'm grateful that my mom and I are early so I don't have to explain my entrance to someone who has never seen me arrive before and gets that look of pity on their face. Seriously, our car looks like a homeless family lives in it. It's bad enough that it's two-toned and violet in most places, but my dad also keeps every receipt he's ever gotten on the dashboard, and they're mixed in with fabric samples and garbage. We are seriously white trash.

As I climb the stairs and get to the quad, groups of kids are in huddles, and several turn around and point at me. I look behind me, but to my disappointment no one is there. I face them again and look for a familiar face to ask. First I check my feet and see that I'm free of toilet paper trails. My clothes seem stain free and buttoned up and my shoes are tied.

Sarika and Angie come running toward me and move me out onto the grass without saying a word. I hear myself yell, "No!"

There's a car on the roof of the gym, a Volkswagen Bug.

It's painted baby blue with sprayed-on daisies in yellow, white, and green. My name is spelled out in green, next to a heart. Beside the car is a sheet with the words, "Jesus loves Daisy Crispin and so do I."

My eyes fall to the pavement, where I see Principal Walker striding toward me, and if I'm not mistaken, he's foaming at the mouth.

"Daisy Crispin! In my office, now!" he yells and turns on his heel.

I hear Sarika and Angie mumble words of support as I follow behind Mr. Walker at a safe distance. I turn around and shrug to let them both know I have no idea what's going on, or who might have done such a thing. My first thought is of Claire. She's standing by the office door and appears as angry as Mr. Walker.

Before I enter Mr. Walker's office, I text my mom. Will she answer? I have no idea, as she still doesn't quite understand the concept of text messaging or how it "just appears like that." I can only hope it's one of her good technology days.

> TEXT MESSAGE FROM: Daisy Crispin
> TO: Molly Crispin
> MOM, help me! I'm in big trouble, come back to school now! Daisy

Max is standing outside Mr. Walker's office, and it's the first time he's met my gaze in weeks. If I had to put words in his mouth, they might be something like, "Throw her to the lions." I stop next to him and open my mouth, but he walks away before I have a chance to say anything. *Just get over it, Daisy!*

112

I will never understand guys. Why can't he just speak?

Mr. Walker is sitting behind his large desk with his hands folded in front of him. He raises his brown knot of fingers to his chin. "Let's pray first. Otherwise I may not be able to hold in my feelings." He bows his head and I do the same. He continues. "Dear Lord, we know that as graduation approaches, spring fever takes over our wonderful Christian students here at St. James. We ask for you to bless my words, and for the students to be most grateful to you and their parents for providing them such a stellar education. Let us get to the bottom of this. In Jesus' name. Amen."

"Amen," I echo.

"Now, Daisy." Mr. Walker sits back in his chair but keeps his hands clasped on his desk. "You have been a star student since you came to St. James. Until this year, I never heard your name mentioned unless it was attached to some kind of educational award or scholarship potential. Suddenly you're having parties, burning down houses, selling trinkets on campus without a permit or permission, defacing school property with those trinkets, and now there's this. A prank that's going to cost the school—should I say, your parents—a lot of money to fix." He lowers his head and shakes it. "I'm at a loss, Daisy. At a loss. Is something going on at home that you want to tell me?"

I assume he means something besides my dad dressing like a pirate with a stuffed parrot on his shoulder.

"Well, I didn't do it, Mr. Walker, and I can honestly say that I don't know who did or why they would have my name attached to it. I was at home last night with my parents. The whole night. You can ask them if you don't believe me. Plus I think that car on the roof is worth more than our current

113

vehicle, so I wouldn't be wasting it on a rooftop. I would have driven it to school this morning."

"Stop talking for a minute. I'm not saying you did this, I'm merely saying that I want you to tell me who did do it. You haven't made the best choices in friends this year, and I'm sure you have an inkling as to who is behind this."

"I have the same friends. They just went through a senior year crisis." I think that's what they call it when your mom returns from Hawaii to find her house burned down and your dad brings home a secret son. It's *some* kind of crisis.

"How do you propose we get this car off the roof, Daisy?"

"I suppose we should ask the people who got it up there, only I don't know who did that."

"It was brought to my attention this morning that you were seen kissing Chase Doogle on the blacktop the other day. You are aware that public displays of affection are not tolerated on our campus—or off, for that matter—between two unmarried students. This is a college preparatory academy. It's not a dating service."

"No, sir."

"So do you think—and I want to make myself clear, do not protect him if you know the truth—do you think that Chase Doogle had anything to do with this car and love profession on the roof?"

"Seriously, Mr. Walker, the only guy besides my father who ever implied he loved me is not talking to me, and I'm certain he had nothing to do with this. Oh, and it's not Chase."

"What a complex life you do lead, Miss Crispin. Who, may I ask, implied he loved you?"

"Well, it was in the moment. You know, prom—he whisked me off into the tango and asked my dad for permission to

114

see me. I think we were both caught up in the romance of the moment."

"Lust can be a very powerful emotion. Stronger than love at times."

Ewww. Is there anything grosser than old people talking about lust?

"Yes, sir. But I wasn't really lusting. My dad was there."

He leans back and opens his desk drawer, pulling out a pen and pad of paper. "Why don't you give me the name of this boy? Does he attend St. James?"

"Uh . . ." I really want to lie. The pull is strong within me.

"Miss Crispin, does he attend St. James?"

"Yes, but like I said, he hasn't talked to me. It wasn't him." I lean into his desk and set my elbows down. "Do you really think that someone who loved me would do such a thing to get me in trouble? Or do you think it might be more someone who hates me and is trying to throw us off their trail?"

"I think you've been watching too much *CSI*. The name, please."

"Max Diaz," I grumble.

"Anyone else you can think of?"

"You should look into Amber Richardson. I heard she wasn't happy about Chase kissing me."

"No one should be happy about public displays like that on a Christian campus."

"No, sir."

Even if Amber could think of something that creative, she is void of the ability to pull it off. Still, I can't help offering my "tip." Maybe they'll find out some of the real garbage she's done to the rest of us, though her senator father will just write another check to the school if they dig something up. Some parents don't believe in consequences for their kids—and the results show. Some, like me, get the consequences anyway.

"I want you to get back to class while we investigate this," Mr. Walker says.

I stand up.

"Just a minute. Miss Crispin, it seems you've been let go from your place of employment."

I nod.

"Mr. Cervantes in the business center has let me know you'll need to take another course for the remainder of the semester to graduate. You won't be getting job credits without employment."

"I'm looking for another job!"

"Be that as it may, I think you need to run some of this extra energy off. Coach Hemper has agreed to let you rejoin the soccer team, and starting sixth period today, you can attend practice."

"But my mom is expecting me—"

"I'll be calling your parents this morning, Daisy. Leave it all to me. Ms. Hemper has extra cleats she can lend you for today. Now get to class."

"It's just . . . how will I find a job after school if I'm at soccer?"

"Someone you know is clearly very ingenious. Maybe you can ask him."

My quest for love and purpose has only driven them both farther from my grasp. Maybe I should aim for something attainable, like world peace.

I exit the office sans help. No doubt my mother will get her text message sometime next week. I should have called her. Technology and my mother do not mesh.

116

"Daisy?" Max is walking alongside me, and now I feel guilty for turning him in.

"Hi, Max!" I say with too much eagerness. I sound like a dog panting for water.

"So who did that?"

"Put the car on the roof? I have no idea, but Mr. Walker doesn't believe me. Contrary to what the sign says, it can't be someone who thinks very highly of me."

"I do." He lowers his dark brown eyes, and my stomach does a twirl. "Think highly of you, I mean."

"You do?" I stop walking and face him. "Really?"

"Maybe we could talk sometime, Daisy."

I nod readily. "I'd like that, Max."

"Catch you later." He takes off the other direction, and I walk out of the hall into the blinding sunshine. Unfortunately, it doesn't blind me from the students who are in between classes and pointing at the car on the roof. Thank goodness no one knows who I am, except for being the girl at the fire—and this goes along with that. Maybe anonymity wasn't such a bad thing after all.

❧ 10 ❦

This is the longest week of my life. Okay, the longest three weeks of my life. I've never been pointed at so much, and have I mentioned having homemade clothing for most of my existence here? Coach Hemper, a steely woman with rough skin and balding, flyaway hair à la Einstein, loves to inflict punishment in the athletic form. I'm sure she sprang cartwheels when she heard Mr. Walker had given her free rein over my afternoons.

The soccer team needs bolstering. Apparently, their midfield needed some shoring up. Sort of like my social life and college funding. Only this promises to be more painful.

My legs are so tired, they're shaking as I try to stand on them. I have to sit down to remove my cleats, and I wish I had my anatomy test today, because I could easily pick out any muscle group. They all hurt.

I'd forgotten how loud the locker room can be, and I jump when my name is belted out. "Crispin!" Coach Hemper shouts, and my name echoes. The rest of the girls quiet, hoping to escape her wrath.

"Yeah, Coach?"

"Take those cleats off for now. You're wanted in the business office." Coach Hemper stands in front of me and points while she speaks. "I want your head in the game. Soccer's a game of wits, and I want to see yours in the game. I took you on, but I never promised Walker I'd play you. I will, however, run you until you don't have time to think about boys or pranks or anything beyond putting one sorry foot in front of the other. You got it?"

I nod. "I—"

She holds up her palm. "'Yes, Coach' will suffice."

"Yes, Coach."

"I don't want your excuses, just want you to know where I stand." I start to speak, but she shushes me again. "Go see Mr. Cervantes." She acts disgusted with me, but I don't know that my head is in any game at the moment. I haven't played anything. The team surrounds me to find out what's going on, but I shrug. I have no clue.

I cross the bright-green Astroturf soccer field and swing by the business building. Unlike in a public school, our business classrooms are equipped with brand-new Macs, gleaming in their silver glory. We get taught by visiting moguls from some of the largest high-tech companies in Silicon Valley. The sight of it reminds me all is not lost. There are opportunities out there . . .

"Miss Crispin, still looking for work?" Mr. Cervantes meets me at the HELP WANTED bulletin board. He has a stack of three-by-five cards in his hands.

"I heard you wanted to see me. Are those new jobs?"

"They're all beneath you, Daisy. People looking for cashiers and the like. Coach Hemper tells me you're not the athlete you once were."

I think I'm offended. "She's tough."

"I've been talking to our visiting businessmen about you, Daisy. They're all interested in your graph and computer skills, but right now all of their internships are nonpaying, so I'm trying to get them to see that not all of our students are from wealthy families."

I don't know why this innocent comment shames me, but I nod compliantly to avoid bursting into tears.

"Something will come up," he says, patting me roughly on the back. "Go practice before you become a statistic." He grins. "A workaholic in Silicon Valley."

I start to walk back to the field halfheartedly when Mr. Cervantes's voice calls behind me. "Daisy!" He's breathless by the time he reaches me, his wrinkled face is red, and he takes a minute. He waves a card at me. "This just came through. I didn't know if it was going to, but it's perfect for you."

"What is it?"

"A graduate student at Santa Clara. He needs a clerk to organize case files and create a database for all correspondence. I told him I had the perfect candidate, but you'll never guess . . ."

He hands me the card and I read the name on the page: Jeremy Winters.

"This—this is Claire's half brother."

Mr. Cervantes nods. "He personally asked for you, but he had to get approval for your salary. I just called him and it's been approved, so he's free to hire. Claire told him you needed a job."

"Claire Webber told him?" I ask. "Is the job feeding me to the lions? Claire's mad at me."

"But she knows you're good at what you do, apparently. Friends fight sometimes. That doesn't mean—"

"I don't know, Mr. Cervantes. There's a lot of water under that bridge."

"Then row quickly. Otherwise your work-study program is pulled and Coach Hemper is going to see how many calories she can pull out of you in an hour." Mr. Cervantes raises his brow.

"Yes, I get it, I'm skinny enough."

"Quit looking for excuses. Go! Listen, in business, you can worry about everyone's feelings or you can get on with it. I advise you to get on with it. You want to pay for college, don't you?"

"Mr. Cervantes?" I hold the card up. "Thank you for this."

"Do St. James proud, that's all I ever ask." He walks back into the business center. I take out my phone before I lose my nerve.

TEXT MESSAGE FROM: Daisy Crispin
TO: Claire Webber
You r talking to Jeremy? Thx for job rec. D

He's going to be a lawyer. Like his father. I'm torn between wanting to know this Jeremy Winters and what makes him tick. What made his mother silence her feelings all those years ago? What made her give up the secret before her death? And what does he possibly think he can get out of me?

I cross the soccer field, wave off Coach Hemper's dirty look, and head back into the locker room, where I pull my BlackBerry out of my backpack and dial Jeremy's number.

He picks up on the first ring. "Jeremy Winters."

"Jeremy, it's Daisy Crispin. I don't know if you remember me, but—"

"I remember you. Didn't you talk to Mr. Cervantes? You're Claire's best friend. Claire told me you were looking for work."

"Claire did? You're talking to her?" I feel out of the loop. Having someone tell me what Claire is doing makes me feel that much more alone.

"Well, we stay to the safe topics of conversation. That's how your unemployment status came up."

"Do you really *need* a clerk? Or is this a made-up job?"

"I need a lot more than that. This law office is going automated, and between that and my caseload, I can't handle all the documentation. Claire told me you'd done that at your last job, and I thought we could talk to you here at the office."

"She told you that?" Seriously, I hadn't known Claire ever knew what I did. I thought she assumed I was just avoiding the group at Starbucks to not have to buy four-dollar coffees.

"I tried to friend you on Facebook, but you ignored me."

"It's complicated," I tell him. "My parents—"

"No need to explain, I'm just telling you why I called the school. So, how about it, can you come in Monday for an interview?"

"I can come in any day. Just give me the address. So you're talking to your dad then?" I venture.

"Mostly to Claire. How's things going with your boyfriend?"

"You might want to ask Claire about that."

"I get it. Be here Monday with a résumé at four o'clock. The address should be on that card with my number."

"Got it."

"You'll meet with the hiring team and, of course, me. It

doesn't pay well, but it will look awesome on your résumé and the hours are flexible. Gotta run." *Click.*

I miss Gil. I want men in my life who know how to get what they want, who aren't afraid to stand up for what they believe in, even if it makes them unpopular. I wish I knew if either Chase or Max was that kind of guy. But right now, they both seem like luminous wimps to me. Which makes looking forward to college all the more important to me. Somehow I hope everything will be different there, that my life will change with a new venue.

I know in a way it's pathetic to think that there's a Prince Charming out there, waiting to steal me away on his white horse. I have no reason other than romantic delusions to believe such tripe.

The car was on the roof for more than a week, reminding me that my own mother didn't even come to rescue me, so what makes me think there's a guy out there willing to do it?

"You joined the soccer team again."

Max Diaz, in all his Argentine glory, is before me. My heart starts to pound at the sight of his dark chocolate eyes and their unending depth. My breathing is shallow, so I nod.

My heart is full of questions. *Why did you stop talking to me? Are you and Claire dating? Did you know you broke my heart? Does this conversation mean you're willing to be my friend? Or do you need closure too? Is that what you meant by asking if we could talk? Just random "how are you" kind of chatter?*

"I heard about your job. I was sorry to find out about your company."

I still can't form words. He watches me for a while and then speaks.

123

"You're seeing Chase Doogle." It's a statement more than a question.

I shake my head. "No."

"But you were kissing him in the quad. Before rehearsals. Claire and I saw you."

"He kissed me." I can tell the difference means nothing to him.

"It didn't look one-sided."

"He caught me off guard. He'd just bought some trings and—" I stop myself. "Why do you care? You made it pretty clear to me that we were finished."

"I don't care." He shrugs. "I was simply making mention of it since you weren't allowed to go to prom, then your dad let you, and then—well, now you're letting Chase kiss you in the quad. A long way to fall, don't you think?"

"Fall? You're assuming a lot, don't you think? For someone who's now dating my best friend?"

"I'm not dating Claire!"

"I guess I confused spending every waking moment with her and kissing her in the school play with dating. My bad."

"Are you jealous?" he asks in that tone that tells me he knows I am. Which ticks me off.

I flip my hair—well, that was my intention, but I end up with a mouthful of hair, so smooth was not the outcome. "Why should I be? You've made your feelings known. I'm not desperate." It comes out more like *desphrat* because I still have hair in my mouth.

He gives the slightest hint of a smile, and it reminds me how much lurks beneath the surface of Max Diaz.

"Have I made my feelings known? I don't remember having that conversation."

124

"Or any conversation, right? Haven't we had this discussion by you ignoring me in Chemistry, as though I never existed? You're not trying to send me a message?"

"You should know me better than that."

"Should I? What about that weird night at Claire's house?"

"I'm in the school play because I needed an arts credit on my transcript. Claire approached me because she thought I could dance. Although I'm not dancing now. I'm playing a crazy man. The play was an answer to prayer, so I don't have to go to summer school."

"So you're hanging out with Claire at lunch so you can rehearse your lines together?"

"You *are* jealous."

"Well, yeah. I've lost my best friend to you."

He frowns. "Ah." He nods his head. "That's what you meant."

"At least I didn't use you to get to her."

"Wait a minute, what?"

"I'm glad our tango was so effective at getting what you wanted all along. I should have known when I saw you two in the mall at work. It was Claire you wanted. That's why you came to her party, that's why you showed up at prom."

"Is it?" His eyes laser into me, and I'm not sure of anything. "If I remember correctly, it was you who decided maybe Bible college wouldn't be the end of the world. Maybe you were as caught up in the romance of the moment as I was. A diversion."

"Meaning what?"

"You stood on Claire's porch and told me all about the great Chase Doogle in all his fake military glory. Well, you got your hero. I'm glad I could be of service in making your dreams a reality." When Max is angry, his accent comes out in full and I can barely understand him. And the fact that he's angry mystifies me.

"I don't understand."

"I went out of my comfort zone. I disobeyed my father to go to the prom instead of work. I did that all for you, only to find out your feelings for Chase haven't changed. Not even when I pointed out that he'd gotten ahold of drugs to ply his date at your party. You still threw me under the bus. I didn't think you had it in you, Daisy. Maybe you don't see yourself as you really appear, did you ever think of that? That it's you?"

"I'm confused, Max. It's *you*. You didn't talk to me. I tried to find out what happened after the dance, and you disappeared from my life. Then, at school, it was as though you'd never seen me before. I—"

"This isn't about my hurt pride, Daisy. This is about you, a beautiful girl who wears her heart on her sleeve, and it's going to get broken again and again by the likes of that player, Chase."

"Do you care if that happens?" I ask.

"I'm a guy, Daisy, and I know how guys like Chase think. I'll leave it at that." His eyes meet mine and I feel their wrath, but also their concern.

He strides away from me, his long legs in dark jeans, leaving me more befuddled than ever.

"So what? You care because, like my father, you have my best interests at heart?"

"Ask your father about why. I think that's best."

"Wait a minute, what does my father have to do with this?" Lord help me, I want it to be my father's fault. I want Max to feel what he felt for me at prom. What I thought I felt for

126

him. If my father put a stop to it, wouldn't that be easier to live with than actual rejection?

Max's strides lengthen and he ignores my question. Yeah, that's more like my reality.

"It's not me, right?" I ask the sky. "I am the sane one, right? Is that my lesson? To walk away from the crazies in life?" Maybe hanging out with Claire has infiltrated my brain. I'm so used to the drama, maybe I've become addicted to those brief moments where I get to avoid who I really am.

I absolutely have to get out of high school so I can thrive in this world and get addicted to good things. Like Jesus.

❧ 11 ❧

"I think I've become a bit of a drama queen," I tell Angie on my laptop through Skype, one of the greatest inventions in the known world, thank you very much. "Could I have missed Max's meaning?"

"He was rude to you, wasn't he? Then he shows up at Claire's and barely glances at you?"

"Thanks, Angie, you always know how to make me feel better."

"What? He dumped you hard. Don't let him turn it around on you now that he sees Chase is interested."

"Yeah."

"Do you like this eye shadow?" She leans into her webcam and blinks.

"It's purple."

"Yeah, do you like it? I learned how to do it on YouTube."

"I guess. I'm not used to seeing you in makeup."

"The guy at MAC said lilac goes with all skin tones."

"Well, he would know, I guess."

Angie brushes on eyeliner in front of her mirror while she

gives me what's left of her attention. "You're not a drama queen, but maybe with Claire out of your life, you're subconsciously craving more excitement."

"I wonder if my dad knows what Max is talking about."

She stops glamorizing and looks at the camera. "If he did, would he tell you?"

"Probably not, unless it involved me going to a convent."

"After professions of love on the roof of the school, maybe your dad has the right idea." Angie dabs on lip gloss. "So I totally think you have a secret admirer. That, or maybe Chase wants you to know he really isn't the dark, twisted soul you accused him of being."

"Are you coming to youth group this weekend?"

Angie tries on a toxic-green eye shadow over the purple. "What do you think of this?"

"You look diseased."

She wipes off the green. "No, I can't go to youth group. My parents have a date night. I have to watch my little sister." She brushes the emerald green on again. "It's supposed to be dramatic."

"Where are you going to wear dramatic?"

"I'm practicing for college. The guys in Boston won't know I've never had a date. Maybe they come from New York and they're used to a more sophisticated type of girl. I have to be ready for it. Just in case."

"But you won't have time to date them."

"True, but maybe there will be someone cute in my dorm. I want to be prepared. I'm just keeping my options open. It would be fun to study with some cute premed student, wouldn't it? Maybe just have someone worship me from afar. I'm not against that."

"Of course you're not." I think about my future in community college and let out a whimper.

"Something will happen, Daisy. Just keep praying. God has your future all laid out for you."

"What a coincidence, so do my parents."

"I think you should highlight your hair. You know, with blonde, chunky highlights. That would give you a new perspective."

"Angie, since when did you become all into beauty regimens? Is there someone we should know about?"

"Just from this angle on Skype, you look kind of washed out. You didn't Skype with Max, did you?"

I pat my hair down. "I did. Do you think he noticed?"

She shrugs. "You never know. I learned that Skyping is a controlled environment. You can get the lighting right, make your eyes pop, outline your lips. That little webcam is way forgiving. It's like having a special mirror, really."

"Who are you Skyping with?"

"Just lots of people, and I noticed when I have makeup on, the guys I help with calculus are just more interested in the math." She leans in so that her dark brown eyes are enormous on my screen. "See the illusions you can create?"

"You look like a goldfish."

She pulls back. "Okay, maybe that was too close, but you can see what you look like in that little box."

"I'm through worrying about image," I tell her. "For the rest of the year, I'm going to play up my assets. My real assets, as in working hard and making the most of my educational prowess. I'm afraid I haven't got much else to go on at the moment."

"I'm telling you, blonde, chunky highlights."

130

As told to me by a girl who has mermaid scales on her eyes.

"Blonde highlights aren't going to salvage my reputation with Max."

"Max? You mean Chase. I mean, you were into Chase all those years and then Max comes along and takes you to the prom. You totally wanted to go, so you feel indebted to him."

"Yeah, that's it. I feel indebted to Max."

"But you shouldn't because you are totally awesome and he was lucky to get to tango with you."

"Yeah!"

"If I ever have a boyfriend," Angie says, "I'm not obsessing about him. It wastes too much energy."

"It does. Especially when guys never seem to waste any emotion on us at all." I sigh. "Guys!"

"I know, right? My mom's bellowing at me for dinner. See ya tomorrow."

"Yeah, I gotta get home. I'm at the coffee shop," I tell her.

I press the camera off, thinking how nice it is to actually talk to someone instead of simply text. Sometimes you miss inflection and empathy. Empathy you might totally need at the moment.

I pack up my stuff and run to the bus stop with just enough time to step onto #54. I scan my bus pass and look for a seat beside someone normal. I find a free seat, slide in, and hold my backpack on my lap like a security blanket.

Some guy with a pockmarked face and greasy hair gets on. He flips his hair as he puts coins in and stares right at me. I actually consider talking to myself at this point, but it's too late. He comes and sits right beside me.

"Hey, how ya doin'?"

I half smile without an answer.

There are a million free seats, but no, I have to be the weirdo magnet. I unzip my backpack and take out my journal rather than endure what would probably be a drug-fueled conversation. I scribble the date and act very important and busy.

April 8

> Maybe finding my true calling starts by naming what I know it is not.
>
> 1. Clearly, I am not cut out for the elite education route, as finances and acceptance letters do not line up. So scratch thoughts of cashmere sweater sets and a plaid-wearing boyfriend taking my books to class. This is not my future.
>
> 2. I am not girlfriend material. Considering I have not been one, the chances of my luck with guys changing at college are extremely slim. If you were to look at the graph of my magnificent failure in this arena, you would see a downward trajectory. Statistically speaking, the gravitational force field will continue to apply here. Since I'm no one's girlfriend, I will probably be no one's wife, and therefore my future as a homemaker is circumspect at best.
>
> 3. Although humiliating myself comes naturally, I have no talent for doing it publicly at the right time. Therefore, my future in the family business of acting and public speaking will not happen. Besides that, the idea of

132

dressing like a chicken in middle age makes me want to vomit my lunch.

I peruse my list and try to hide these words from my heavily breathing neighbor, and Jeremy's name and number fall out of my binder.

Maybe I'm supposed to be a lawyer. Maybe this job has been brought down from heaven to give me a sign. Although I'm kind of a dorrmat, so I guess being a trial lawyer is out. I guess I'll need further study, God.

"You spelled doormat wrong," my seatmate says.

Just what the world needs, a homeless editor.

"Thanks." I slam my notebook shut and exit the bus. I'm a stop early, but close enough. I sprint home as fast as my weakened soccer legs will take me, but I'm thinking about the chunky, blonde highlights as I run. Maybe if I had highlights, it would instill confidence, and maybe that would scare the hobos from my life.

I'm out of breath when I get home. I slide my key into the lock, but before I can turn it, my dad yanks open the door. "Daisy!" he bellows.

I clutch at my pounding heart. "You scared me, Dad!"

He pulls me into a giant bear hug. "Welcome home, dolly!"

"First the bus and now this? Do I have like six weeks to live or something?"

"Ha-ha, you're such a joker. Get in here, your mom's got dinner cooking. Low-salt, tasteless chicken. Hmmm. Good for us, with no trans fat or flavor."

"Pierce!" my mother shouts. "Cut that out. It's good for your heart. Hi, Daisy." My mom comes over and kisses my cheek.

"Are we on a sitcom or something? What's with all the fantastic greetings?"

"Your dad's right. You're so funny," my mom says. She wipes her hands on her apron, a self-made project that has a bulbous red heart in the proper place and iron-on letters that read, "From Mom's heart to yours."

"Nice apron, Mom."

"I just finished it today."

"I like the heart," my dad says. He pinches it then kisses her.

"Eww! No PDA in front of the children. It's a rule!"

Then I notice my grandmother and grandfather sitting on the couch. They both smile at me and stand up. "We've been waiting for you," Grandma says.

"We thought you'd never get here!"

Ah, that's it.

I stare back at my mom and dad. "No PDA in front of the parents either. Do you have no shame?" I face my grandparents again and grin. "Hi, Grandma. Hi, Grandpa. Sorry you had to see that."

I walk toward them into our small living room, which is now overpowered by dark, wood furniture shoved up against the walls. If we had rafters, the furniture would reach them. As it is, they only reach the popcorn ceiling. My mother's fabrics drape off of Grandma's dining room table. The house almost looks normal, even with the furniture resembling an Ethan Allen showroom, and the house is cleaner than usual. Like a real family lives here and we're not a retail outlet. Well, not a crafting retail outlet anyway.

"Hey, kiddo!" My grandfather slaps his knees and bends over—although I'm taller than him now—as his signal to me to run toward him. "Come and give Grandpa a kiss!"

I drop my backpack and comply. Grandpa envelops me in one of his painful hugs while I try to talk with my cheek scrunched up. "Hi, Mmpa."

He releases me. "Say hello to Grandma. You're such a stranger we barely recognized you. Don't have time for your old grandparents anymore, huh?"

"Hi, Grandma." I bend over and kiss her cheek.

"You're never here when we come by anymore. Too busy of a social schedule now that you're in high school, is that it? Too busy for us? You'd think we lived a hundred miles away instead of ten."

"No, Grandma. I'm working all the time. Well, not now. Now I'm doing soccer, hopefully not for long, but I'm home for dinner, so that's different."

"Well, it doesn't matter. Now we're here to stay. We'll certainly be up to see you off in the morning."

Suddenly the appearance of their furniture in the living room clicks. "You're here to stay? I thought that was—"

"It was supposed to be tomorrow. We didn't get a chance to tell you that Grandpa and Grandma arranged to have their stuff moved a little early," my mom says. "Which means we finished your room today while the movers brought in the furniture, and Grandpa paid them extra to take your stuff into the garage."

"Oh. That's great. Wait a minute, did you move all my stuff?" Everyone is staring at me, so I temper any response I might have.

"We moved all of it," my dad chirps. "We didn't want you

to have to worry about it with that load of homework they give you."

Thank goodness I took my journal with me. It's much better to have a spelling-bee-champion hobo looking at it than my parents.

"I'm so excited for you to see your room," my mom says. "Mom, we've kept Daisy out of there so it would be a surprise for her. You know how she likes to control everything."

My mom leads me through the house to the garage, and my nightmare—I mean, new bedroom—comes into view. The garage is cleared to the right side, or passenger's side, as you might call it. To the left, or the driver's side, are all of my mother's crafts on industrial steel shelves beside the household goods and Costco stash.

My bed droops forlornly in the corner underneath my dad's tool bench, which is only partially cleaned off. Okay, it's clean by my mom's standards, so I should not complain. She is very clean—it's clutter she struggles against.

"I'm sleeping under the hammers? Is that safe?" I wiggle the shelving units. "Are these earthquake-secured against the wall?"

"We'll have that all taken care of soon."

"So I just have to hope the big one doesn't hit tonight, is that it?"

"I know it doesn't look good now," my mom says apologetically, which naturally makes me feel guilty. "We had to work fast, but we'll make this a nice room for you, Daisy. You'll love it out here, with all your privacy and freedom. See, your laptop is on Dad's tool bench. We thought you could use it as a desk for now. You'll have everything you need out here."

"Including toilet paper." I look at my mother's Costco stash. "Plenty of that."

136

My mother's face droops and I feel another pang of guilt. "We'll get it cleaned up, Daisy. It's just for one night like this, and you can make it your own. I'll work on it tomorrow while you're helping at the church, and you can have the rest of the weekend to put the finishing touches on it. Now, get all this out of your system. We don't want Grandma and Grandpa to think they're intruding."

"Yes we do," my dad deadpans.

"Pierce!"

"No, it's great, Mom. It's just change. Give me some time, I'll adjust."

"She doesn't like it, Molly. Can you blame her? We're treating her like a dog, putting her out in the garage. I told you this wasn't a good idea. Your parents could have rented a house. It's not like they don't have the money."

"Shh!" my mother hisses, her hands flapping. "They'll hear you. We are not treating Daisy like a dog! This is the best for all of us, and you agreed with that, Pierce. Daisy will have her college fund climb, my parents will have their meals made for them, and we'll all be one lovely family."

"My house looks like a rest home. And I thought *they* would stay in the garage, not Daisy!" my dad says.

"Pierce! Look, I put your David Beckham poster on the garage door," she says to me.

My David Beckham poster has been defaced and wrinkled by the move, and David's nose now looks more like Barry Manilow's. The poster is stretched over a small portion of the garage door in a feeble attempt to disguise the fact that there's a garage door in my room.

"Sorry about the hole. I accidentally opened the garage door and didn't realize it would rip the poster."

137

"It's all right, Mom." I stare down at the concrete floors, which are covered by green carpet squares splitting apart at the seams and buckling with giant cracks of concrete showing. My new room looks remarkably like a badly designed mini golf course or an IKEA warehouse. My desk is in the corner farthest from the bed, covered with my mother's stuff, near the makeshift castle of craft ware and miscellaneous toiletries. It looks like I live in the supply room of a Dollar Tree.

"Just like home." I grin.

My mom pats my back. "You'll get used to it. You can use your decorating eye to make it all yours. Maybe Claire can help you. She's always good for that type of thing."

"Yeah."

"We haven't seen Claire in a while."

"She's rehearsing for the school play. She has the lead."

"She never told us. When's the opening?"

"I'll have to check on that." I flop on the bed, and my mom sits down beside me.

She pats my leg. "What's the play?"

"It's up for political debate at the moment." My cell beeps.

"Sounds like you have a message. I'll leave you and your room to get acquainted. Dinner's in ten minutes." My mom leaves the room singing.

I look at my phone and I have a text. It's been so long since I received one, I wonder if my BlackBerry isn't simply having cardiac arrest.

TEXT MESSAGE FROM: Chase Doogle
TO: Daisy Crispin
Hey sweet girl. Looking at my tring and thinking of you. Pizza tomorrow? What say u?

"Why do I feel like you want something?" I ask my phone. I wake my laptop up from sleep and look in horror as I realize my free wireless (courtesy of my neighbor for feeding her demon cat when she's away) doesn't reach the garage. This just keeps getting better. I move it around until I see the signal does come through, you just have to sit a certain way.

The phone buzzes again and another text comes through.

```
TEXT MESSAGE FROM: Chase Doogle
TO: Daisy Crispin
So pizza's the plan. I'll pick you up at
church. 7:00. You have grocery packing tomor-
row, right? Wear something that shows your
legs.
```

Seriously? I wonder if Chase hasn't texted the wrong girl. Legs? I mean, what? My legs are like two toothpicks with cement blocks at the end of them. Bulgy, coltlike knees and bony limbs. I look down at my legs, just to make sure they haven't suddenly turned into the gams of some pinup girl— but nope, same stick legs. Same big feet. He's got to have the wrong girl.

I know guys. I hear Max's words in my mind, and my heart sinks at the warning. Why can't Max ask me to pizza? Do I say yes to the wrong guy just because he is a guy? And how does pizza-by-text fit into my dad's no-dating rule?

```
TEXT MESSAGE FROM: Chase Doogle
TO: Daisy Crispin
You there?
```

I turn my phone off. Am I here? That's a good question.

❧ 12 ❧

The longer days of spring have arrived, and with them comes hope. Not because anything in my pathetic life has changed, but because the sun makes everything look brighter. I texted Chase back. What's a little pizza between friends? It's not like it's a date. And I wore jeans, just to let him know I wasn't buying into his smooth talk about my legs. But I did shave. No sense in being ridiculous.

My church has an active ministry feeding the working poor in the Bay Area, one of the most expensive places to live in the country. The first Saturday of every month, the youth group is in charge of the rotations for packing the food for the weekly distribution. This is about the extent of my participation in youth group, since everything else requires one to act girly or athletic. Neither persona fits me when guys are around. I'm more SpongeBob with a side of Patrick.

Once a month, the youth group takes the church's Saturday rotation. Every Saturday before youth group events, we come and bag groceries so they can be distributed on Sunday morning. Its purpose is twofold. High schoolers are motivated to be there for the fun activity afterward, and shamed if they show up without helping. A perfect plan. Not that the shaming bothers the popular kids. They stroll in when they feel like it, right before broomball or Great America, sweeping guilt off their shoulders like dandruff.

Since I'm early, as always, there's no one at the tables yet, so my job is to set everything up and get the assembly line moving as the kids arrive. Productivity and order, my specialties. I set up each of the stations: fruit, vegetables, dairy, meat products, and nonperishables, and then step back to survey my handiwork.

"Looks great!" Pastor Andy pats me on the back, stands beside me for a second, and then jolts. "You've got this. I'm going inside to finish some paperwork. Call if you need help."

I happily start to stack the plastic bins filled with food in their rightful place when Max approaches the tables. His hands are shoved in his pockets. "Hey."

"Hey."

"You need some help?"

"You want to help me move the meat over there? It's the heaviest."

He grabs a plastic bin and takes it to the far side of the table. "I'm sorry about yesterday."

"You don't have to be. You're entitled to your opinion."

He laughs. "Even if you disagree with it?"

"Yes." I grin.

Out of the corner of my eye, I see the popular girls heading toward the tables. Amber is more hateful of me than ever, now that I know she went up to the bedroom with Chase at Claire's party. It's like I've outed her, and she cannot stand that I believe the truth about her. She misses no opportunity to slam her shoulder into me in the hallway or comment on my bland, trendless clothing or mock me in any number of ways.

She *never* comes to help with the food pantry. In fact, her presence here makes me wonder if her dad's political campaign is up and running. This is probably nothing more than a photo op. But I try to channel my mother and think in terms of loving everyone, including my enemy.

"Hi, Amber, Britney, Rachel. Did you come to help?"

"No," Amber says with a flip of her long, blonde hair. "We're here to have dinner."

Britney and Rachel giggle at her joke.

Ignoring. "It's just that you're not usually here on Saturday nights, but I'm happy to have your help. Britney, why don't you work in vegetables, and Amber can take fruit. Rachel, how about dry goods?"

"How about they just deliver all this food to your house? Are you trying to act as though you didn't start this ministry for your own unemployed daddy?" Amber asks.

"Nice," Max says. "Does your daddy know you talk like that? I guess we know which party he runs with, huh?"

"Shut up!" Amber spits. "He doesn't need the votes of illegal aliens, that's for sure."

"Amber!" I shout. "That was cruel, even for you. Max is not illegal. And he's not an alien."

"He is if he was willing to go out with you and dance like a fairy onstage in front of the whole school. Why don't you just swallow your pride and own up to the fact that you don't belong at St. James Academy and you never did?"

"Like you do, Amber?" Claire appears behind me. She's dressed in hot-pink cotton shorts, black tights, purple leg warmers, and sporting a new copper-auburn bob. "Give me a break. If you didn't have Daddy's money, your academic probation would have ended a long time ago. You'd still be a freshman, and we all know without that new Richardson wing, your graduation would never happen. Those popping sounds in your head? That's the brain cells dying off at a record pace from all the blonde dye. Or is it the fake hair extensions tugging on your skull? You should really go organic."

Britney and Rachel look at Amber, waiting for some smart response, but let's face it, no one is quite as quick as Claire. It's all that debating she does with her parents at the dinner table.

Me? I'm tired of the drama. Period.

"We're at church. Can't we at least act civil?" I ask, sounding too much like my mother, but I'm so weary of Amber and her gang. I mean, get a life. I suppose it's true that idle hands are the devil's workshop. "You should get a job, Amber. Maybe if you had more to do, I'd be less fascinating to you."

"Trust me, you're not the least bit fascinating to me, Daisy. Don't flatter yourself."

"How's everything going?" Pastor Andy comes out, his football-toned muscles stretching a ministry T-shirt. "Small turnout tonight, huh? Well, girls, it's nice to see you. To what do we owe the honor?" he asks Amber.

"We're just here to help, but it seems we're not good enough for Daisy."

"Daisy?" Andy looks at me and I shrug.

"I gave them a job. Is it my fault if she can't follow directions?"

"Daisy! Did you make them feel welcome?" Andy asks me, like I'm in kindergarten.

Claire begins to tap-dance in her crazy outfit. I've just now noticed she's wearing a green backpack purse, as though to don all the colors of the rainbow. Claire starts singing as her body genuflects—she can't wait for the applause. "If I knew you were comin'—"

"You'd have baked a cake?" I ask.

"Yes," Claire says, clearly upset I've ruined her song. "Do you feel welcome now, Amber?"

I force back a laugh while I continue to busy my hands by stacking the boxes and readying the stations. I try to ward off the bad mood I feel coming on. It ticks me off that Amber has the power to change my mood. Only because I give it to her, which makes me madder still. I'm grateful for Max's and Claire's appearance, but also weary.

"Amber, what is it you want from me?"

"I don't want anything," she says to me while looking at Andy. "I came here to help with the food pantry for the poor, and Daisy makes me feel like my friends and I don't belong. We're not good enough for her."

I roll my eyes. Andy, clearly overwhelmed by the catfight unfolding before him at the table, focuses on the task. "Girls, I don't know what's going on here, but I know we all want to feed the working poor so that they can make it to the end of the week. So I suggest we all focus on sorting the bags. Daisy, start the boxes, will you?" He physically moves each girl to their station and brushes his hands. "Great. I'm going to get the van and you can load them when you're done." He leaves.

Maybe it's because I don't have sisters, but I don't understand what Amber and her friends get out of picking on others.

Max walks up beside me, and I hear Amber make a comment under her breath.

"Why do you think she's so fascinated by me?"

"Uh, please!" Amber says with a hand thrust to her curvy hip. "I couldn't care less what you do."

"You're not stalking her?" Max asks. "How often do you come help with the food pantry?"

"How often do you?" Amber sneers. "Do you even go to this church?"

"Nope," Max says. "I'm here because I was hoping Daisy might have dinner with me."

This provokes raucous giggles from Amber and her friends. "Geek love," Britney says.

"I'd rather be a geek than mean," I tell her.

"Of course you would. You have no choice," Rachel says.

"Ignore them," Max says. "So?" He looks over at Claire. "I thought if Claire came with us, it wouldn't officially be a date and therefore all right with your father."

Claire smiles at me as she puts bunches of broccoli florets into the boxes.

"You're here for me?" I ask her.

"Consider it a sales award for your trings."

"Trings," Amber scoffs. "It totally makes sense that Lady Gaga here would come up with such an idea."

I'm confused by Claire's and Max's appearance and their sudden turnaround. I want to trust them—this is my best friend, after all—but Claire hasn't been herself.

"So what do you say to dinner?" Max asks.

"Wait a minute, you asked my father if you could date me? After prom?"

"Of course I did. He said no," Max acknowledges. "Claire said if I hung around long enough, he wouldn't have a choice."

"But then you decide I'm stealing your boyfriend, so I thought why bother telling you," Claire says.

145

Call me paranoid, but I'm still not sure she wasn't trying to steal Max.

"Daisy can't go out. She has a dinner date." Chase stands behind Amber, and I feel the air rush out of my lungs as my head wags back and forth. As I stand here, seeing Max and Chase beside one another, there's no question in my mind who rocks my world.

"I do?" I stammer.

"She does?" Amber asks.

We're all staring at one another with giant question marks for expressions. Right now I just want everyone to go away so I can have Max to myself.

He asked my father to date me! See, if I'd known that, would it have mattered that he hadn't called me? Sure, it would have, but not nearly as much. Just because it never happened doesn't mean he didn't want it to, right?

April 9

Random fact: Rio de Janeiro is the world's happiest city. Even though Max is from Buenos Aires in Argentina, it's the same continent. And he makes me happier.

I changed my mind. I don't want to be known. I was much, much happier invisible. It seems the car fiasco was more difficult than I'd hoped. And lasted a lot longer than I'd hoped for—it almost made me wish people were pointing at my bad clothes again. And it took nearly a week for my anonymous profession of love (hate, haze, whatever it was) to come down. Add another two weeks

146

and you'd think the drama would be over by now. I mean, they could have taken the sign down at least, am I right? But no. It was as if Mr. Walker thought I personally drove the car on the roof, and I was starring in my very own Salem witch hunt for flying vehicles without a license. For a week! So wrong.

Now Amber and her friends have taken a renewed interest in me. And, as if to punish me, Chase. But as I stared at Chase and Max side by side, and Max and Claire side by side, I knew how incredibly inconvenient my feelings were. I look at Max and my stomach surges until I feel it in my toes. Because regardless of how he's acting right now, I know what we shared was not just my very active imagination. One glance at me and it's like I see what's inside. His words don't match his actions. I could say the same thing about Chase, but in the opposite way.

Why? Why do I have to feel this way about a guy who is planning to attend college in South America?

Sigh. I'll get over it. Right? Right, God? I'm too young. He can't be the one. Chase kissed me . . . and I felt nothing. Chase commented on my legs . . . and it felt like a lie.

Max looks at me, and there's this innate, heartfelt connection that makes me trust him. Not in the way I trusted Chase, like he was some kind of perfect god set on earth for me. But in a real, "I accept you" kind of way.

I'm special because Max looked at me with love in his eyes, and even if I never see that look again, I'll know that God put Max here just to give me an idea of his love for me. My heart is aflutter at the thought.

❧ 13 ❧

My mom sewed me a suit for my job interview. It's not as bad as it sounds. It's a deep-violet wool gabardine, and my mom modified the pattern from a 1970s bell-bottom pantsuit into a cute pencil skirt and a jacket with three-quarter sleeves and black piping at the collar. And cauliflower, ruffled sleeves. My mom could totally go on *Project Runway*, except if I hadn't overseen the entire thing, she probably would have added bows or lace in unfortunate places.

I'm pairing my new suit with a pair of black boots that I borrowed from Claire, and a black business briefcase—from when Claire was trying out for *Our Town*. As I stare into the full-length mirror, it's almost like a stranger is staring back at me. And she is not dressed like a Denny's hostess.

"I look like I'm ready for *Celebrity Apprentice*."

"It looks like you're going to be late!" Angie says, looking at her watch. I rush into her vehicle and talk to myself the whole way downtown. I never even see any of the scenery, and before I know it, we're there.

"How'd I sound?"

"Crazy, like you were talking to yourself. But good. Just remember," Angie says as she slows down her car by the curb, "play it cool. Lawyers don't like a lot of emotion. Text me when it's over." She holds up her crossed fingers. "I'm praying for you."

I hold up my crossed fingers and tug myself and my brief-case out of the car. I'm looking at the massive glass doors and fail to see the light-rail—ahem, *rail*—and I go down without noticing I'm falling. I hit the concrete and metal hard, but I bounce up like a pogo stick, because as much as that hurt, getting hit by the train would be worse.

"Smooth!" Angie yells out her car window. "Shake it off and get in there!"

My heart is pounding in my throat as I approach the law of-fices. Unlike my former office housed in the derelict warehouse section of town, where our only excitement was the honk of the roach coach, Jeremy's office is downtown in a marble-faced high-rise. Its pink marble greatness looms over me, making me feel smaller than ever and my suit more homemade than ever. I start to turn back to Angie's car, but she's gone now.

"This is stupid. If I can go to St. James in homemade clothes, I can do this."

I step into the echoing foyer, and toward the back of the wall are three gold elevators.

"Can I help you?" A young man in a security uniform stares at me, but his eyes are warm as I walk toward his desk.

"I have a job interview at Tyler & Finch."

He takes out a nameplate that reads Visitor and swings a clipboard toward me. "Fill this out and attach the visitor pass. Tenth floor."

I sign my name, and I can see my hand shaking as I try to remember simple facts like my address. I clip the badge to the bottom of my jacket. "Thank you."

"Knock 'em dead," he says with a smile.

"Thank you," I say again, letting out my breath.

"Breathe," he says. "They're just lawyers. They only eat their young for dinner."

I laugh and step into the open elevator. "Thank you!"

He salutes, knowing just what I mean. The elevator is so fast, I nearly lose my footing in the heeled boots, and I reach for the brass rail to brace myself. No sooner do I do so than the doors fly open and I'm standing in the law offices, which smell like new carpet and stale books.

Jeremy is standing at the entry desk and reaches out his hand. "Daisy, welcome. It's good to see you again."

"You too. Thank you for this opportunity." I trip on the carpet as I try to keep up with Jeremy's long strides, and as I pass each office, I'm shocked at the amount of money I see around me. Each office is equipped with a dark mahogany desk, a collection of leather-bound books, and leather furniture on wheels. In fact, it makes St. James look like the poor part of town.

The downtown office building is so elegant compared to my past work environment. Gone are the 1960s metal desks from Checks R Us and the carpet that still smells like cigarette smoke, though it's been illegal to smoke inside since before I was born, so why it smelled like that I don't even want to know. It was a constant reminder that expectations were low and that my outfit that day had very little bearing on the quality of my employment status. I can see if I get this job, my output for clothing is going to have to increase.

Oh my goodness, maybe at my inner core I'm as cheap as my mother. Maybe it's in my genes that I will be wearing homemade clothes for the rest of my life, and I've only been kidding myself that it was my mother's fault.

Jeremy stops abruptly and I slam into his back. "I'm sorry. So sorry." I nervously reach for my bangs and brush them off my face.

"Daisy, relax."

Nodding my head, I try to agree verbally, but nothing comes out of my mouth. He opens a door and stretches out his arm. "After you."

I walk into a room where there's a large black conference table with mints at the center beside a pitcher of water with several glasses. It's supposed to supply an aura of comfort, I suppose, but all I can think of is my parched throat that has closed up at the sight of the fancy office and the desperation for a job that I currently feel.

"Have a seat. I'll get the team and we'll be in for the interview in a few minutes."

"Jeremy!" I say desperately.

"Yes, Daisy?"

"Anything I should know going into the meeting?"

"You should know that I've learned I'm nothing like my father, and neither is anyone in the office. So relax. Just be yourself. You made a big enough impact on me after five minutes. You're a natural. I saw a lot of promise in you that night as you navigated a very difficult arrangement."

By leaving, I think. *Not exactly conflict resolution expertise.*
"Thank you."

Be myself. Not that! I can't even pack food for the working poor without some kind of conflict. If a dirt cloud follows Pig-Pen, that character from Charlie Brown, I think a cloud filled with all those symbols follows me. Maybe in heaven, God sees that little bubble all the time.

Work is the one arena where I felt confident. Now, in front

of this giant table in my homemade skirt and other people's accessories, I feel as self-conscious as I feel walking down the halls of St. James Academy. I tap my foot on the dark Berber carpeting and try to release some nervous energy. I'd pick up the water pitcher and help myself, but I'm too nervous I'd drop it.

I start to pray for peace.

"Miss Crispin, I assume?" A large man with an affable face and a navy suit greets me. "I'm Mark Finch."

"Nice to meet you, sir." I shake his hand firmly and remain standing while another interviewer comes into the room. She's a brunette, midtwenties, with her hair pulled back so tightly in a bun she looks as though she's had a face-lift. Her suit is gray and cut perfectly to her curvaceous figure. Definitely not homemade. More Ann Taylor. I find myself wondering if my mother could have sewn around those curves and still made the suit fit me. Luckily for her, I'm more angular than rounded.

"This is our senior paralegal, Jenna, and you already know Jeremy, our law clerk."

Jeremy comes into the office, and I feel myself sigh within. A job at McDonald's would be a lot less intimidating, and suddenly I'm not feeling nearly as confident in business as Gil always made me feel. Everyone sits down, but I'm still ill at ease.

"Now, most law firms wouldn't be bothered with interviewing all the interns at this high school level, but I'm led to understand that you have computer expertise that would help our office to organize some of our case notes."

"Yes, I computerized my last place of employment, and I can write programs if necessary to make your case notes work for your company."

"And how about privacy? Can you make your system confidential?"

"Yes. I wouldn't suggest taking your system onto a public network, though. There's still far too much code that can overwrite what I know, and it's being written every day."

"You don't talk like a high schooler."

"I'm an only child and I'm a nerd at school, so I don't doubt that's true."

Mr. Finch laughs. "Nerds rule the world, Daisy. Don't forget that."

"That's what my father has always told me." Of course, my father doesn't even rule his own living room, so it's not a phrase I took too seriously.

"Daisy, if you could do anything with your future, what would it be?"

"I'd like to go to Pepperdine, to the school of business there. I was accepted, but it looks like the economy has overridden my goals."

"I'm sorry to hear that, but community college for two years can allow for a lot of growth in a student."

I nod my head to fake my agreement.

"You don't agree?" he asks.

"Was I that obvious?"

"Let's just say you shouldn't go into trial law."

"That's what I said!" I exclaim with a tad more emotion than he's probably used to. I slink farther into my seat.

"So if you're planning to go to college in the fall, that means you'll only have until August to complete this project?" He puts his hands together, and I have to face reality. In front of people I barely know.

"I doubt I'm going to college in the fall. Most likely I'll be part-time at West Valley Community College."

"You act like that's failure, but there's no shame in saving money for what counts. If you want to go to Pepperdine, then two years seems a small price to pay. We all have to make choices in this world, and in this economy especially. No one is going to hand us life on a silver platter."

I nod, unrepentant. He's forgetting about the twelve years of schooling and the grades that got me into Pepperdine. Another two years is just like the seven years Laban added onto Jacob's workload when he realized he'd married blah Leah instead of beautiful Rachel. It's the point of it. You have certain expectations, and they're sucked out from under you by the very people who are supposed to keep their promises to you.

"It might seem that way." I feel my jaw tighten. "But it's the principle of the situation. It's being relegated to the garage. It's taking care of my parents. It's my dad dressing like a duck." I look up, and with horror I realize I've said everything aloud. I slap my hand over my mouth. "I'm sorry, I—"

"You sound a bit entitled, Miss Crispin. Perhaps your parents are trying to teach you gratitude and to appreciate what you've been given." Mr. Finch stacks his papers back into his folder. He doesn't look nearly as affable as I took him for. "Thank you for your time, Miss Crispin. We'll be contacting you with our decision."

"You didn't ask me anything!"

"I'll give you one word that will go further than any degree you might earn: humility. Learn that trait and you will never be in want of anything." Mr. Finch leaves the room, and the tight little paralegal follows him.

Jeremy sits across from me, drumming his fingers on the table. "Well, that went well."

155

"It did?" I ask, wondering if I've missed some inner lawyer dialogue.

"No, it didn't."

"I'm still unemployed." I am incredulous.

"What's wrong with community college?"

"It feels like failure to me. Do you know how hard I've worked in high school?"

Jeremy shrugs. "If community college feels like failure, maybe that's why God wants you to go."

My stomach plunges and I shake my head. "No, I learned to stop being a perfectionist already. My prom didn't turn out anything like I thought it would, so I'm good there."

"Maybe you're not."

"No, I have the journal and everything. I wrote it down. It's right there in black-and-white." Granted, it *was* in black-and-white. Now it's just black since I burned it to a crisp in the fireplace.

"What if you need an extra helping of humility?"

"Jeremy, I am living in my parents' garage, I am unemployed, I dress like a twelve-year-old, my mother made this suit, and I can't even feed the poor without enduring the wrath of the rich girls at my church. I could teach the subject of humility!"

"Anyone who says that doesn't know a thing about humility." Jeremy rises from the table.

"Jeremy, wait!"

"You think because of who you are, you deserve more than these other people. Mr. Finch worked his way from nothing. He went to community college before getting into a state school."

I look at the door. "Oh no! I offended him."

156

"What I think you fail to understand, Daisy, is that you can be a snob without being wealthy."

His words sting. "I'm a snob?"

"You might be. Here's the thing. Mr. Finch is all about second chances, so if you change your mind and plan to be in the area in the fall, come back and talk to him. Tell him what you've learned."

"Jeremy?"

"Yeah?"

Now's my chance. I have nothing to lose here. "Jeremy, do you know why your mother didn't tell Mr. Webber about you?"

He grimaces at me and checks around him. "Why do you ask?"

"I can't really explain why. I just had this feeling that if I knew, I'd understand my own life better."

"Is that why you're here?"

"I guess now it is."

Jeremy's brows are furrowed and he's clearly annoyed with me, but I'll get over it. It's a feeling I'm used to. "Come on." He grasps my elbow and leads me out into the hallway by the elevators. "Is that why you screwed up the interview? This was about my mother?"

"Oh no, I screwed up the interview completely on my own. Trust me, that wasn't planned."

He heaves a sigh. "My mother knew my father well. Even back then, he had aspirations. He wanted a life different from what she could ever give him. She wasn't—" He pauses a minute and his eyes fill with sadness. "Like Mrs. Webber. She thought he'd always be ashamed of her because she enjoyed the simple things in life. She said she worried that he'd think she got pregnant on purpose." Jeremy shakes his head. "When in fact the reality was she was always too good for him."

"I'm sorry I brought it up. I just thought—"

"My mom always said suffering in this lifetime is a given, but wallowing in it is optional."

"She never regretted her decision? Did she know your father became a wealthy lawyer?"

Jeremy snorts a laugh. "She did. It confirmed her decision. He wanted something different from her."

"What if he wanted to be a father? To take responsibility?"

"What if he didn't?"

"It seems unfair to me for someone to make that decision alone."

"Maybe, but that's how life works when you make a mistake. You pile one on top of another if you don't fix the first one from the outset. She planned to tell him when he graduated, but then he got married, then he had Claire, and the further along Mom's secret got, the easier it was to just embrace it as her own. Raise me to be a good man and sort it all out later."

"Only she didn't get a later."

"No," he says solemnly. "Why do you care so much about my mother? Did Claire ask about her? Did my father?"

"No, nothing like that. It's stupid, really." I cover my face, ashamed. "Do you really think Mr. Finch would have me back if I decide to go to West Valley?"

"I can't promise anything, but I can say it's a possibility if you're willing to apologize. Bosses like to know the character of their employees is impeccable. In this economy, they can afford to be choosy."

"Yeah, I guess," I say, the wind sucked clear out of my sails.

I didn't get the job. It's going to take some time to digest this. I mean, failure in the social world—I get that. But this? This is what failure feels like—failure at something I'm good at, not failure at getting dates or social invitations. I don't like it. Not one bit.

"I'll let you know when I'm ready for another interview, Jeremy. Please thank Mr. Finch for his time. I'll send a letter doing the same thing."

"That's my girl."

I stare back at him and force away the uncomfortable feeling I get. I'm sure it's my own failure talking to me.

❧ 14 ❧

"It's a wonder you complain about school at all, Daisy. You never seem to be there." Gil, my old boss, sits across from me at "his" Starbucks. The one that knows his orders, where the churlish barista girls giggle at his presence, and where he orders me their version of an Arnold Palmer so he doesn't drink alone. *I'm just that kind of girl. Won't do the hard stuff, but won't let the man drink alone either. I should give etiquette lessons.*

Gil taps his empty cup, which he just drained in record time, onto the table, and there's another rush of appreciation from behind the bar.

"What is that like?" I ask him, leaning in. "I mean, everyone should get to experience that for one day in their lives."

"What are you talking about?"

I roll my eyes, annoyed we inhabit the same planet. I change the subject and jam the straw into my drink. "So, I quit the soccer team. But I didn't get the job at the law firm. It appears my brilliance did not translate to the law offices of Tyler & Finch. So now I have to crawl back to soccer to get the credits I need to graduate. That's going to stink."

"It sounds like a disease anyway. Consider yourself lucky."

Gil slaps the table. "I can't believe you made the senior soccer team without working for it. You shouldn't have quit. Do you know I tried out all four years for my football team and got cut every year?" He groans. "Maybe things come too easy for you, Daisy. Did you ever entertain that thought?"

I stare at him in disbelief. "Yeah, that's it. Things come too easy for me. Excuse me, have we met? Because I think you've confused me with one of your Porsche-driving frat buddies." I pause for a drink. "Name one thing that has come easily to me, Gil."

"Grades. The BlackBerry my company bought you. Getting into any number of universities with no donations made by a wealthy father . . ." He taps his finger on the table. "Oh, and your prom date. Which you said you'd never be able to get. You went without a date and ended up dancing with some hot foreign guy. That's right, isn't it?"

"Easy? You're leaving out a few pertinent details. Like I don't have a wealthy father so bad grades were never an option, and my father was at the prom with me, after Claire and I set her house on fire and had to make amends by running the Breathalyzer. Does that sound like a dream night to you?" I feel my shoulders tighten at the accusation all over again. "Did you not witness my yearlong internal struggle as it played out in the office?"

"No, because women always have drama. I've learned to ignore it." Gil smiles, and one of the young women, a blonde, brings him a new cup.

"Americano with room?" She grins. "I took the liberty of adding the half-and-half. That's what you use, right?"

He pulls a Starbucks card from his left shirt pocket and hands it to her. It's gold. Like his life. Casually, he checks out her name badge. "Leslie, you are amazing. Thank you so much!"

"It's nothing. I see you come in here all the time, and you always get a second one when your meetings run long." She smiles at me and then skips back to her counter.

"Am I sitting here?"

"They know who you are, don't be ridiculous. As I was saying, I didn't notice your prom drama because it's like all women's drama and I've learned to shut my ears to it."

"Even though you're the one who causes most of those women's drama."

"You never miss a chance to let me know where I stand, do you?" He looks over to the ladies behind the counter and offers them up a smile, as if throwing a dog a bone. The lone male rolls his eyes.

The sad thing is I only resent this, as that kind of power will forever elude me. Having the X factor is either something you have or something you don't.

I sigh as Gil looks back at me with that magnetic gaze of his. "Are you saying you think I'm rude for noticing you're a womanizer?" I ask.

"I think for someone as bright as you are, Daisy, you can be dim. Every time you get stuck in this mode, where you act like you don't know what you want for fear you won't get it, you flounder. Whereas when you want something and go after it, I've never seen you fail to make it happen."

"What did you want to see me about? Why am I here? I have places to be, you know." Not really, but I like the way it sounds.

"For two years, we listened to you go on and on about one Chase Booger."

162

"Doogle," I correct him.

"What have you. I prefer Booger."

"I don't believe men with Ivy League educations are supposed to use the word *booger*."

"You would know."

"You're supposed to be the adult here," I tell him.

"As I was saying, for two years I listened to those cackling giggles as you entertained your co-workers with the latest Chase news. Then one day he's no more. Banished from your existence. He did something wrong and you moved on." He stirs his coffee. "Not that I'm saying Chase Booger was worth your devotion, but you seemed to give him up easily enough. Now just substitute Pepperdine and your job. You've moved on."

"What are you getting at, Gil?"

"I'm seeing the very same pattern with a certain Latin lover and my girl Daisy. That's my point. I don't think you ever wanted a boyfriend at all. I think it's the chase you're after, and not the one with the goofy last name."

"You're saying I'm a flirt? I don't even know how to flirt."

"I'm saying you have the makings to be a fine tease. With boyfriends, colleges, jobs . . ."

I gasp. Being called a tease is one thing, but being called a tease by my twenty-four-year-old former boss, a known Lothario, is offensive at the very least. "I'm not even allowed to date or go to the college of my choice, so I fail to see your point. Why am I here again?"

"Which is why being a tease is so easy for you. You just blame Daddy when things get too close."

"I'm not a tease. I would love to have a boyfriend. In fact, a date for grad night is—"

"Another one-night affair. How many sermons have I endured at your hands about my lack of second dates? Maybe I've taught you more than you hoped to learn." He raises his brows.

"I'll have you know that Max Diaz asked me out to dinner, and—"

"You turned him down because Daddy says you cannot date."

"No. Well, not only because of that. I turned him down because . . . because . . . because he was hanging out with my best friend Claire."

"And that's against the girl code. Question for you. Wasn't Max your prom date before he started hanging out with Claire, thus making the girl code broken by Claire originally?"

"You are way too interested in my social life, which is pathetic, and I can't imagine why you'd be interested. One more time, why am I here? I have homework to do. Don't you have a job to be at?"

"I'm trying to get into the minds of all these women who go out with me once and never want to see me again. Maybe you, my pseudo little sister, hold the key."

"I highly doubt that, since their IQ is probably equal to my age. That's why you asked me here?"

"I don't know why I ever took your back talk. A complete lack of respect toward your employer. No, it's not why I asked you here."

"Gil, Michael from *The Office* could give you pointers on workplace boundaries. Please. So why did you want to meet me?"

"I heard you weren't working yet, and I have some work in my new office. It's nothing official, so I can't promise you

164

hours, but I thought if you had nothing better going on, I'd show you the location and use your computer skills on an on-call basis."

"My father thinks our relationship is inappropriate. I doubt he'd like to hear that I was working for you again."

"See? There you go again. When the fire gets too hot, you pull out the Daddy card. Unfortunately, Daisy, I know you listen to Daddy only when it's convenient for you, or you wouldn't be sitting here now in the coffee shop. With me."

I look around me. "It's a public place." But if I expect all the weirdos who inhabit this place to protect me . . . I mean, if I want the guy wearing the black, shellacked hairpiece to provide my safety net, I'm hallucinating. "I respect my parents and I know you're trustworthy, Gil. As long as I'm not dating you."

"So when he said you couldn't go to prom, you just accepted that."

"That was different. That was ridiculous."

"Everything you want and they don't is ridiculous. All I am saying is that you can respect them when it's convenient."

"That's not true!" I feel the need to defend myself against these false accusations. "I'm a good girl."

"I never said you weren't. I just think you know your own mind, and every time you venture into doing something for your own future, you feel guilty and try to shove it under the rug, but it comes and rears its ugly head in ways you can't imagine. So you may say you're not going to college at Pepperdine. You may accept your fate and be willing to work at a local law firm, but I'm only saying you are more defiant than you think. More like me than you think."

"Point proven. I'm not trustworthy, is that what you're

saying? Because if that's the case, why would you trust me to do the numbers on your business? Numbers I should have fudged so that we all might have our jobs now."

"Except you wouldn't have done that."

"True."

Gil leans in, and he makes me wish I were older. That I could talk as easily to guys at school as I can talk to him. Maybe I wouldn't be relegated to the brains crew, and people would know my name for more than setting fire to my BFF's house and a rogue VW on the school roof.

"I'm saying that you may mind the rules, but I don't think you mind them outright. I think you find a way to do exactly what you want to do and stay within the boundaries of your parents' requests."

"You're saying I live by the letter of the law?"

"Maybe I am. Don't be offended, Daisy. I know you to be a good Christian girl who cares about others and only wants to do the right things, but I also see you struggle with minding those rules when you'd like to do something else."

Within a few days, two different men, both well out of high school, have told me that I'm not who I appear to be, that I might be in desperate need of some humility. That's disheartening. I mean, if I'm not humble in my circumstances, what am I?

"The important thing is you're known at school now. You won't ever be able to leave St. James without everyone knowing you were the girl someone confessed their love to with a vehicle on the roof."

My mouth goes dry.

"Daisy, everyone knows you now, right?"

"Gil, you didn't! Do you know how much trouble I got into

for that? I had to join the soccer team again or get a job. I'm losing credits because your company failed and Mr. Walker was determined to keep me busy. I might not have graduated!"

"But you will. Because you're a fighter." He pulls out his BlackBerry. "So, I can't give you work credit because we don't have an official status at the school, but I can give you six hours starting next week at $16.50 an hour. What do you say?"

"Gil, you can't just let me take the fall for that stunt. My own best friends think I had something to do with it, or that I'm hiding a boyfriend somewhere. Max and Chase both think I've been playing them. How could you do that? You have to tell Mr. Walker!"

Gil shrugs. "They can't trace it. I hired some guys from the junkyard. You're safe."

"Why would you do that?"

"You said you wanted to be known. Someone did that to a friend of mine in high school. He was known forever."

I let my head fall on the table. "Aren't adults supposed to act mature?" I feel my hot breath on the table when I speak. I stare at Gil. How could I have dropped youth group, soccer, choir—anything high school related—and expected the outcome to be any different? "I should be focusing, mapping out my new future, and instead I was trying to get known. Who cares if I'm known at high school? God knows me."

"What you need, Daisy, is to be honest with yourself. Stop putting values on what you want and just admit you want them. You know, you won't always get what you want, but I'll tell you, learning to fail is a lot better than lying to yourself."

"I fail all the time!"

Gil shakes his head. "Nope. You quit before you fail. Analyze it if you think I'm full of crap. Your parents say there's no money for Pepperdine, and you just give up. That's it. No more college for Daisy. If she can't have exactly what she wants, she'll settle for whatever. Sign her up at the community college and give her any guy to marry. Why fail?"

I feel my nose sting, and I blink desperately to keep Gil's words from invading my heart. It can't be true. It simply can't. "I fail. I fail all the time!"

"You fail on your own terms. What really matters to you, Daisy? Do you even know?"

I think about Max and how willingly I handed him over to Claire. I practically gift wrapped him!

"God's got the world in his hands," I say firmly. "He can handle my future. I'm just a realist. If I don't get to go away for college, I need to find something, or I could get lazy and end up here for life. I could be a manager of a fast-food restaurant and think, 'Hey, this is fine for now.' And one day I wake up and I've got three kids and I'm still the manager of Burger Barn."

"How you get from quitting soccer to three kids and 'would you like fries with that,' I will never understand. I thought you'd solved that perfectionist, all-or-nothing thinking. You're still trying to bend what happens into your wish come true. Sometimes, Daisy . . . sometimes life just sucks and we don't know why. But I gotta run. Are we on for next week or not?"

I narrow my eyes at him and wipe my cheek with the back of my hand. "No."

"So, you're mad. It's my fault you're back to being a high school freak?"

"Precisely."

"You could have lied. You could have played along."

"I couldn't have."

He pushes a letter in front of me. "Here's your letter of recommendation. I put my cell number on there if you get any interviews. You're young. Go easy on yourself. We all make mistakes. It's how you recover that determines character." He winks at me. "Ask one of my exes about my character."

I pick up the sheet of paper. "You hide behind that, but Gil, I know your character. I just wish you'd share it with the rest of the female population instead of hiding behind the mask of a jerk."

"It always does me good to drain a little of your excess energy. Reminds me not to get complacent." Gil's eyes are fixed on the door behind me.

"Thank you for this," I say after having scanned the contents of the envelope. "And Gil?"

"Yes, Daisy?"

"I want to go to Pepperdine. I want to kiss Max. I want to find a job and quit the soccer team."

He grins. "Didn't that feel good?"

I nod. "It totally did."

Gil's gaze is still transfixed on the door.

"Do you mind? Look, I know I'm not your date or anything, but no girl appreciates a guy checking out other chicks when they're with them."

"What?" Gil shakes his head. "Isn't that the guy you were chasing? No pun intended."

I turn around and see Chase with Amber beside him. The two of them look incredibly cozy and haven't even noticed me, so I turn back to Gil and shrug. "That's him."

"You don't seem too upset."

"He's told me who he is one too many times for me to be upset." I don't want to confess I'm so over Chase. It makes

169

me too much like Gil. I'm trying to be a good witness, for crying out loud. Though I guess we are allowed to change our crushes from kindergarten to senior year.

"Good, because he's coming over here. Should I confess to professing my love for you on the rooftop?"

"Please don't."

I feel myself straighten in the chair, and I smile when Chase makes his presence known. Amber sneers at me as if she's won the lottery, and as far as I'm concerned, she's won fair and square.

"Who's this?" he asks, not recognizing Gil in his casual clothes outside of my former office.

"Gil, meet Chase."

Gil stands up so that he towers over Chase, and the somersault my stomach does at the sight makes it worthwhile. Even if Gil does think of me as his painfully misunderstood little sister, Chase and Amber don't know that. I imagine Gil, from their vantage point, looks like a sophisticated older man (ooh, I so wish they could watch him get into his Porsche) on a date with *moi*. And who I am to correct them?

I stand up and step a little closer to Gil. But then I remember I'm supposed to be acting like a Christian. Like the adult I'm about to be.

Chase's cheek flinches and Amber notices. Her eyes flash. "I'm Amber." She steps in front of Chase and turns on her purring voice. Gil is polite but reserved in his attentions toward her, and I could kiss him for that. Even if his brain does need a healthy dose of human growth hormone.

"Well, Daisy, I have to head out. You need a ride?" He takes out his keys and lets the Porsche chain dangle.

"I told you, my father hates to see me in that Porsche."

170

He makes a clicking noise and points at me. "That's right. I always forget how young you are, princess. You act so much older." He brushes his fingers down my cheek and gives me a look that I can only assume he's used many times in his singles' scene. "Call me about what we discussed." Gil pecks me on the cheek and strides out the door, like the cowboy he is (in my head right now, anyway).

I smile at the happy couple as their eyes follow him out. "What are you two doing on this side of town?"

They both look at each other and stammer for an answer.

"Is that the guy who left the car on the roof for you?" Chase asks.

"No one is in love with me, Chase. That was a prank on me as well as the school."

"So you're really not dating anyone then?" Chase asks, and Amber socks him in the arm. "What? I didn't mean anything, I'm just asking if she's dating someone, that's all."

"That depends," Amber says to me. "Is the rest of your social-loser group planning to get boyfriends?" She turns to Chase. "Geeks travel in packs. I think it's so no one beats them up."

"Would you two cut it out?" Chase says.

"Me? I didn't say anything. Call off your girlfriend, Chase."

"She's not my girlfriend!"

"Pardon me?" Amber crosses her arms. "Look, Chase, I've had about enough of your games. Is this on or isn't it? You're not at the Air Force Academy yet, you know, but you should be by now, shouldn't you?" Her eyebrows flicker, and her meaning about her father's recommendation is made more than clear. "I don't need to put up with this. In case you haven't noticed, I don't need your attentions. If you want to be friends with

Little Miss Dateless here, you go right ahead, but I've got bigger plans for my life than to hang out with life's losers and feel like I've done my good deed for the day." She stomps off and turns around when she gets to the door. "You can both find yourself a ride home. Looks like there's a bus stop out there."

I hate to tell her it's how I got here and I can get myself back.

Amber storms out of the coffee shop and I watch her go. "I can't believe someone would say those things out loud. What's going to happen to her when someone stops saying yes to her every whim? Did you ever think about that, Chase? Because that's your future right there. That is not a happy chick. All I'm sayin'."

Chase grins sheepishly. "I guess we're in trouble."

"It's not funny, Chase." Sure, he can laugh. He won't be stalked in the hallways by the mean girls. He won't have his Facebook wall graffitied or, worse yet, an "I hate Daisy" page created. Such a sorry scene at a Christian school, but like I've always said, St. James is more about money than faith. "Thanks a lot."

He laughs again, as if I've said something funny.

"I'm not kidding, Chase."

"Amber's harmless. What's she going to do, douse you with lip gloss?"

"If she's so innocent, why does she hold her father's recommendation over your head?"

Yeah, he doesn't have an answer for that one. I, on the other hand, have been told time and time again who Chase Doogle is. He is Gil without the charm or years of using experience behind him. This time I choose to believe it. I won't fall back on an image I created in kindergarten. I will embrace reality in all its ugly truth. Chase Doogle is a tool.

❧ 15 ❧

As if taking the bus home from school every day didn't remind me that my family is not like the others at St. James, my neighborhood drives the point home. I imagine most of the students at St. James aren't even allowed to drive into my neighborhood.

It's your standard, California ranch neighborhood, dwarf sized compared to the mini-mansions and full-sized ones of my friends. In fact, I think Angie's bedroom is bigger than my entire house. I once asked her if she had the master, but she took me into her parents' room and showed me the size of theirs.

Honestly, as someone who has to vacuum the house? I am not impressed—it would be like vacuuming the soccer field. My first thought was how ridiculous all that wasted space is. Thinking about the families we feed at church, I wished I could donate some space to their plight. That's the thing about being rich that I've noticed. It takes you far away from the people who really are needy—that's my opinion anyway. Since most people never drive in the neighborhoods where some of us actually live, they have no idea that people are actually hungry. That families work three jobs and can't put food on the table.

Silicon Valley has five types of neighborhoods. Your standard California rancher, the mini-rancher built after World War II, the deluxe rancher with three-car garages, the Mc-Mansions, and the full-size mansions.

I live in a sensible two-car garage rancher—or maybe I should say four bedroom sans garage, since that's currently my digs. Our neighborhood is not skeevy, nor is it elegant. The houses around us are fine, if not large. Ours is the bigger one, really known more by its holey screen door and peeling paint, but it's void of the bars on the windows, which seem to be a staple in my neighborhood.

My mom keeps up the garden, but otherwise the house looks like an expansive double-wide. Especially right now, with my mom and grandmother waiting for me on the flat porch (no step up) in two camp-style rocking chairs.

"You're home," my mother says. "Did you have soccer? Where have you been?"

"I had to meet someone after school."

"Who?"

"Gil," I say as I think about the repercussions of lying.

"Daisy, you know we don't like you meeting up with him. What is wrong with that man that he doesn't have friends his own age?"

He does. But they're definitely friends with benefits, so I'm not telling my mother that.

"Who's Gil?" my grandmother asks.

"He's her *much* older, former boss who sold his company right in the middle of Daisy's school day. She takes the bus to work and finds out from a stranger that she doesn't have a job!" My mom sits upright in her chair. "Daisy would have lost credits for her work program, but luckily she was allowed to join the soccer team."

"But I quit, and now I have to go begging to get back on the team or find another job quick, so when Gil contacted me, I thought—"

"She was going to get a job at Claire's brother's law firm, which we thought would be great, but that didn't work out. This old boss pays for her cell phone, and I don't like the way that looks."

"Yeah, I didn't get the job at the law firm," I say sheepishly.

"So now she's not doing soccer and she's not working and she's meeting boys twice her age after school. Daisy, what am I going to do with you?"

My mother has a way of making everything sound so sordid. She says this like I've just announced I've made plans to cross-pollinate with a melon. An avid horticulturist, she believes all breeding outside one's realm of understanding is vile. She thinks Gil is vile. Which, if I were his girlfriend, he would be, but as his employee, I thought he was a great boss.

"Mom! I'm not interested in Gil. I'm interested in work so that I can pay for college and help with the fund. Those last two years are still going to be incredibly expensive. I figure we have to make 8 percent interest on what we have and grow the fund by 75 percent by the time I start my junior year."

"Don't 'Mom' me. We've been waiting all afternoon for you. Grandma had a surprise for you, and I had no idea where you were, and now she has to hear you were where you had no business being."

"Why didn't you call my cell phone?"

"That's another thing, Mom," Mom says to Grandma.

"This Gil fellow bought her a BlackBerry phone, which is very expensive compared to a regular cell phone. He's paying for it until she goes to college!" My mom tsks. "I told her father to make her give it back, but he thought it was a fine thing since she takes the bus by herself. I was quiet out of respect, of course, but I think it sends Gil the wrong message. It puts her at his disposal."

See, sordid.

"Well, I wouldn't necessarily say it puts her at this boy's disposal," Grandma says.

"Can I go in now? I'm hungry."

"What were you doing with Gil?" Mom prods.

"I met him at Starbucks. He has some part-time work for me, and since the law office didn't work out, I'm looking for other possibilities to fulfill my work credits at school. I need to get a job, Mom."

"I put my foot down over this, Daisy. I just don't trust that young man." She looks at my grandmother. "He drives a foreign sports car!"

"Scandalous, huh, Grandma? It's a Porsche too." I can't help myself. I start to giggle but try to hold it back, which only makes it worse. "I'm sorry, Mom."

"You think this is all a joke, but Daisy, your father and I have lived more life than you. We may have learned *something*. First we tell you no dating and your father lets you dance at the prom. Now that boy will not leave your father alone, trying to take you out. It's as if he doesn't understand our meaning of courting. Your father has tried to explain it to him, that you don't date without the thought of marriage and that you're far too young—"

"Wait a minute. *Who* is bothering Dad?"

My mom clamps her lips around her teeth. "Never mind. Go and set the table for dinner. We'll discuss this later."

"Mom, Gil is seven years older than me, and he was my boss. Who are you talking about at school? Because if there's any chance I have a courter, I think I should know about it. I mean, now we have Grandma's three-person courtship couch and everything. Let the games begin!"

My grandmother starts to laugh, which infuriates my mother. "Mother, this isn't a joke. This is an adult male around your granddaughter!"

My grandmother tries to raise herself from the flimsy rocking chair, and I hold it still while she gets up and braces herself against the small picket fence at the edge of our porch. "Molly," Grandma says, "you always did worry yourself into a frenzy over the smallest things. Daisy's a responsible girl."

"And I want to keep her that way."

"She's not dating this man Gil. She's told you that, so why must there be all this arguing? My blood pressure is going through the roof. Daisy, when your mother was little, she dated many boys in high school."

"Which is exactly why I don't want her making the same mistakes I did."

I cross my arms over my chest, waiting for my mother to tell her mother exactly what that means, but she doesn't. *Oh, sure, rat me out and then take the fifth on yourself.*

"Now, Mother, we are raising our daughter to—"

"She's raised, Molly. Look at her. Are you seeing the same grown woman I am? She's responsible for her own homework, she gets to work and back, she makes her own dinner half the time, and she gets a bag lunch ready on most days." My grandma smiles at me. "Well, most days before I got here. Tell her what she does right once in a while, that's all I'm saying."

"She's seventeen. She is not grown. Even the law is with me on that one."

"But she's nearly off to college, and that poor boy . . . What Pierce is putting him through is torture. Your father wanted to run after him when he saw his disappointed face."

My eyes go wide. *What boy? What disappointed face? There was a disappointed boy face? Over me?*

My grandmother continues. "I understand the worry. It's a terrible worry raising a daughter, especially in this age, but I don't think you give Daisy any credit, and she's a beautiful young woman." Grandma kisses my cheek. "I'm going inside before the mosquitoes come out." Grandma exits through the screen door and it crashes against its aluminum frame.

I look at my mom. *Yeah. What she said!*

"Mom, are you talking about Max? Has Dad talked to Max recently? Was he here? Because he's seeing Claire from what I can tell, and if you know anything different, it would explain a few things."

"So that's why Claire hasn't been around." My mother takes this information as though it will be filed and used against me later to prove a point. "Daisy, you know we love you, and it's not that we don't trust you. But we don't trust Gil."

"Who does? Mom, his own parents don't trust him, but I'm telling you, he's not like that with me. He's like a big brother."

"Perhaps he is, so that you let your guard down. Your father is doing what he must to protect you, but you don't make it easy for him. You led that boy on at the prom and your dad didn't want to embarrass you in front of your friends, so he let you have your dance. Which he claimed was ill-advised and slightly obscene."

"Mom! Have you watched *Dancing with the Stars*? Because seriously, Donny Osmond was a lot dirtier than my innocent tango. It's the dance of his land, you know. It's cultural!"

"Your culture is Christianity, and I don't see room for the tango in that. I know your father and I are old-fashioned, but you can't say we don't have your best interests at heart."

"No, I suppose I can't." My voice is defeated. "That doesn't mean it doesn't suck."

"I hear you."

"Mom, this is a Christian school, and everyone else got to go to the dance. I don't understand why—"

"Did Sarika go to the dance?"

"No, but she didn't want to go. She's going to grad night, and there will be dancing at that!"

"What good is going to a high school dance for your future?"

"What good is getting accepted into all the best colleges only to go to my local community college?"

"What happened to my sweet, compliant child?"

"She thought the rules would change a little as she got older," I say.

"I'll talk to your father about grad night. Is that what you want?"

I nod. "I'm supposed to grow up and leave the nest. I'm not an axe murderer, I'm just in love with a guy who makes my heart pound a mile a minute."

"In love?" My dad whacks open the screen door until it hits the peeling paint on the wall, and a few more pieces of paint crumble to the cement floor. "Molly, do you know who professed his love to your daughter on that car at school?"

My eyes widen. Does he?

"It was that tool she worked for."

"Gil?" my mom asks.

"Gil. That's who. He paid a group to do it, probably because he knew I could sue him for messing with my underage daughter. When I think about him coming here in his sports car acting all innocent, I could—". My dad's hands roll into fists. "I will take matters into my own hands. I just got off the phone with Principal Walker. The school seems to think this is some kind of joke, but I certainly don't, and now that I know who is responsible, I'll handle it myself." Dad reaches into his jeans and pulls out his keys. "I'll be back."

"Where are you going?" I ask, my voice shaking.

"I'm going to defend my daughter's honor!" He throws his keys up into the air and grasps them tightly as he walks to his Pontiac.

"Dad!" I call after him. "I don't have any honor to defend."

He stares at me in horror.

"Wait, that came out wrong. I mean, I haven't done anything to defend my honor. No, I mean, I haven't done anything to harm my honor. Gil is my boss, nothing more. If he did this, he only did it as a favor to me. He must have thought it was a good thing."

"He's nothing more yet. I plan to make sure it stays that way."

I take my cell phone out to call Gil and give him fair warning, but my mother snatches it from me. "And that will be enough of this. No more gifts. No more jobs with Gil. No more contact with that man at all, do you understand me?"

I feel physically ill as my mother takes away my BlackBerry. My one sense of normalcy in an otherwise crazy-rich world, where I am the poor one, the lone girl who's happy enough to have a pair of jeans, regardless of any label. The only one who this harsh economy seems to hit at St. James.

God? When I ask what makes me special, I mean it in a way that doesn't imply mentally disabled. Are we clear on that?

"I have to call Claire." I pull at the screen door, but my mom smacks it shut.

"No, you're banned from using the telephone. You're not going to call that man, or Spype him—"

"Skype."

"Whatever else you do. Text message, call, any form of communication is banned for you right now."

"You're holding me prisoner!"

"You'll thank me one day."

"I don't think I will," I tell her honestly. *I think, at the moment, that I'll rejoice in putting you in a subpar nursing home.*

My mom walks into the house and collects the phones, my laptop, and anything else that I might use to contact anyone outside the home. When she puts my BlackBerry in the trash can, that's when I know I need backup. I look at my grandmother and she shrugs. Then I look to my only hope. Besides a random miracle, that is.

"Grandpa?"

"What's the matter, pumpkin?" He drops the newspaper.

"Grandpa, would you drive me to my friend Claire's house?"

"Dad," my mom says. "Claire lives in the hills. You don't want to be driving those roads. Daisy needs to set the table anyway. If I don't want you calling Claire, why would you think I'd let you go hang out there?"

My grandpa snaps the paper, folds it shut, and puts it in a leather holder he brought with him, at the side of the sofa.

"I live in the hills too, Molly, and I've been driving them since before you came into being. I can drive her to Claire's. Besides, if she doesn't go, I'm worried my wife's blood pressure is going to go through the roof with all this tension. It makes sense Daisy would want to go to her friend's big house in the hills rather than be relegated to the garage here in her own house."

"Dad, you make it sound like she's abused or something."

"I just know that what my princess wants, Grandpa gets." He winks at me. "I'll set the table for her when I get back. If your husband would look for a real job with the kind of motivation he left here with, you wouldn't be working your hands to the bones making sock puppets."

"They're oven mitts." Mom turns to me. "I thought you and Claire were fighting. How are you going to get home, Daisy?"

"Claire will bring me when we're done. We're going to celebrate her lead."

"Fine, go. It will be good for you to not think about what your father is going to do to that Gil once he finds him. Why can't you just do what you're told? Your father's health is still not good." My mother makes the sign of the cross over herself. Which is odd since we aren't Catholic.

Grandpa and I walk out to his Buick and get in quickly as if we're both making our escape. "Step on it, Grandpa. I gotta call Gil before Dad makes a terrible mistake."

Grandpa squeals out of the driveway and has us on Claire's street in record time. He maneuvers up the road with mad skills.

"I can't believe Mom worries about you driving."

"Your mother worries about everything. Even as a child.

If something could go wrong, she'd find a million ways to worry about it. Your grandmother tried to show her it would all be all right, but I don't know that she ever believed her." Grandpa takes his hand off the wheel and pats the console between us.

Grandpa and I have a magic connection. From the time I was little, I remember him coming to get me to take me out for ice cream, just him and me. Unlike my own parents, he's always fully there with you. Present in the moment as if he abandons all outside worries when you come into his presence.

"I know you're not involved with your boss. It's utterly ridiculous."

"It is?"

"Daisy, you are a normal teenager. Boys come into play nowadays and your parents don't want to admit that you're a normal teenager. They don't want to lose you. That's the trouble being the only child, I suppose. How many times in your life have I given you advice?"

"I don't know. Never? Well, there was that time you tried to talk me into the green dress and I really wanted the purple one."

"Green's just my favorite color. I don't think I'd count that as actual advice."

"Then never. I can't remember you ever giving me advice."

"I'm going to give you some now."

"You are?"

"Daisy, I would have never moved into your house, not even for a month, had I known your parents planned to put you into the garage like a dog. I don't like that one bit. Your grandmother and I would have been happy to stay in the garage, but we should have rented a house like I wanted to do in the first place."

"Grandpa, that makes me feel worse."

"Your parents love you, but they are so concerned with doing the right thing, they sometimes make the wrong decisions in trying to be perfect."

Ack! That doesn't sound familiar or anything.

"Ya think?" I say with sarcasm. "Like my dad running off after my old boss—who knows how to drive his Porsche. Somehow I think the oxidized Pontiac, even propelled by my father's anger, is not going to cut it."

"You're not staying home from college. You're going to Pepperdine, and if you make one step toward that community college, your old grandpa here will quit golfing and lose his will to live."

"What?"

"You heard me. You're not going to community college. I haven't told your father this, but I found that bill and I paid it. They just drop their bills on the floor, like they're garbage."

I laugh. My grandfather will never understand the laid-back way my parents live their life. Laid-back as in cleanliness, not structure.

"Now you sound like Gil, and my father is off to kill him."

Grandpa laughs. "I can hold my own with your father." He pulls into the driveway of Claire's luxurious mansion. "That's what you two did?" He nudges his chin in the direction of the scaffolding.

"Actually, the whole school did it. We were just the ones responsible. They took down all the burned stuff, so it doesn't look so bad now."

Grandpa whistles. "That makes our kitchen remodel look small by comparison."

I lean over and smack his cheek with a kiss. "Thank you for the ride, but Grandpa, I don't want to go to Pepperdine if it's going to cause a rift the size of Africa's."

"Which is?" he asks, playing to my knowledge of numbers.

"Nearly four thousand miles stretching from Lebanon to Mozambique."

"That's my girl. Stay out of trouble, and get ahold of that poor boy Gil before your father does." He chuckles. "You know, getting a car on the roof is a great prank. All we did back in Montana is grease a pig and let her loose in the hallways. We thought we were something."

"If everyone had a grandpa like you, there would be no war or famine." I kiss him on the cheek again and run up to Claire's massive front doors. Usually I'd walk right in, but not today. Not knowing where we stand.

❧ 16 ❧

I wave my grandfather off before pressing the doorbell, but he's Grandpa, so he goes nowhere until the door opens. The doors, which resemble something out of an English castle—and for all I know, they could be—creak open until Claire sticks her head through the crack.

"Yeah?" she says.

"I came to congratulate you on getting the part in the play."

"No, you didn't. You came to call Gil before your dad finds him and makes a fool out of all of you."

My mouth drops open. "How do you do that?"

"It's a gift." She swings the door open and I walk into the familiar museum she calls a home. Claire waves at my grandpa and he gives a short honk of the behemoth horn.

"Can I use your cell?" I ask frantically.

"I already called him."

"You already called who?"

"Gil. I already called him. He's been warned. He's on his way to Tahoe with some chick, so he's not remotely worried." Claire smacks her gum with her tongue, and like clockwork her mother snaps at her.

"Claire!" she yells from the kitchen. "Stop doing that! It's so unladylike. No wonder you can't even get kissed in the school play."

"Nice." Claire rolls her eyes. "Yeah. I'll never catch Mr. Right with my behavior."

"You seem to have done fine with Max."

"Would you stop? I tried to tell you a million times what that was about, but you just never heard me. You had to get your paranoia on and made sure I was pulling a fast one on you. Max is leaving, Daisy. At the end of the year. I just don't want you getting hurt, all right? I have watched you pine over Chase for years, and I won't go having you get attached to a guy who is leaving the country. That's all I need, you forever locked in a battle for unrequited love." She sighs. "I'm doing you a favor, whether you're ready to thank me or not."

"Okay, definitely not ready to thank you."

"I didn't think so."

"In my defense, that's what you've been doing my whole life. We just normally don't have the same taste, so how was I supposed to know first Greg and then Max?"

"Wait a minute, Greg?"

"He was on my prom list until I found out you were all into him. Which I never would have known, but you started dressing like Michelle Obama and I knew there was a conservative in your future."

"Well, I was into Greg until I understood how much he liked to play with fire. You should have seen what the police hauled out of his garage after he set the field on fire with his physics project. Total pyro. And I'm not going to tell you again, I'm not into Max! I'm into you moving on with your life and not getting lovesick over another Chase. Understand?"

"Maybe if you were still dating the pyro at the party, he

would have known how to douse the fire. Seemed to have some experience with it."

"I was still dating him. I think what fire has taught him is to run."

"Oh. Guess not then. How did you know about Gil?"

"Your dad came over here, mad as a dog because his friend at the junkyard told him about the great prank at St. James and pointed out the car. Why does your dad hang out at the junkyard?"

"He uses the scrap metal for his art. What's more humiliating? The fact that there was a dead car professing love for me on the roof or that my dad hangs out at the junkyard?"

"That's a toss-up. He came here to find out if my dad knew if he had any legal recourse against Gil. I overheard and called Gil on his cell phone."

"Which you got . . . ?"

"Every time you called to tell me you were in a Porsche."

"Oh, right." I'm letting her off way too easily. "Claire, why aren't you our friend anymore? You just drop the trings off with Angie, Sarika, and me, and that's the last anyone's heard from you, but I'm supposed to believe you have this great love for us all of a sudden?"

She starts to walk toward the stairs. "I do have a great love for all of you. I just show it differently. Look, you're all going to fancy colleges. You all have your whole lives planned out and I'm going to be stuck here if I don't get that ACT internship. So I need to learn how to do it on my own."

"I'm going to be stuck here too."

"You will not. Who do you think you're kidding? This is me, Daisy!"

"Can I please call Gil? I'll just feel better if I talk to him."

She shrugs and hands me her iPhone, which I can never dial, so she does it for me before handing it off. "Suit yourself."

Things are strained between us. Now, with all the years we've been friends, Claire and I have gotten into so many fights it's not even funny, but this is the first one that I thought—still think—might have done us in forever. She's different now. Hard to reach. I long to just have her look at me, laugh, and say the whole thing is behind us like she usually does.

Claire's mom appears in the arched doorway in the cavernous entry hall. She's wiping her hands on a towel and would look almost domestic if she didn't have a full face of makeup, pearls, and a Nanette Lepore skintight dress that falls above her knees and is paired with some rockin' heels. I only know it's Nanette Lepore because Mrs. Webber tried to explain to me how the stitching was done and what made the dress worth as much as three birthday appearances by my dad in a chicken suit.

I found it comical that Mrs. W was the one to explain to me the art of sewing when my own mother's business is sewing, and she truly could make anything someone wanted. Granted, Mom might add some googly eyes for fun, or maybe a fringe of fur, but she does know her way around a sewing machine.

"Well, Daisy, it's good to see you." Mrs. Webber tosses the kitchen towel over her shoulder, and I race to her side and grab it.

"That's silk."

She laughs, a tinkling, fully female laugh that seems to bring out the guys like it's her own whistle only men can hear. Looking at her now, and the smile on her face, I find it hard to believe that she and Mr. W ever had any difficulty at all staying married. She's the picture of health and looks

189

like she could be starring in her own antiaging ad with her dewy-pink complexion and bright coral lips.

"I know it's silk, Daisy. We're having a dinner party tonight," she says as she snaps the towel back. "Claire, you should run up and get dressed."

"Another dinner party?" I ask.

"Oh, you know Mr. Webber, he's always got someone he needs to impress."

"Well, that dress should do it. You don't have to feed them, do you?"

"Daisy Crispin, it's sounds like you've been hanging around that boss of yours. Your words are as smooth as butter. If your father has his way, it sounds like his backside is going to be as smooth as butter."

"But my words are true. I don't stand to get anything out of you. Unless it's an invitation to dinner." I look at the phone. "It went to voice mail."

"Try again! In answer to your question, Mom," Claire says, "no, we haven't made up. Daisy is still accusing me of stealing her boyfriend, and now she's telling me she meant to steal mine."

"Before I knew you were dating. What kind of best friend dates her best friend's crush? Or, for that matter, likes someone and doesn't share it with her best friend?"

"Daisy, is that you?" Claire's dad appears in his office, which sits alongside the entryway. It's hard to tell if he's ever in there because the room is covered from floor to ceiling in different elaborate woods. It's really kind of ugly if you ask me. But no one did.

"Yes, it's me. Hi, Mr. Webber." Gil answers the phone, and I'm torn, but I hold up a finger to Mr. Webber. "Gil, you there?"

"Daisy, don't worry about your father. What's he going to do, beat me to a conversion? The second Spanish Inquisition?" He laughs, and I hear a lady—and I use the term loosely—laugh behind him.

"I just wanted to make sure you knew he found out about the—" I look at Claire's parents. "You know, the prank. You said no one could find out."

"Well, apparently, your dad has a few friends down at the junkyard."

I'm mortified. "I'm sure he does."

"Don't worry about me, love. Let me know what happens with soccer." I hear him click off and I'm face-to-face with Mr. Webber again. Who has said all of one hundred words to me in my lifetime of being his daughter's best friend.

"Come into my office for a minute. Claire, you can come too if you like."

Claire, being the nosiest person on earth, shirks whatever she was doing and follows her dad into his office. I follow her. "I don't think I've ever been in this office when you've been home."

"Maybe not, but I know by the amount of makeup sparkles I've found, no doubt you both have spent some time in here."

I sit down in the burgundy leather chair across from Mr. W's desk, Claire beside me. Mr. Webber sits at his desk and clasps his hands in front of him. Just like Principal Walker did. The action sends a wave of revulsion through my body. "Am I in trouble?"

"In trouble?" he asks.

"Did Claire and I do something?"

Claire holds up a hand. "I am completely innocent for once in my life. I even called your boss for you."

"I guess that's true."

"Girls!" Mr. Webber grabs our attention. "I only have so much time before the dinner party. Can we get on with it?"

"With what?" Claire asks.

"Daisy, it's come to my attention that you've been interviewing for a job with Tyler & Finch, my son's law firm."

"I have," I say, feeling suddenly guilty. "Is that bad? Because they didn't hire me, and I don't think they're going to unless I stay here and go to community college. My grandpa told me that he'd pay for real college just to get me out of here, so I don't know that—"

"Daisy!"

"Yes?" I respond.

"How did you find out about the job at Tyler & Finch?"

"Jeremy called the school business office and asked for me specifically," I say with pride. "I'm very good with writing Excel programs and organizing office information, so he heard—"

Mr. Webber raises his palm. "That's fine, you don't have to go into detail."

"Am I in some kind of trouble, Mr. Webber? Besides the car on the roof of the school, I mean."

"Daisy, you've walked with our family through a lot of crises, and I want you to understand something. Whatever mistakes Mrs. Webber and I have made, we are making up for them now."

"Yes, sir."

"But I want to tell you a lesson I learned long ago, which I never really understood was a lesson until now, since I'm older and I can see it being repeated in my son."

"Sir?"

192

"I grew up in a Christian home. Did you know that, Daisy?"

"No."

"I was a rebel from the start, and though I had a longtime girlfriend in school, ultimately I made a big mistake on grad night during a three-day cruise for seniors."

"Dad, gross. Do you mind?"

"Thank you, Claire!" I say.

"What I'm trying to say to you is that you haven't known the kind of people we were brought up to be. You've seen Mrs. Webber and me as members of the country club, but that's not who either one of us is. We were both raised to be working toward the Lord's work, to fulfill a higher calling. Jeremy coming back really rocked us to the core because we had to look at who we'd become." He taps on his desk. "I know, you fail to see how this concerns you."

"Sort of, yeah."

"I'm going to tell you why I fell away from the church, and it's not the church's fault, mind you. I take responsibility for walking away and holding people to God's standard, but it's my story and I want you to hear it, because I think you, Daisy, are in the most danger of following in my footsteps."

"Me?"

"Yes, you. Because you're a perfectionist, and as such, you will always be tempted to do things in your own power because you can. You're a girl who creates her own weather pattern, whether you know it or not, and you don't play to the masses."

"Well, that's not really a choice, Mr. Webber."

"I almost lost my whole family because I never dealt with some very ugly truths in my youth. It was time."

Okay, I am seriously uncomfortable with the oversharing

and deep Mr. Webber. I think I like the shallow, rich one who ignores us much better. I try to stare down Claire as if to say, *Make it stop, make it stop!* I mean, seriously, if I want a freakish parent handing out TMI, I'll just go home. But she's fascinated by her father's words and that he's just not barking out orders, so I'm out of luck.

"Do you mean—"

"Mrs. Webber and I are coming back to the Lord. We've wandered in the desert long enough, and we've both decided to give it another try with God at our side."

"Oh my gosh, that's incredible. Claire, isn't that incredible?" I'm overexcited, sure, but how else does one react to the sensitive Mr. Webber? It's creepy, quite frankly. I'm thrilled if what he's saying is true, but that doesn't mean I'm not uncomfortable.

"So now I need to tell you the truth as I see it fitting to your situation," Claire says. "Is that what you're saying, Dad? That you're willing to hear me?"

"That's right, Claire. I'm willing to hear it."

I tense immediately, and if there's a muscle in my body that isn't firmly locked into position, I'm not aware of it. Or it has stopped working altogether. Claire's family is usually so eerily polite, this is alien.

"Are you sure this concerns me?" I ask him.

"This concerns you immensely. It's why I'm doing this, Daisy," he says in a Darth Vader voice that doesn't invite argument. "It's about Jeremy and you."

"Are you worried I'm after your son? Because I can assure you, I'm after a job, and—"

"Daisy," he says firmly.

I stop talking.

194

"Jeremy's mother was a lovely Christian woman back in high school. She had a lot of fight in her, a lot of passion, and she really wanted what the Lord wanted of her. And she was a good listener. As good as any I knew back in the day."

"Uh-huh," I say, trying to sound blasé, because the truth is, if we're going into Claire's dad's sex life, I am so out of here.

"You've heard about our grad night trip and what happened. I'm sure I don't need to go into details."

"No!" Claire and I say simultaneously.

"As you know, I didn't realize that Helen was pregnant back in the days of my youth, but that's no excuse. Had I called her or made any effort to contact her after the cruise, I would have known everything. I chose ignorance and she chose pride."

"I'm not pregnant!" I shout. "No one thinks I'm pregnant, right?" I jump out of the chair. "Is that what this is about?"

Claire starts to giggle. "Yeah, we were all really worried about that. Not!"

"Sit down, Daisy. This has nothing to do with you and boys. I'm well aware of your nature and I know you are not pregnant."

"Okay, good. Because my dad is mortified that's going to be my problem, when really he should worry about his having grandkids at all because I'm like guy repellant."

He looks at me again in reproach and I shut up. No wonder Claire never talks back to her father. He has that way about him that commands respect. Real respect too, not the kind you fake to please him.

"Shut up and let him finish, Daisy," Claire squeals. "Seriously! I want to get out of here."

"As I was saying, Jeremy's mother was a lovely young girl, and she wanted to do everything right, but her version of Christianity had a dark side, and I'm seeing it in our son as well. I tell you this because I know you've been talking to Jeremy about a job, and I wanted to offer a word of caution. I don't want you to take that job at Tyler & Finch. If you need work, you can come to my law firm until you leave for college. I would greatly prefer that you not enter into a relationship with Jeremy, professional or otherwise, at this time."

I swallow past the lump in my throat. "It's all right, Mr. Webber. It didn't work out at the law firm. Jeremy's boss didn't like me, but if you have a job, that would be great. I'm trying to get as much put away as possible so I can enter the school of business. I hope it's not the school of business at community college, but at this rate—"

He's staring off into space. "The church," he continues in a closing statement kind of way. "The church is filled with people. People are sinners, and so ultimately, it's impossible to stay in fellowship with any group of people and not entail some hurt in one's life—even at the hands of Christians."

"Mr. Webber?"

"Where I went wrong was blaming God for my own sense of shame and anger at the church. Once you head down one path of sin, it seems easier to go down others, until you've forgotten you were a Christian altogether."

I nod again. I'm looking like a bobble-head doll at this point, wondering what on earth he's trying to say and wishing it would be over soon.

"The type that got to me was the type that manipulated to get people to do God's will. They spoke in pious ways while they were secretly working to get exactly what they wanted, not God's will. Oh, they called it God's will, but ultimately, it was just what they wanted."

"I don't understand."

"Dad, can we go now?" Claire whines.

"When someone speaks to you," he goes on as if we're really interested, "as an active listener, you listen to their opinion, even if it's different from yours. As a mark of respect, you must give the other party a show of respect because their life experiences differ from yours. Their experiences add up to a different sum."

"You're not making any sense." Claire's annoyed.

Mr. Webber clears his throat. "You give people the right to their opinion because their life hasn't been the same as yours. Their life experiences are going to equate to a different point of view. Isn't that right?"

"I guess. Are we talking God's truth here?"

He holds up his hand again. "Jeremy wants to know me as a part of his history and makeup. To know his father. I can appreciate that and I love that. I want to win back the years that the locusts have stolen. I want him to trust me as a father, even though I haven't been there for him for the important moments in his life."

"Well, sure. Only a monster would want to push away his own son." I want to be encouraging, but what the heck?

"How do I put this?" he asks.

"Quickly. You put it as quickly as possible," Claire quips.

"I don't want to sound like a victim here, because I was a willing participant to what went on that night of the cruise, but Helen had an ulterior motive, and it's the reason I never called her again. It's also the reason I didn't want to marry her."

197

Now it's getting interesting. Maybe this is the reason I'm guy repellant. I lean in toward Mr. Webber and I'm taken aback by how good-looking he is. No one should have a father who looks like this. It's not right. It's like Hugh Jackman being a daddy. Some things just don't go together.

"I still don't understand why you think—"

"Helen lured me into her room that night. Her plan was to have happen exactly what happened. In her defense, she came from an emotionally abusive home and she was ready to move on, but after that night, I saw how easily she could manipulate me into getting her way. When we both said we would wait until marriage, I knew I couldn't fight her for the rest of my life. If I gave in after that night, I would be giving up my dreams for the rest of my life, under the control of the quiet and conniving Helen. It seems I didn't know quite how conniving she was, though my own behavior can't be excused."

"It does sound a bit like you're blaming her."

"I realize it does, but Daisy, you've always had a good sixth sense about people. What's your sixth sense about Jeremy?"

"I like him. I thought it would be really good for you to have a Christian son and be exposed to all of his beliefs. He was very nice when I met him here. He came out after Max came inside. To say goodbye to me."

"And when you met him at the office?"

"Well, that was uncomfortable. I accidentally offended his boss. But I guess it was God's will. Though Jeremy would like me to try again."

He stifles a smile. "If one really believes in God's will, they let God do the deciding."

"Right," I say, convicted about my own decisive nature.

"I have reason to believe that Jeremy may be grooming you. Do you know what that means?"

"I've heard it in molesting terms. That's not what you mean, right?"

"No, what I mean is that I think he may be putting you through the same tests his mother put me through, to see if you're worthy enough to stand next to him. After the first series of tests, he'll advance them until you forget what you think altogether."

"That's kind of dramatic, isn't it?"

"Do I strike you as the dramatic type, Daisy?"

"No, sir."

"Would you do me the favor of staying away from Jeremy? At least if I'm not around him to protect you."

"You don't think he'd hurt anyone—"

"I don't think he'd hurt a fly. Knowingly. But I do think he's got a manipulative spirit, and I want you to surround yourself in prayer. I will do the same, praying for the shield of faith to guard us in God's truth." He sits back in his chair. "You can go now."

I sit there, unable to move until I feel Claire lift me out of the chair by my arm. "Let's go," she whispers.

We get outside the office and Claire shuts the door.

"That was random."

"Just don't go to work for Tyler & Finch. That's all he's saying."

"Well, he's saying more than that. Did your brother do something?"

"He's just different. Intense. Dad's been having him over a lot, but they always go into his office, and Mom and I take off and watch *The Bachelor* or something."

I nod, staring at the door. I can't tell which way is up any-more. When Claire's dad starts sounding more religious than my own, there's some serious stuff going on. "I need a drink."

"I've got some of your iced tea in the fridge."

"You knew I was coming?"

Claire always made me iced tea after school before I had to work. It's a true act of warmth for a girl who doesn't know what happens to her own laundry after it hits the chute.

"I knew when your father found out about that car and Gil, it was only a matter of time until you were cut off from the free world."

"They took my BlackBerry and my laptop."

"You poor baby. Let's go highlight your hair. Maybe that will get their minds off it."

We giggle and get our iced tea before escaping into Claire's massive travertine-covered bathroom, which is only half as massive as her parents' bathroom. I think about my carpet-squared garage and wonder how it is that we ever became friends in the first place. I think I just rediscovered my best friend and I couldn't be happier, because part of what makes me Daisy is my best friend Claire. Without her, life is much less exciting and, well . . . lonely.

Claire has a lot of talents. Cosmetology is not one of them.

"You gave me stripes. My mother is going to kill me!"

"Oh, hush up. We have all weekend to fix it. Besides, you're already in trouble."

"How did you get the stripes to go the wrong way? I'm like an albino raccoon."

"Remember how cute it looked when Drew Barrymore dyed the ends of her hair to match her Alexander McQueen dress? I thought it would go faster if I twisted your hair up while I did it. But it sort of made it go all swirly. I thought it was closer to your actual color than it is."

I stare into the mirror and my stomach buckles. "I have paisley hair." I pull at the tips. "Paisley!"

"Just give me a minute to think. I'll fix it."

"No, don't touch it. You did this on purpose. Because you're interested in Max."

"Would you cut it out with the Max drama? I am not interested in Max!"

"I'm going to ask your mom if she has something to fix this before her dinner guests get here." I let the towel flop over my shoulders and run down the circular staircase frantically. When we were younger we always had Scarlett O'Hara moments on these stairs, but interestingly enough, the reality of these stairs has been more like the burning of Atlanta.

It's then that my nightmare becomes a reality. "Max!" Instinctively, I halt on the steps, and my hands go to my hair and smoosh it down until it's as unnoticeable as possible. My voice echoes through the cavernous foyer, and Claire's mother looks up at me.

"What did you girls do to your hair?"

"Daisy, what are you doing to your hair?" Max echoes. "Have you ever seen a red ring-tailed lemur?"

"I haven't." But I have. I just don't want him to tell me that I look like one. "It was a look I was going for. Didn't quite work out." I walk to the bottom of the stairs.

"How many times have I told you not to let Claire fiddle with your hair? Don't you remember how all her Barbie styling heads were bald?" Mrs. Webber sighs. "Go into my bathroom—no, never mind. I don't have time for this now. Go up to Claire's room, and I'll come fix you after the dinner party. Don't let my daughter touch your hair." She clicks her heels away into the kitchen.

Max pulls my hands off of my head. "Let me see it." He walks slowly around me, and in the bottom of my stomach I feel his presence. I feel the way he looked into my eyes when we tangoed and the connection that unites us, and I'm more confused than ever by his actions.

"I can't be the only one who feels this way." I stare him straight in the eyes and he meets my gaze. "That's not physical attraction. There's more to this and you know it." I keep staring at him. "What do you see?"

202

He leans in. "I see the most beautiful woman in the world. A soul—" He exhales.

"I can't take any more secrets. Everyone is full of secrets and I need to know the truth. Even if it hurts. If you love my friend, my best friend, more than me. If you want her more than me, I want you to be happy. I just want to know."

His palm comes to my cheek and slowly slides down to my neck. He starts to hum a tango, and I grasp his hand while his other one comes to the small of my back. We fill the room with our own shared music.

"Why can't you trust what your heart tells you? Why do you always look for something different?"

"I need to hear the words. What are you saying?"

"Look into my eyes and ask yourself the same question. You want the easy way out and I can't take that. If you don't understand why, I'm sorry for that. But look into my eyes and tell me I don't feel for you."

"I don't know what to think!"

"You do."

Claire comes down the steps and sees us embroiled in the dance we've come to love. "You two! Get a room!" Claire says. "Has my mother seen you?"

"We have one," I tell her with a wink. "Do you mind?"

Claire cracks up. "I do, actually. Remember? My parents are having a dinner party."

I don't want this moment to end. I don't want Max to take his arms from around me, and I don't want to go to this place of ignorance where I don't understand my best friend or the guy I've fallen for. One look from Max and I'm overtaken by thoughts of the future and being whisked away to a foreign country, leaving behind everything I know, including all the number facts and business acumen. Certainly it makes me pathetic, but nonetheless it makes me honest.

"You want what I can't give you," Max says.

"Meaning?"

"You want words and I can't give you words. Not yet."

"Why not?"

He stops moving and drops his arms to his sides. "What do you think I feel?"

"I only know what I hope you feel."

"Then stick with that."

"Max, my mother is not going to be happy to see the two of you dancing in her foyer when her guests get here," Claire says. "What do you want?"

"I need that script we marked up."

"Fine. I'll go get it." She climbs the steps again, and Max looks me in the eyes until I feel like I'm wearing my old, homemade slacks and every part of me is self-conscious.

"I feel so lost without the words. Why can't you just tell me what's going on? Why all this secrecy? What's with you and Claire if you're not interested in her? Claire's never let a day go by without telling me anything vital to my life—how badly I might be dressed that day, or what's wrong with my lack of makeup—so why hasn't she said anything about this? There's only one reason. You two have a secret that doesn't include me, and what else could that be?"

"What else could it be?"

"Stop answering me with questions. You're frustrating me. I'm a simple girl. I speak in math, not this blasted subtext you all find so mesmerizing. I'm not you. And I'm not Claire. I need things spelled out."

He leans in. I feel his warm breath on my face and I feel

his lips press deeply into mine. He pulls away and keeps his eyes focused tightly on my own. "You'll figure it out."

But I don't think I will. Not before my hair grows out anyway.

April 15

Random fact: Kissing increases the heart rate and adrenaline, neuroscientists say. From my experience, only when that kiss is with the right person.

Longest day of my life.

Most romantic kiss of my life.

My heart is in need of permanent surge protection, and though I am no closer to knowing what makes me special at the moment, I am closer to understanding that another person can lift you up on wings of eagles and make you feel as if there isn't another living person on the planet.

I trust Max implicitly, and yet I can't help wondering if I should. The quiet moments, the awkward pauses, the outright ignoring me. Is he a game player, or are his words secondary to the way he looks into my eyes?

It can't be secondary. A guy who is embarrassed to be with you in public doesn't deserve to be with you in private. Hasn't my father always told me that?

But then my mind goes to what Claire's father told me. To trust my instincts. To stay in prayer.

205

I break out my Bible, which I'm embarrassed to say hasn't been seeing enough light of day. Granted, it could see more if I just lifted up the garage door. Probably more sunlight than any bedroom Bible is used to.

I open my Bible to the love passage. *Love is kind. Love is patient.* Claire and Max certainly haven't seemed all that kind or patient in the last few weeks, and I'm left with my original thoughts.

What makes me special? My distinct inability to understand why the world can't just work the way God designed it, with spectacular engineering skills and math, the interplanetary language of love. I am certain that God is anti stealth communication.

ᘓ 18 ᘗ

Saturday, May 14

The spring play at St. James Academy is a citywide event. The drama team is not made up of your average theater nerds and poets. On the contrary, St. James has a very prestigious performing arts school. Claire has been in the drama club since she was a freshman, but she's never garnered more than a bit part. She's a good actress, but when she's competing against daddies who will write checks, it's more political than it should be. This is her first lead and she means business. Her father was even willing to get out the checkbook for this event. Her last, since she's a senior.

It's a social event marked by parents who drop huge amounts of cash for the team. Our drama team is like a who's who of high school life. And it's the bane of my parents' existence that not only am I not a member of the drama team, I would rather pluck my eyelashes off one by one than join.

Acting doesn't evoke warm fuzzy feelings of a job well done for me. It reminds me that my dad has never gotten a real job because of his love for "the arts." Again, if you want to call dressing up like a chicken and offering marriage proposals to strangers "the arts."

Many of the kids grew up in church choirs and performing arts to keep them busy—as opposed to football (too danger-ous) or soccer (hard on the knees)—so playacting allowed all that excess energy out without the corresponding bodily injury.

As I approach the theater, the irony is not lost on me that I'm standing in line with Angie and Sarika, paying for the privilege of seeing Claire alongside Max onstage. After a political wrangle at school the size of the Gaza Strip, *West Side Story* was abandoned, but in the new play, written by the drama coach, Claire is still supposed to kiss Max. She made it a point to tell me.

The fact that they have the leads is not lost on us in terms of popularity contests. Most often the lead roles go to the most popular kids who will pull in their friends and make the show worth watching. This year the rumor is that Claire got the part because she's best friends with the girl whose someone professed their love via a VW on the roof. Which would be totally funny if it weren't me, and if it had been the actual reason. Apparently I'm old news. They didn't plan for that.

Never underestimate the fickle students when it comes to what's in and what's out. The tring is already long forgotten, as is Gil's prank. Replaced by doorways that were glued shut and toilets wrapped in saran wrap.

Usually the playbill is as professional as anything you'd find on Broadway, with paid advertisements and glossy, full-color spreads of the actors. This year it's one step above a color copy because of the changes and politics about the play.

The new theater teacher is an "ar-teest," and as such, he and Principal Walker could not agree on a play that satisfied his artistic freedom while not causing parents to clamp their checkbooks closed. The result was a self-penned *One Sorry Chick*. Anyway, with a title like that, none of the standard popular girls wanted the role, so it was all up to Claire, whose love for the arts transcends any humiliation factor. Not that Claire has ever possessed a humiliation factor. The more attention she can garner, good or bad, is fine with her. You learn sometimes that it's safer not to ask.

Anyway, now the play is about a homely girl with braces and bad clothes. It's basically *Ugly Betty* as written by the new theater director and the setting of St. James Academy. Claire was careful not to tell me more. Or let me in on the dirty little secret of whether she and Max kiss onstage, which I'm still hoping the director has put a stop to over parental protest (hopefully, my parents).

We all make our way into the auditorium behind Amber and Britney and their peons. They are giggling, dressed in tiny, hip-hugging minis, and doing their level best to make their own entrance bigger than anyone's onstage.

"Oh, I know!" Amber enthuses. "Can you imagine taking this part? The makeup alone is enough to keep a real actress off the stage."

"Real actresses call themselves actors now," I interject as I feel Sarika pull me back by the shirt. "Remember Angelina Jolie in *Girl, Interrupted*? Real actors are willing to strip bare emotionally for the right part." Naturally, I've never seen that movie, as it's rated R and my parents haven't yet let me graduate to PG-13, but I can mimic Claire with a skill all my own.

"Whatever it takes to make yourself feel better about your

friend playing a geek." She pauses. "Hey, isn't that typecasting? How is she acting again?"

"I wonder if she'll have one of her trings on for the show!" Britney says, and all of them cackle to attract as much attention as possible.

My mouth is open, but now both Sarika and Angie are pulling me back. "Forget them. Their skirts are marring their brain cells."

"I don't understand why they have to be so mean like that."

"Because they know it bothers you. Don't let it."

I'm incensed, though. "Claire deserved this part. She has been trying to be the lead for every play since freshman year, and she totally deserved a lot more than this one play, but Amber's daddy always takes out the checkbook."

"Let's go find our seats," Sarika says. "Life is not fair, Daisy."

"That doesn't mean we shouldn't try and make it so. We can't let the bullies win all the time."

"They don't win all the time. Eventually karma comes back to haunt," Sarika says, pulling from her Indian heritage. "Or, as my father says now, one reaps what one sows."

"Amber's dating Chase now. Tell me that isn't reaping," Angie says.

We pad down the steep staircase to our seats in the second row, and as we climb over anxious stage parents who arrived early, it dawns on me that this is not a show where I desire orchestra seating. "Joy. I get to see their nostrils while Claire seduces the man of my dreams."

"They're acting," Angie reminds me as she takes the last of the three seats available in the row.

"Exactly, so what if they're so believable that I can't tell the difference?"

"You can tell Max he has to convince you of the difference after the show. Sit down." Sarika motions her arm toward my seat, and I try to remember the benefit of having Max kiss Claire versus Amber.

"I haven't seen Claire's parents," Angie says.

"They'll come, won't they?" Sarika asks. But if Sarika gave an oral presentation in Biology, her parents would be present with expressions of wonder, as though she's just uttered her first word.

"I sure hope so. Mr. Webber said things were going to be different from here on out."

"When did he say that?" Angie asks.

"I had a talk with him. It sounds like he and Mrs. Webber are trying to work things out and even bringing God into it."

"That's awesome!"

"My parents have been praying for them every night. They'll be happy to hear there are some results," Sarika says.

"My parents are here somewhere," I say. "Hopefully not close enough to divulge acting secrets and tell me if Claire meant it or not."

"There's your dad," Angie says.

I look down in the row before us and see my mother, father, grandfather, and grandmother. "What are you all doing here? I'm not in the play," I tell them, thinking my grandpa must have expected I was or he would not have left the golf channel. Oh, one benefit to my grandparents being in the house is they brought cable with them. It's a sad day when your grandparents are the ones all about moving forward and being progressive.

"Well, you knew we were coming."

"But I saw your seats, Mom. You were way in the back."

"We changed them when we got here. Not all of the more expensive seats were sold, so we were able to get these for the same price as the mezzanine."

Thank you for announcing that tidbit of frugality for all my friends to hear.

"Besides, we love Claire like she's our own, so of course we'd come to see her and we'd want the best seat in the house."

As long as you didn't have to pay for it.

"Hello, Mr. and Mrs. Crispin." Angie is wearing her new, toxic-green eye shadow with neon clarity, and my mother forgets about me and focuses on her.

"Well, Angie, it's good to see you. That's interesting makeup you're wearing."

Please don't say it. Please don't say it.

"Your mother lets you wear makeup?"

"Molly," my dad interjects. "It's none of our business if Angie's parents allow her to go out in public like that."

Shoot me. Just shoot me now.

"Maybe we should go," I say to Angie and Sarika.

"Our best friend is starring in the school play," Angie points out. "What kind of friends would we be if we didn't support her?"

"The human kind?" Sarika says.

"My legs are cold," Angie says. "Can I borrow your hoodie to put over them?"

I hand her my sweatshirt. Sarika's mother has this odd ritual. I'm not sure if it's cultural, religious, or just plain obsessive behavior, but she makes us wash our feet and legs to the knees when we come in the house. I've never had the courage to ask why, but I wouldn't have gone to Sarika's house to pick her up had I known her mom would be there.

Now my feet are cold too. Which makes me wonder if *cold* water is part of the ritual as well. All I know is the admission has my mother throwing coats and sweaters at us like she's preparing for a winter storm. But at least she's quiet and makes no mention of Sarika's eyeliner.

The lights begin to flicker on and off to give fair warning, and since my parents are avid theater fans, they shut up immediately. The lights dim one final time, and the orchestra makes a warming-up sound. We usually have no orchestra for the plays, but the new drama coach thought this would be a way to add excitement to the opening.

As I get situated and put my cast-off purse from Claire on the floor, I freeze. The strings have stopped practicing now.

As the curtains go up, the backdrop looks startlingly like St. James Academy. I realize we're at St. James, but I mean the outside of the school . . . the part that . . . I hear myself squeal. I am mortified to see they've painted the building with a car on top of it. With MY name plastered on the set. "You have got to be kidding me."

"That is so going in the yearbook." Sarika shakes her head.

My dad finally sees what everyone is murmuring about and whips around until I think he might have thrown something. "Do you see what that guy has done! I told you not to hang around worldly people, but all you did was say, 'Dad, he's not like that. Dad, I'll protect him.' And now look. Now look at how you're remembered because of Gil. Your boss." My dad's seething.

"Shhh!" a bunch of people hiss at my father, but even in the cast-off light from the stage, I can see he's having none of it.

"That boy is going to pay."

Characters shuffle onto the stage, and I clap at Max and

Claire's entrance. They take their place at a table set in the forefront while the rest of the extras pretend to dine at other lunch tables in the background.

"I thought this was supposed to be *West Side Story*!" my grandmother yells, since she's not conscious that the rest of the world still hears. "This isn't *West Side Story*! Why's Daisy's name up there? Daisy, are you in the play?"

"Mom!" My mother leans over and whispers (for everyone within ten rows) that it's part of the set and the play got changed at the last minute.

"I wish you'd told me that. I can't hear them."

The lights brighten again, and the new drama coach, Mr. Carroll, comes out center stage. "Ladies and gentlemen," he says loud enough for my grandmother to hear. "Tonight is our opening presentation of *One Sorry Chick*, and our actors are bound to be slightly nervous. If you would please refrain from talking and ensure all cell phones are completely turned off, we'll get on with the show. *One Sorry Chick* was written by me"—he places his hand on his chest—"as a commentary on what happens in our high schools today, and how tolerance is preached but still not acted upon. Even in a Christian high school."

Mr. Carroll clasps his hands and waits until the rumbles die to a murmur and then silence ensues. He stretches out his arm. "And now, please enjoy the show." He's not effeminate. He's the angry, tortured theater sort. The kind who could easily play Holden Caulfield without a great deal of acting. He doesn't seem to understand why the world doesn't embrace his obvious brilliance or why he's stuck teaching in a high school—an elite high school with a strong performing arts program, but a high school nonetheless.

214

Claire and Max are the first ones onstage, and I can see Claire is in full character, absent from herself. She delivers her first line from the diaphragm. "You're breaking up with me?" She makes a sweeping motion with her head. "Here?"

Max's character looks sheepish. "It's nothing personal, Marisa."

"Nothing personal! How can you say that to me here? Now?"

A beautiful goddess-type character comes onto the stage, and I do not like how Max's eyes follow her. I do not like it one bit.

"That's why you're breaking up with me?" Claire squeals.

The voices become muddled, and I fall into my own thoughts of how Mr. Carroll decided to use St. James as a backdrop for the play, my public humiliation as the scenery. Even in their best efforts, teachers don't get it. In his efforts to depict how cruel high school taunting can be, Mr. Carroll has only succeeded in making my own taunting stretch on for eternity—to live forever in yearbook photos.

"They could have warned me," I say to Sarika. "About the scenery."

"They probably didn't know until today when they ran through dress rehearsal," my mother tells me, turning around.

The play is long, boring, preachy, and laughable. I imagine Mr. Walker is wishing they'd gone with the tried-and-true *West Side Story*, or even *Romeo and Juliet*. Because *One Sorry Chick* is no Tony winner, and Mr. Carroll is no playwright. It's really just my life onstage—constant hazing and belittlement by the rich, popular kids, which is not the least bit entertaining. Little flares of acceptance, only to be wholly dumped into a pit like Joseph by his brothers.

It's so easy to say it's all for my own good, that God will use all my high school memories to grow and stretch me, but as I sit here watching my best friend about to go in for the kiss with Max, I wonder if there's something wrong with me that I can't remember the good times. Sarika and Angie had similar experiences at St. James, and neither of them seem to look at the downside as I do.

When Max does go in for the kiss and Claire's lips meet his, it's but a second. It's chaste, almost like you'd give your grandpa. And while it makes the play's ending completely unbelievable, it rocks my world that truly there isn't anything between Claire and Max.

They all come onstage, grab hands, and take a bow. The audience is clapping, not wildly but politely. And not because they didn't enjoy it but because there was too much reality in it to be taken lightly.

Mr. Carroll seems to think the three curtain calls were for his play and not the actors who suffered through it. He comes onstage as if to accept an award. "We regret that all of this was done at a Christian school, where one expects to be slightly sheltered from the hardships of the world, only to find Christian-inflicted pain is even worse because Christians should know better. We have changed the names to protect the innocent."

I clear my throat loudly. "I don't think we changed all the names."

I look around for Amber and Britney, and their jaws are set, their arms crossed. They may feel guilty, but it's clear that the wounds they've caused haven't penetrated. They seem unsullied by the performance and unwilling to take ownership in anything they might have done. From the dark look on Amber's face, I almost wonder if she feels like us, the victims.

"Thank you for attending our show and for giving your attention to this very vital issue. As bullying becomes more prolific than ever with the use of mixed media, Mr. Walker and I felt that we must take on this problem in our school. Especially as a school that represents Christ. Now, Daisy Crispin?" He shields his eyes and looks out into the crowd, but it's dark so I sink into my seat. "Daisy Crispin, are you out there? If you'll notice, we have a name on our set—Daisy Crispin, and she is a real student here. Daisy, can you come up onstage please?"

"She's right here!" Angie yells. She stands and yanks my hand up in the air, waving it like I've won the lottery. The harder I try to yank it back, the tighter she squeezes.

"Daisy, would you come up here, please?" Mr. Carroll asks again.

Unlike Claire, the very last thing I like is to be in the spotlight. Suddenly I'm a little girl in tights with ribbons on my hair and my parents have just performed a ridiculous song of some sort, and I can see all the strangers' faces looking at me as though I were vermin. And my parents may have been dressed as rodents for all I remember, but I see the penetrating, judgmental gazes and my stomach churns. I want to run, be anywhere but here.

I was wrong. I never wanted to be known. I wanted to be accepted. Nowhere is it more apparent that you are not accepted than in front of a group. Look at them all and it's a sea of colors and a mishmash of emotions. Look at the crowd individually and you're aware of the hard stares, the knit eyebrows, the narrowed eyes. The judgment seat of humanity.

I walk down the stairs toward the stage, but as soon as Angie lets go of me, I bolt back up the stairs as fast as my legs will carry me. Two burly guys from the football team lift me, and my legs bicycle as they carry me toward the stage. Laughter erupts in the crowd. Once on the ground, I climb the stage steps like it's the gallows and await my dark fate.

Mr. Carroll reaches out with both hands and pulls me between Max and Claire, then twists me around so that once again I'm facing the crowd. The roar in my ears goes silent and I'm that little girl again. Watching people laugh at my mom and dad, screaming, "Don't you laugh at my daddy! Don't you!" That particular incident ended in me biting the wrist of an old man, and my parents' expulsion from that particular rest home.

I see my dad in the audience and my throat is full. My tears fresh. Why did he do it? Why didn't he care that they laughed at us? At me? I still have no idea why I'm onstage, and my whole body is trembling. Max reaches for my hand and clasps it tightly, then he scoots next to me, allowing me to lean on him.

"It's all right. I'm right here with you," he whispers. His arm comes around me, and for a moment my mind goes blank and I forget about the hundreds of faces staring at me.

"I brought Miss Crispin up here because recently she has been the strong speculation of undercover behavior and questionable morals. The reason I chose to use her real name on the scenery is to highlight Daisy's commitment to purity before marriage and her innocence in some of the vicious rumors leveled her way."

I'm gonna die. Just carry me out right now. I'd run, but my legs feel too shaky to hold me. I look into Max's warm

218

chocolate eyes and forget that I am currently experiencing the most humiliating moment of my life.

"Because of Daisy's character assassination this year, she has engaged in behavior that isn't becoming, including a party at her friend's house that got out of hand, serving alcohol, and ultimately burning down part of her best friend's home. In short, often gossip can make a person act completely out of character. This is just one of the dangers in loose talk."

Speaking of character assassination.

"As a way to say thank you to Daisy for inspiring the story line of tonight's play and her commitment to the school's honors program, Mr. Walker and I would like to announce that Daisy Crispin is our first annual queen of grad night."

The audience squeals.

"Our grad night will be in celebration of the quiet saints who march boldly along in their walk—like Miss Crispin, who takes time from her busy schedule to pack food for her church's grocery ministry, make straight As, and even move out of her bedroom temporarily so that her grandparents can move in during a remodel. As a tribute to Daisy and her parents' strong devotion and commitment to the purity-before-marriage ministry, the first grad-night queen will host Celibation, a fun and nondrinking alternative to wild parties that Christian graduates have no business being at. So will you join me in giving her a congratulatory hand!"

Smiling maniacally. *Celibation?* No. So wrong. Awkward and wholly life-defining. I walk down the steps toward my mother.

"Mom," I say numbly, "I'll see you after the party. I'm going home with Claire." My flat tone tells Sarika and Angie there's no room for argument.

Still, I do my best to rise above it all. I'm not the kind of friend who can't congratulate her longtime best friend on a job well done. I head backstage with my head held high. No one even points at me. No one has to. My story is known to all now.

The cast all surrounds me. "You were all great," I say halfheartedly.

Claire stares at me. "Are you mad?"

I shake my head. "About the play? No. Celibation? Maybe a little."

Max comes beside me. "It will be great, and you've had such a fun year and maintained your cool. You've got a lot of grace, Daisy."

"I do?"

"Someday I'll explain how much."

"In the near future? Or twenty years from now?"

"Huh?"

"I wondered when you planned to tell me. Because I could really use hearing something nice about myself right now."

"How about I tell you at the cast party? You coming?"

I look at Claire. "Yeah. Yeah, I'll be there."

"Cool. I'll see you there. Gotta go get changed," he says and strides out the door.

"Oh, shoot!" Claire pulls her wig off and scratches her head. "I left my hairbrush and makeup in my locker in the gym. Can you run over and get it while I get changed, Daisy?"

"Sure. No problem. I'll be right back." I push through the exit door and enter the gym, which sits adjacent to the theater. The lights come on automatically as I enter and jog to the end of the blue lockers. Claire's is just next to mine. I do her combination and lift the latch, and a gym bag half my size tumbles out, splaying Claire's makeup all over the floor. It takes me so long to pick it all back up, the lights go out on me, and I have to wave my arms to get them to turn back on again.

I push the door to get back into the theater, but it's locked, and when I bang on the door, no one answers. I can hear the murmur of people behind the door, but it doesn't appear they can hear me. I pound for a solid half hour until the murmur stops and the lights go out again. Clearly, Claire is reveling so much in her adoration she's forgotten she has a best friend. I pound again—she wouldn't do that. This time the lights don't come back on when I wave. I. Am. Left.

I think about Max waiting for me and wondering why I didn't come back right away. My heart is in my throat. The last thing I need is another misunderstanding with Max.

"Not now, God. Please, I'm begging you! Not now!" I wander through the gym to find another exit that leads outdoors, and run my knee straight into a bench. "Ow!" I wail, grabbing my knee and jumping around on one leg. I'm so annoyed, I kick my foot into the lockers, and now that hurts too.

I finally see a green exit sign that's lit at the end of the gymnasium. I push through the door beneath it and with relish feel the cool night air on my face. My relief is brief, as the darkness extends into the empty parking lot and there is no sign that anything at all happened at St. James that night.

"Where is everyone?" I ask the stars.

❧ 19 ❧

The parking lot is dark and my car feels a million miles away. Everyone has left, and I still feel red-hot from humiliation. *It's nothing*, I tell myself. *It's all going to be over in a month*. I'll be out of school and off to college, whichever four-year will give me the best scholarship. Somewhere in a big city, where I can find a job and get lost in the crowd. No one will know my history. I'll start over. It will be easy.

"Daisy."

I scream when Claire's brother Jeremy steps out of the shadows.

"Jeremy, you scared the life out of me. What are you doing here?"

"I was waiting for you. I think you were the last one out."

I look behind me, and there's no one. Not a straggler hanging about, no cars in the parking lot but mine. It's just me and Jeremy. For some reason I feel no safety in his presence and look about to find a sign of anyone I may have missed.

"Yeah, everyone's gone," he says. "I didn't mean to scare you."

I look into his eyes, the ones tinged with pain, and there's a darkness cast upon them now, a gaze more sinister than

I remember. Of course, it's night, and we're alone, but if I didn't know better, I wouldn't even recognize the Jeremy I met at Claire's house that night.

"What are you doing here?" I ask him.

"I told you. I was waiting for you. I wanted to talk to you, and you haven't been answering your phone."

"My parents took it away," I tell him, wishing to God I hadn't given him that information.

"You said you were coming back for another interview."

"Not exactly. I said that if I decided to stay in the area for community college, I'd come and apologize, but the more I thought about it, I wasn't really sorry for what I said. I've worked hard and I don't want to go to community college. It's just not my dream. No offense is meant to Mr. Finch or anything, but I have a different idea."

"Mr. Finch is a great man to work for. You know, I told him you'd be coming back."

"I'm sorry about that, Jeremy. Do you want me to call him and explain?"

"I'd like you to do what you said you would."

"I didn't think I'd fit in there very well anyway. I'm used to a very casual work environment, and I don't have the clothing collection to work in an office where everyone is wearing suits. My mom sewed the one for my interview."

"You fit in fine there." His voice is strained with a tinge of anger that makes no sense whatsoever to me.

I shrug under the orange glow of the one light still left on in the parking lot. "I think that the job wasn't right for me. I hope you don't mind. I really appreciate you getting me the interview. I know you went out of your way for me."

"Is this how you plan to live your life? Giving up on anything that presents a roadblock? Sometimes things worth having require a fight."

What I wouldn't give for my BlackBerry at the moment. To have anyone, even my parents, at my disposal right now. I take the slightest pleasure in the fact that if they find my body somewhere, they'll lament taking away my one shot of normalcy in this life. "The BlackBerry might have saved her life!" my mom will wail.

"You're making me uncomfortable, Jeremy. I didn't want the job and Mr. Finch didn't want me."

"I'm making you uncomfortable!" He's clearly agitated. "I told my boss that you were coming back."

"Well, you shouldn't have told him that."

"I assumed, having met you at my father's house, that you were the responsible type. Claire said you were. My father said you were, but I come to find out that's not true at all. You have everyone snowed into believing you're a mature employee."

"I am the responsible sort. I showed up at the interview on time, got a lecture from your boss on how I should think, and didn't get the job. I wrote a proper thank-you for the interview anyway and left it at that. What did you expect me to do? Beg?"

"I thought you'd humble yourself for a good job. People are having to do a lot worse in this economy."

"Look, I didn't happen to agree with Mr. Finch's philosophy on life, and while I respect his viewpoints, they're not mine. I don't want to go to community college. Not that I see anything wrong with people who do, it's just not my wish, and I felt like my viewpoint was snotty and not acceptable to him. It may be snotty, but it's still my opinion and I'm entitled to one."

"So it doesn't bother you at all that I told him you could set up our database and that you'd be back."

"I've dreamed of college since I was in first grade. I'm not like other kids. I want to make something of myself, and I want to be able to call the shots in my life. Haven't you ever had a dream that you need to see realized?"

I stare at my father's car, isolated in the dark parking lot, and think of my options. My heartbeat floods my ears and adrenaline pumps through my system as I try to think of a way around Jeremy. St. James is at the top of a hill, its own solitary compound, away from the noise and distractions of the city below. Away from anyone who might come to my rescue at the moment.

"I have to get home." I take a step around Jeremy, and he grasps my shoulders. I can feel his sharp nails biting into my arms.

"You don't care that you've made a fool out of me, do you?"

"I'm sorry. Of course I care, but there's nothing more I can do about it. Not without lying about my principles."

"Principles! Ha! What does a little rich girl in a fancy school know of principles?"

"Jeremy, I'm not rich. You know I'm not rich. I'm here to get a good education so I can do what I want in the future. There's no saying Mr. Finch would have hired me regardless of what I said. We didn't seem to mesh."

"Mr. Finch will hire you. When you tell him what he wants to hear."

"Did you hear me? I don't want to tell him that. I don't believe it. College, a four-year degree, is my dream. I mean, I worked hard all these years. Community college feels unnecessary."

"You humiliated me." His jaw is tight. His words come out tinged with spit.

"Besides, I've got a job. Your father's law firm is going to hire me part-time until I graduate and over the summer."

"My father?"

Apparently, this is not what I should have said. "Please let go of me. My parents are expecting me."

He grabs me roughly by the arm. "Come with me."

"Jeremy, I can't. I have to—"

His grasp tightens and he thrusts me in front of him. "My car is over here."

All I can think of is the advice not to let someone take you to the second location. The second location is always the crime scene. It's where things happen that aren't good. Things that are shown on the nightly news that make you want to move to the country.

A thousand thoughts go through my mind, but I act on the first one. I watch Jeremy crumple into a ball after I "kick him where it counts," as we said in grammar school. I make a mad dash for my father's car, but I can't get the keys out fast enough. My dad and his stupid ancient car! *Automatic locks, Dad! A BlackBerry. All this technology that could save my life right now.*

Jeremy grasps me from behind and I can't move my arms. He twists me around in front of him. "Walk! And don't try anything funny!"

"What do you want from me? Your father is going to find out about this, you know. Is this who you want him to know? You're a Christian, Jeremy. You told me so. God can see us right now. He's watching you and he wants you to do the right thing. He wants you to act in love, like your mother always did." He pushes me down to the asphalt and I feel the gravel cut into my face.

"Don't you dare talk about my mother! She lived her whole life doing right when my father abandoned her. She never told him about me. She knew who he was. Who he would be if she told him he was a father. She was right about him! All he ever cared about was money."

"No, Jeremy, he's so proud of you. He's so excited to have a son. He always wanted one."

"He said that?"

"Oh yes." *God, forgive me for lying, but get me out of this mess. Please. I won't whine about wherever you send me to school or even if I dress like a dork for the rest of my life. Just get me home to my beloved garage.* "He said that you were working at a very important law firm, and I should take that job first if it were offered to me."

Jeremy's car is nowhere in sight, and I wonder where he's taking me as he roughly pushes me forward. I dropped my father's keys when I fumbled with him, and my hope of getting away is dwindling. I can only hope that the Jeremy I met at Claire's house that night comes back before Mr. Hyde hurts me in some way. I try to look into his eyes under the streetlamp and see a sign of the warm eyes. I look for some way to connect, but his stare is vacant, his face wrinkled with a quiet, seething rage.

His car is hidden in the garbage dump station, and he opens the door and pushes my head down and in, like I'm on a cop show. I get in without a battle, because here at the school without even a janitor, I can't help but think of escape opportunities. Even down the hill, I could jump from the car and roll onto a neighbor's yard with shouts for help. I sit in the passenger seat, put my hands in my lap, and close my eyes in prayer.

I worry my journal will be found. (Probably the reason I burned the last one!) You know, I don't even worry over anything racy. That's just it—I don't want to be exposed for my pathetic desperation. For it to echo throughout history in my journal. My first kiss with Chase—that was blech. My first kiss with Max, which was magical and lit up every part of my brain like fireworks.

Jeremy gets into the car, which is your basic Toyota Camry with nothing special to differentiate it from a thousand other cars on the road, but I look at his arms and wonder if I could take him.

His expression is still knotted with pain. "Why would you kick me?"

"You're taking me somewhere against my will. I tried telling you I didn't want to go. What would you suggest?"

"You lied to me. You have to make it right."

"What does that mean?" He starts up the car, and my mind starts racing again with ideas. "It's almost eleven. My dad is going to come looking for me."

"Your dad should know he's raised a Jezebel."

"Jeremy, your dad should know where you intend to take me. Why don't you call him?"

"My father is a selfish leftover from the eighties. He has no moral consciousness, nor is he living for the Lord."

"You're kidnapping me," I wail. "How is that living for the Lord?"

"Like yeast in the dough, we are to cast out those not living for the Lord."

"Cast us out where? From the church, right? Are you taking me to see my pastor? Is that where we're going?"

He turns and grins at me. I can see the white of his teeth

228

in the darkened car, and as we head down the curvy road toward the flatlands and people, I start to think of ways he might go, places I might jump out. As if he reads my mind, I hear the doors lock.

Why didn't I think to leave some sort of clue by my dad's car?

"I don't understand what you want from me," I say in a wrecked voice. "Do you mean to hurt me?" I figure I have nothing to lose with straight honesty at this point.

He doesn't answer.

"Jeremy," I plead. I stop when I see houses. We've reached the neighborhoods below the school. The car doesn't slow to a reasonable speed and he doesn't stop at the corner, he just wheels around the edge. I close my eyes and pray like I've never prayed before. I apologize to my parents, my grandparents, Max, Chase, Amber, anyone I've ever wronged . . . until we're in downtown San Jose. I look at the people on the street, who, quite frankly, don't look much safer than the lunatic next to me, and soon Jeremy pulls into a parking lot filled with revelers for the Saturday night restaurants and bars.

"What are we doing?"

"You're going to start the program I asked you to."

I look up at the marble office building. "I'm not."

He steps out of the car, locks it again, and comes around to my side of the door. He unlocks it, and I smack the button and lock it again. We play this game until it gets ridiculous. I notice a pair of policemen on horseback and wait for him to unlock the door once more, then kick my way out. He's flat on his back when I run to the policemen and flag them down.

"I've been kidnapped!"

"Kidnapped?" they ask.

Jeremy sees me talking to them as I point. He scrambles up and gets back into his car. One of the officers gallops to the vehicle and the other stays with me. Funny thing, how a horse intimidates a Camry.

"Do you know him?"

"He's my best friend's brother. Well, half brother. He just came into their lives two months ago." I've confused the officer. But that doesn't stop me from rambling.

"Are you hurt?"

"Well, no, but I didn't know that he was thinking of hurting me at the time. I tried to get free of him and kicked him, but then he got up and he got angry. I shouldn't have stopped, but I had nowhere to go, really. Everyone had left. You would think there would have been at least one straggler, right? But nope. Then he grabbed me and—"

"Slow down. We'll need to get a statement, and given your age, it's best that we go down to the station."

"But aren't you going to arrest him? Because he wanted an apology, but he didn't deserve one, and you can't really kidnap people to get an apology, right? Isn't that like coercion or something illegal like that? And he thought I was a snob, but I'm not a snobby rich kid. We live on the east side of town, and I only go to St. James because my parents believe in a Christian education—"

He rubs his forehead as though I've given him a headache. "Stop. We'll get your statement later. Stay here. Don't move until I come back."

"Excuse me," I say to a group of friends going to a comedy club. "Can I borrow someone's cell phone just for a minute?"

One of the women takes out an iPhone and hands it to

230

me. I can't call Claire. How do I explain having her brother arrested? At least I hope they're going to arrest him. The officer never did answer me on that. But Claire is a trip I need to make in person. And my dad will kill me for not being where I said I'd be—with Claire—so I call Max.

"Hello?"

"Max, it's Daisy. I'm on Second Street, downtown across from the Improv. Could you come pick me up? I'll explain everything, but you know I wouldn't ask if—"

"I'll be right there." He ends the call.

"Thank you," I say to the woman, handing back the phone.

"No problem."

As I look over, I spy Jeremy being handcuffed, and my mind races to the future. To explaining this to Claire, to her father. Ugh. To my parents. I have nothing to feel guilty for—Jeremy's actions brought on his own consequences—but that doesn't stop me from realizing how they will hurt people I love.

Then there's my school. I have finally been reinstated as "good" again, only to find I'm wrapped up in yet another inexplicable drama with an older man, a car, and a lack of common sense. Don't even get me started on hosting Celibation. It's just a fact: things are not meant to go right for me.

❧ 20 ❧

Three police cars, with sirens blaring and lights whirling (which there's no need for, so clearly the officers just want to make a statement to the downtown crowd), pull into the parking lot behind the Camry, behind the horses. I want to crawl into the sewer grate and disappear. I've given my statement, but I still have to go down to the station. Some nonsense about being a minor and alone in the middle of the city by myself. Whatever. I keep praying Max will get here before they cart me off to the station. Even if I can't go with him, his presence and a ride home might convince the cops to let me go.

With the comedy show about to start across the street, the parking lot has filled to capacity, and I pace the sidewalk counting as I try to make time pass. Finally, Max pulls up in his father's car and rolls the window down when he spots me.

"Are you all right?" He reaches his hand out toward me.

I nod and force myself not to burst into tears.

"Get in. I'll get you home. Your parents must be worried sick." He looks over at the police cars. "You don't have anything to do with that, right?" I can tell by the tone of his voice that he knows I do, and that says so much about my world.

I nod. "I have to go down to the station, but I'm hoping if they see I have a ride home—"

"Daisy!"

"It's not my fault!"

"It's never your fault, but drama follows you like a sick puppy." He laughs when he says this, but that doesn't make me feel any better.

I frown. "I know, but this time—"

"I'm kidding, Daisy. I'm only glad you're okay. Not the best time for a joke, sorry. I'll go park the car and be right back. Tell the policeman I can take you home." He smiles before he slowly pulls the car away.

I watch his taillights and feel myself relax after the barking of his orders. I needed someone to tell me what to do in this moment. "Even when you're annoyed with me, Max, you're still adorable."

The policeman on the horse clip-clops back over to me, and it makes me wonder why they never get off their horses. A street cop on a Segway reads Jeremy his rights. It's hard to take anyone seriously on a Segway—the balance is far too precarious. It's like a video on a skateboard on *America's Funniest Home Videos*—you almost know it's not going to end well. I stare at the police car as a cop presses Jeremy's head down and maneuvers him into the car. Jeremy glances at me, and his expression is creepy and unforgiving. My body shudders as the police car drives off.

"We've called your parents. Your father will meet us at the station. We like to have an adult present when a minor gives a statement." He writes something on the pad.

"I've already given a statement. Will it really help to give another one at the station?" My voice comes out whiny. Hate that.

"You'll just repeat what you've told me here and we'll have your father sign that he was present during the statement."

I sigh. Another adult who thinks I'm inept. "My dad's health isn't great. Is it all right if my friend brings me home and I make another statement in the morning? I mean, I'm not in trouble, right?"

"No, but we do need your cooperation and would appreciate procedure. I'm sure your father would want us on this case as soon as possible."

"Yeah," I say in defeat. "Can my friend drive me?"

The officer stares at me.

"Look. His name is Max Diaz. He has a job. He's a good student and he's eighteen . . ." Max is walking toward us, and I can't stop my face from exploding with a smile. I'm trying to be subtle, but it's no use.

"And he's a lot better looking than me." The officer laughs. "Fine. Here's my card with the address of the station. If you're not there in twenty minutes, I'm coming to get you personally."

I nod with so much enthusiasm I could double as a bobble head. I turn as Max comes closer, and if I could skip into his arms, I would, but his walk is brisk and his expression cold. Dang, he looks so cute even when he's in protective mode. I snuggle into his arms, even though they're robotic and parentlike at the moment.

"Can I touch her?" Max asks the police officer.

The cop bursts into laughter. "That's between her father and you."

"Not what I meant," Max says. "I didn't know if—"

"Never mind, kid. Just get her to the station and stay out of trouble. This the first time that guy has bothered you?" the cop asks me. "I mean, he doesn't have any friends who might put you in jeopardy?"

"No." I shake my head. "I wounded his pride, but I won't do it again."

"I'm going to suggest you file a restraining order against him."

"It's my best friend's half brother."

"We'll talk about it down at the station."

I look at Max and we start to walk to his car. "I had to park kind of far away. The lot filled up for that show."

"I know. They all walked by me wondering what I did."

"What did you do?"

"I didn't listen to my gut and I should have. Claire's half brother has issues."

"So does Claire." Max snorts.

"No, I mean real issues. Like, they tell his story on an episode of *48 Hours Mystery* issues."

Max turns serious as he opens his car door. "Where's your cell phone?"

"My parents took it away. They were worried that—never mind." The last thing I want to do is explain my parents' distrust of Gil. Or why I had a cell phone in the first place. It's not going to make any sense to a guy like Max. Or anyone whose parents see a cell phone as a necessary part of communication.

Max pulls his phone out of his back pocket. "Take this. I don't want you without a phone in case this guy gets out."

I shake my head. "I can't."

Max slides his phone into my hand. "I'm not taking no for an answer, so there's nothing for you to argue about. Get in the car. We need to get to the station." Max waits for me to get in and shuts the door. I look up and see the concern on his face, and his protection fills me with warmth. Regardless of all the things that go wrong in my life, there's a lot that goes right.

Max gets into the driver's seat and looks directly at me with his warm, deep eyes. They radiate concern, if that's possible. "What happened tonight?"

I feel myself shaking as I think about the night. "After everyone left to celebrate, I think they forgot about me." I stare at my lap. "I know, it's strange."

"No, I just wondered why you weren't at the cast party."

"But not enough to actually check?" I try to keep the edge out of my voice.

"I should have."

"After you all left, I sort of got locked in the gym. I eventually found my way out, but Claire's brother was waiting in the dark parking lot. The lights go off at a certain time, and I guess I overstayed my welcome. Jeremy pushed me into his car—"

Max raises his eyebrows. "Against your will?"

"I don't think you get shoved into a car you want to enter."

"Sorry. Stupid question." Max turns the key and starts his car. He pats my leg. "I'm so sorry, Daisy. I wish I'd been there. I should have been there."

"Jeremy felt I had wronged him at the job interview. He wanted me to make it right so that he could hold his head high in his office. A pride thing, I guess."

Max's expression softens and he grasps my wrist. "You're trembling."

"I'm still cold, I guess."

He tears off his jean jacket and hands it to me before putting the car into drive. I pull it around me and sniff the collar, which smells like Max, woodsy and spicy.

"You were fabulous in the play," I say to change the subject.

"It was a subject close to my heart. A beloved, sweet girl who is mistreated and gets back up to fight another day. A true heroine. Who wouldn't want to date her?"

I lay my head on his shoulder and relax as I feel the beating of his heart. It's so steady and consistent, and though Max's actions haven't been this year, somehow I know there's more to it. I pull away.

"I'm going to start college as a redhead."

Max gives me his look, with the cocked eyebrow.

"Because I've tried being a mousy brunette, and I've tried being a blonde without much better luck, so I'm thinking red for college."

"Can I call you Lucy?" he asks. "And get exasperated in Spanish when you drive me loco? Because maybe, just maybe, you should be a redhead."

"Max."

"Yes, Daisy?"

"Again, you were fabulous tonight in the play. I'm sorry I was such a baby about the whole thing. I didn't realize that you and Claire were—you know, were there for me after all."

"I had to do the play to get the final credits. My dad would have killed me, and your father made my pursuit of you off-limits. I thought it was best to ignore you rather than face looking into those eyes every day. Seeing what I could not give you."

"It would have been better than thinking you were interested in Claire."

"Claire scares me."

I laugh. "She scares most people, but I thought of you as superhero material. Certainly not put off by the difficult tasks in life."

"Some mercurial types are worth fighting for. You, Daisy, may change like the wind, but I don't. When I ignored you in Chemistry, it wasn't because my feelings changed, it was because your father told me to stay away from you. I thought if I had any hope of a future with you, I'd best stay on his good side until you turned eighteen." He grins. "I'm not Chase. Don't make me pay for his games. Look in my eyes and tell me if you can't trust me."

"Then why didn't you look at me?"

"I knew my eyes would betray me."

"I won't make you pay for Chase, for my own ignorance. I wish I knew what was happening with you is all. Why didn't you tell me what my dad said? I feel like I've wasted so much of the year on trying to figure out what was wrong with me."

"Maybe that's the issue. Maybe it isn't you and you're always looking within, rather than believing someone else has the issue. Sometimes other people suck, you know?"

"Yeah," I agree. "I guess there's a time to look for the best in people, and a time to just pray for our enemies and call it a day. Pearls before swine and all that." As we drive through the city, we pass a homeless man, lumpy from jackets and blankets. He's pushing a grocery cart with an overflowing mound of stuff. "I wonder what leads to that kind of life. Choices? Lack of family? Friends? Mental illness? Drugs?"

"Could be any of those things. Or maybe a combination. So . . . back to us."

238

"Us? Is there an us?"

"I'm not going back to Argentina for college."

"You're not?" I try to feign disinterest. No one wants a girl who is too eager. Not that being less eager has helped me all that much, but a girl has to try. "Wh-where would you go?" I stammer.

"My dad wants me to do the basics here before I transfer home. I think he's still hoping to talk me into changing my choice of careers. Seminary is something I'm going to have to move my father into slowly."

I laugh. "Too bad you're not my father's son. He'd mortgage his life to send you to seminary. So you're not leaving?"

"Not yet. Are you anxious to be rid of me?"

I giggle nervously and bite my lip until it hurts to regain my composure. "No, not at all. It's just I've had it in the back of my head that community college was for losers, that being a pastor wasn't really a noble calling, and you totally convict me, Max. I'm an intellectual snob and, to top it off, wrong."

"What makes you come to that conclusion?"

"You're willing to fight to be a pastor. It's your calling. You're not doing it just because you can't do something else. And community college? The truth is, it's a better value in this economy. I've been a snob, so convinced that the right school would make all the difference in my future, but that's up to me." Secretly I think I'd follow Max to community college. I'd do it with zeal, which perhaps makes me more pathetic than I thought. I'd give up my dreams so easily?

"I don't know that any pastor fits anything but that description, other than dedicated. You wouldn't do it for the money."

"Maybe it's my calling to give up some of my prejudices."

"My own father thinks it's a waste of time."

"Your mom's okay with it?" I ask him, knowing she's waiting back in Argentina.

"It's a longer story than you have time for." He pulls into the police station parking lot. "We're here. You want me to come in?"

"No, don't do that. My father will think you had something to do with this. If I have any hope of convincing him you are worthy of my courtship time, I have to put off instant gratification." I reach for the door handle, but he tells me to wait and comes around and helps me out of the car.

He cups my face with his hands and stares at me as if he can see everything inside me, like one of those see-through fish. "It's okay that you don't have your whole future laid out right now. Maybe something better will come along. Maybe that allows for God to tell you where to go." He kisses me with force, and I'm lost in the moment as everything around me dims and fades from my vision and ears. "Call me when you get home. I don't care what time it is."

"All right."

"Daisy, you may think this is all some crazy trip, but every journey has a purpose. Even Moses's journey for forty years in the desert."

"I hate when you talk like you're an old man or, worse yet, like you just finished *The Iliad*."

Max kisses me again. "You're hot. Amazingly, supremely hot. And I liked *The Iliad*."

"That's better." I shiver. "Do you mind if I keep your jacket?"

"No problem, but how are you going to explain it to your father?"

I sniff the collar again, and it soothes me like a warm bath. "I'll figure it out."

He turns away from me, which some might say is his best view. I wouldn't say it. I might think it, but I would never say it. *But dang!*

❧ ■ ❧

My dad rushes toward me in the police station as if I've lost a limb.

"I'm fine, Dad. No more drama, all right? I've had enough to last tonight. Even for me."

"You were supposed to take Claire home and come right home after the party. We've been frantic!"

"I would have called you, but I didn't have a cell phone."

"Why weren't you with Claire like you said you would be?"

"She got caught up in the cast party and forgot about me."

"Then why didn't you come straight home?"

"I tried to, Dad."

The familiar officer waves us over. "We've got a room in here for your statement."

"Claire had all that stage makeup on, you know? So I waited a long time for her, but in the excitement, she ran off and forgot me. I was waiting like an idiot, not realizing all that noise was people leaving."

My dad rolls his eyes. "How is it these things happen only to you?"

Because I don't want every place in the world to look like our living room? "No idea. Take it up with God. I don't know. I finally found a door without an alarm on it and let myself out. When I got out there—"

"Save it for the statement." Officer Barillas leads us into a room with mirrors and sits us down at a table. My father is a nervous wreck, his face is beaded with sweat, and his hair

241

is greasy looking and uncombed. He looks like a hobo, and I know with us being at the police station, it's really not an issue right now, but . . . *Gee, Dad. Do you think you could try a little less?* Some of my mother's costumes don't look as realistic as my dad's natural hobo look.

I give my statement again ad nauseam, and then there's a knock on the door. Officer Barillas gets up and opens it to Claire's father, who is dressed in a striped, point-collar shirt. Which only makes my father look more homeless and hopeless. I know he's the one with the son in jail for kidnapping, yet one would never believe it by looking at the men side by side.

"Daisy, are you all right?" Mr. Webber looks haggard and sounds out of breath. He's not his usual coiffed self, even in the dress shirt, which makes me feel a little better about my dad the hobo.

"I'm fine," I tell him honestly. "Is Jeremy okay?"

"This is all my fault." He looks at the officer and clamps his mouth shut. Apparently the lawyer in him is stronger than his desire to help at the moment. "Jeremy's fine."

"Officer, if you'd excuse us, I'd like to have a talk with our lawyer," my dad says, indicating Mr. Webber. The tension in the room is frenetic, and I wish I could escape with the officer.

My dad waits for the door to close and points at Mr. Webber. "You knew this kid was a crackpot and you didn't tell me? You told my daughter? What did you expect a seventeen-year-old girl to do about it?"

"You've got it wrong." Mr. Webber brushes off any guilt, and the old Mr. Webber I remember, the one who lets responsibility slip away, is in the room with us. "I never thought he would be violent in any way. I only warned Daisy that he

242

seemed to have trouble with boundaries and taking no for an answer. I didn't want her to take the job at his law firm so she wouldn't have to be around him."

"Listen, I've put up with you ignoring your own daughter and blaming her for having a party when there's not a parent in the household to stop her, but this has gone too far. You have a responsibility to these girls—"

"I agree," Mr. Webber says. "I've abdicated my authority and it's come back to haunt me in serious ways."

"But it's still about you, isn't it? You can't see what you've done to your daughter, or mine for that matter. It's uncomfortable for you."

"Dad!"

"Stay out of this, Daisy." My dad turns back to Mr. Webber. "Those parents at St. James didn't sue you for throwing a party where beer was served. They sued you for not even knowing it happened. They tried to get through to you that you weren't acting like a parent, and yet you're still doing damage control instead of fighting for what matters, while you let innocents take the rap." My dad has spittle coming out the side of his mouth, and honestly, I didn't know he had this kind of fire in him. In my whole life, I've never realized what a hero my father really is, and I'm shamed by my previous thoughts that money and a good job make Mr. Webber a "real" man. "I'm pressing charges against your son, and I won't be manipulated into any deals or sweet back-room bargains. He belongs locked up, and if I had it in my power, I'd have you locked up with him for negligence."

"I agree," Mr. Webber says. "I came down here to tell Daisy I was proud of her. She did the right thing turning Jeremy in to the police. I'm not a great father, Pierce. I admit that. I'm absent half the time and distant the rest of the time. I'm working on it, but I swear, I never meant to put Daisy in any danger."

My father's stoic expression doesn't change. "She didn't have a choice. Your daughter was supposed to be with her but went to another party and left her alone at the school. You can't simply live life as one giant escape from reality and expect things to turn out right!"

Considering my dad hasn't had a real job in years and generally dresses up as a pirate or furry animal during his workday, this doesn't speak well for his lecture on escaping reality, but maybe the difference is my dad has always taken a safe trip away from reality. And he's never left others to clean up after him.

"You can't blame Claire for this. She's not Daisy's keeper."

"I would have happily stayed at the theater had I known my daughter would be alone. I also would have preferred you told me, not my daughter, about your son's manipulations. That would be how adults handle things."

I can see Mr. Webber's face reddening with anger, but he remains calm and his voice is even as he responds. "You have every right to be angry with me. I've let my family down, and yours as well, in more ways than I can count, but I want to make it right now. I'll do what I have to do to earn back your trust." He thrusts out a hand, and my father pauses before clutching it. Mr. Webber steps out of the room.

"Dad, be kind to Mr. Webber, please. He really is trying to make things right. I don't want him to get discouraged. His faith is shaky at best."

My dad nods and the tense hold on his shoulders relaxes. "All right, Daisy. You've always been a good reader of people, so I'll take your word for it on Mr. Webber."

"I wasn't very discerning about Jeremy, that's for sure. But the guy I saw tonight was not the guy I met at Claire's house. It's very strange. I mean, he was weird when I went to the job interview, but tonight it was like his very soul was missing. So creepy."

My dad puts his chin on my shoulder and hugs me around the chair. "I'm so proud of you, Daisy. God did this for me. So I could see you're growing into an adult and it's time to let you take care of yourself a bit. I blamed Mr. Webber there, but I don't really. I don't want anything to happen to you, and it's easier to blame someone than believe it could happen."

"Really, Dad?"

"Your mother and I have even decided to let you date that Max character. Before my phone rings off the wall with his requests. I'll give him credit—he's persistent, and he tells a father what he wants to hear. I do believe it's real. He has an honesty and a respect about him. Unlike that Chase character you followed around for so long."

This makes me smile.

"Besides, he earned the right tonight."

"Tonight?" I snuggle Max's jacket around me, wondering if my father noticed. I wear so much of Claire's clothing, I can't imagine that he knows what's mine and what isn't. Unless, of course, one of my mother's homemade tags is sticking out of it.

"The police weren't the first ones to call me with your whereabouts. Max Diaz was."

"He was?" I feel slightly betrayed.

"I like this young man. He has your best interest at heart." My dad wags his finger. "But if I find out he's playing games, I'll send him back to Argentina on the first plane, got it?"

Grinning, I give my dad a kiss on the cheek. "Thank you, Daddy."

"You mean the world to me, Daisy. I know I don't always trust everyone around you, but I've learned to trust you. Even when you have the worst possible luck, you manage. God looks after you and you manage well. I'm proud of you, sweetheart."

"Really, Dad? You think that?"

"Right now I think it. We'll see how I feel when Max comes to pick you up for your first date. I can't exactly keep you home from a grad night called Celibation now, can I?"

"What do you think is going to happen to Jeremy?" I ask.

"Nothing, if his father's law office gets involved."

"Dad, give Mr. Webber the benefit of the doubt. Please?"

"You're right, Daisy, that's the Christian thing to do. If you say he's changed, I'm going to believe you until proved otherwise." My dad takes my BlackBerry out of his shirt pocket and hands it to me. "I think you need this."

"It's all charged up!" I cry. I rub it against my cheek, feeling its velvety smoothness, missing its small radiation glow. I kiss the face of it and notice the magic red light beeping. "Daddy, I have mail!"

He laughs. "I remember the day when a cookie would make you that happy."

"A cookie still makes me happy," I tell him. "But my Black-Berry makes me much, much happier. At least 537 percent happier."

"I took the contract over from Gil. Or at least I will when it's over in six months. That way you can keep your number. But you'll have to pay the bill."

"I will!"

"And I don't want you working for Claire's father. At least not yet."

"I don't think I'm cut out for law anyway. I'm too precise with my love of math, and the law's version of truth is relative at best."

"You can take the job with Gil after school."

"You trust him?"

"I trust *you*. I understand that he was only trying to help you. Though I've told him we'll be needing no more of his kind of assistance."

Wonders never cease.

❧ 21 ❦

"We're graduating today!" Sarika, usually the calm one of the bunch, is jumping up and down in her turquoise sari with tiny silver and crystal beading all over it. Whenever I see Sarika in her colorful saris, where bling is acceptable in the middle of the day, I'm jealous. I just look bedazzled and tacky when I do that.

"We look so hot!" Angie chimes in. "Today we can tell all the guys who thought us unworthy how *un-wor-thy* they were. Look at us and weep, boys. When all those bodacious girls have put on a few pounds at our reunion and we still look twenty and have great jobs, life will look different!" Angie is wearing a sage-green satin gown with brown tulle over the skirt and gold beading at the hemline, which falls just above the knee.

"You do look hot," I tell her. "But then how was anyone supposed to notice with your head in a book all the time? I give you props, Angie, you showed us how it's done, this high school thing. You never worried about what others thought."

Claire twirls in front of us, and she is once again the belle of our ball. With a mother like hers, it's to be expected. Although Claire has always had excellent taste when she chose to showcase it, rather than try to stand out with a spider nose ring or purple stripes in her hair, she always looks best when she isn't acting a role but simply being herself. Claire's mother bought her a marine-blue Badgley Mischka silk organza dress. The underlayer is a navy form-fitting mini with a sheer organza top layer in a classic ruffle, so it's both cute and hot. It's cinched in the middle by a ruched pleat, and she's wearing four-inch bronze, strappy heels.

"Dang, girl!" Angie says.

"No kidding," Sarika adds.

It's impossible to look at Claire now and think she didn't always have the power to go home again—or in this case, be popular. The fact that she always chose us over appearances says a lot about the real Claire. The one who is under that trouble-making, attention-seeking, mercurial actress. She's steadier than I gave her credit for because she could have left us a long time ago.

And me? I didn't do so badly myself. My mother made me a cream-colored, flirty, girly dress with several small rosette appliqués along the bust. Streams of silk chiffon fabric burst from the empire waistline like a tulip's petals. Mom made the skirt a bit longer than I would have preferred, but in the end it hides my scrawny legs, so it works. I tried to borrow a pair of Mrs. Webber's heels, but I couldn't walk in them very well. Having to make a speech at tonight's grad party, I decided my ballet flats were best for the occasion.

"You all look so beautiful!" Mrs. Webber cries as she videotapes us and walks around each of us, detailing our entire look with a drawn up-and-down motion. "Okay, now get together, everyone!" We huddle, she films us some more, and then she narrates what each of us is wearing. "Stay here. I'm going to get the camera." She leaves the room, and Chelsea takes out her own camera to capture her work.

Chelsea is Gil's sister and an elite hair and makeup artist in a fancy Los Gatos salon. Mrs. Webber hired her for this momentous occasion so that we all might have swept updos and perfect makeup. With our grad night called Celibation and me as its official host, I'm wondering if we shouldn't have donned Amish bonnets and called it a day.

Chelsea blots Claire's lips and motions us to stand by the great marble tub in the corner. "You all look like an international beauty show. You're all beautiful and you're all ready!" she announces.

Sarika, Angie, Claire, and I check our reflections in Mrs. Webber's massive bathroom mirror. "Your mom was so cool to do this," Angie says.

"I think she got worried when she saw your rainbow eyes that you might do that and ruin the pictures," Claire says.

"Claire!" we all yell in unison.

"Just saying."

"It doesn't seem real that we're actually going to graduate," Sarika says. "It seems like yesterday we all started in that sorry freshman choir."

"It's not real until we walk across that stage and Mr. Walker hands us our diplomas," I say. "Until that happens, I am not counting my chickens because one never knows what could occur with me in the middle of it."

"Weird how high school sucks in the day-to-day. Nothing but agony of homework, rejection, and hazing, but if I look back on the whole of it, life was pretty good," Claire says. "We had a pretty good run."

"We did," Angie agrees. "Claire, you started out in the

250

B-list choir and ended your senior year as the lead in the final play."

"Angie," Claire says back to her, "you started out in that pathetic chorale group, ended up lead piano in the advanced orchestra, missed out on most social functions—including burning my house down—developed your first crush this year, learned makeup is your friend, and you're off to Stanford. Not bad."

"What about Sarika?" Angie says. "She started in the choir, ate nothing but vegetables, and managed to be class valedictorian. She got early entry into Harvard and was never sidetracked by a guy because she still trusts her parents to pick out a husband for her. That is delaying instant gratification and avoiding all the male rejection the rest of us faced."

"No kidding, and I faced all that rejection for nothing because my parents wouldn't let me date anyway." I laugh. "Like I was a glutton for punishment."

All three of them look to me. Chelsea starts packing up her makeup. "Daisy, my brother said it best. You have an old soul. Maybe you were too good for all these childish high school boys. God has better things for you."

Chelsea's comment makes me feel a hundred feet tall, but the rest of my friends are silent.

"You're all at a loss for words," I say. "It's okay, I'll help. I started out in chorale, wanting nothing more than to garner a boyfriend in high school. I . . . I made a list in a prom journal that led only to historical accuracy on my many, many rejections. I lost my job, but that was okay because I got it back again. My parents moved me to the garage, but that led to a little more freedom and better access to my neighbor's wireless internet. Of course, I had to change neighbors, but it was worth it in the long run. The best date of my life so far turned out to be Max picking me up and taking me to the police station to make a statement. And my first real date is one at an event tonight called Celibation, which I will host as the symbol for all things pure. Or as the symbol for rejection, depending on your outlook."

Chelsea zips up her case and walks over to me. "I hate to tell you girls this, but high school is hard for most people. The world lies open to you now. With those fabulous grades and prestigious schools, you won't even remember the bad times—only how they made you better people and helped you evolve into the you that you're supposed to be."

Mrs. Webber comes back into the room. "Girls, huddle together so I can take your picture."

We huddle together, smile our biggest "we're outta here" smiles, and head to St. James Academy. My only thought is, *It was the best of times. It was the worst of times.*

Mr. Webber got us a stretch limo to take to graduation. Once we're all in it, I think of my parents and grandparents huddled in my dad's Pontiac and feel slightly guilty. Albeit only slightly. The rest of me is thoroughly enjoying Pellegrino sparkling water, which will not stain my dress if I spill it.

I'd like to say that all eyes turn toward us as we roll up in the great white limo, but it's a sea of limos—some Hummers, one pink—so we're low men on the limo totem poll. Again.

Still, the driver gets out and opens the door, and we emerge from the car like we are new creatures in our silk and organza, our makeup ready for the red carpet.

As I step out of the car, Max greets me with a hug and takes my hand in both of his, and all is right in the world. "Can I talk to you a minute?"

"We'll see you in there," Claire says.

"We'll save you a seat," Sarika adds.

As I gaze into Max's deep brown eyes, a thousand thoughts rush through my head—and none of them are good. There is goodbye in his eyes, and I wonder if my whole life will be like this. I wait for something great to happen, for life to sail like a great ship cast upon the sea, only to find it smashes into the rocks onshore, breaking into a billion bits.

"You're leaving again," I say to him.

"How did you know?"

I look at my feet and suddenly wish I'd risked the heels so that I felt more confident gazing at my pedicured toes between the stilettos. I'm like a child in my ballet flats, and my toes instantly turn inward. "Your eyes tell me. My father finally said we could have our date tonight. Official and everything, and now you tell me that you're leaving the country. Is it me?"

"Look into my eyes. You seem to see right through me. So look and tell me that I want to leave. That I wanted any of this to happen. All of our time together is not wasted."

My heart swells as I look into his eyes. He's not like other guys. He's not lying, and yet he's leaving me, so essentially the results are the same. These feelings are worse than the daily rejection I've faced here at St. James, because Max matters.

He places his hand on my jaw, and his touch makes me forget my fears about his leaving and drown myself in the moment. Which I don't ever want to forget. "You look absolutely beautiful today."

"When are you leaving?"

"After grad night. My mom's expecting me and sent me a ticket to Argentina. She wants me to start at her alma mater this fall."

"You're not coming back?"

"I don't think so. I plan to study in Buenos Aires. It's cheaper there and my mom wants me home. She says my father has been here long enough. It's been two years since I've lived with her."

I force myself not to whine out loud, *What about me?* The words are stuck in my throat and I can't say anything else, but then the infantile voice comes bubbling out of me. "I wish I'd never met you!"

He nods. "It would have been easier. Had I known how your father felt about dating in the first place, maybe it would have been better not to have let each other in."

"Does that make it easier on your conscience?" I ask him.

"My conscience is sick right now, Daisy. I understand that I'm young, that everyone thinks this is nothing more than puppy love, but I know you know differently. What we have we'll never be able to explain to others. Not your father, not Claire, no one. We seem ridiculous because most of what passes between us is silent, and even though we've had no time together this year, that hasn't stopped the feelings. Not for me anyway."

"Me either," I admit. "I know you love God. I see it in your actions."

"Because he first loved us, we can love others."

"Don't go."

"Don't ask me to stay. My mother gave me up for this education, for me to help my father get the business going, but it's time to go home."

I nod, choking back tears lest I ruin my professional makeup. I don't want Max to remember an ugly cry as the last face of Daisy Crispin.

254

Max starts to walk and holds my hand in his. I can feel my grip tighten and I can't bear to let him go. I've thought about my education and my future for my entire school life, and now I can think of nothing else but following my heart to Buenos Aires.

The crowds are sparse in the parking lot as I catch sight of my dad's Pontiac.

"Daisy!" my father calls out to me. I stop. Max tries to let go of my hand, but I clutch his and won't release him. Let my father see. Max is leaving and I don't plan on letting go until I have to.

"Dad, aren't you in there yet? You're going to get terrible seats."

He films my words and keeps the camera high and focused—I'm assuming this is so there is no sign of Max in the movie. My head will be giant, but Max will be nonexistent. Something my father has hoped for my entire life when it comes to guys and me.

"Molly, get in there with her," my father barks.

My mother comes and stands between Max and me. He releases my hand and waves at me. "I'll see you inside."

Max waved at me! Like I'm nothing but an onlooker in a parade. My grandparents stand beside my mother and we all smile for the camera, while my heart is breaking inside. I don't expect anyone to understand. What everyone saw, what was apparent to the rest of the world, is not what we felt.

"Daisy, smile! My, you have a lot of makeup on," my dad says. The camera's lens droops toward the asphalt.

"Pierce, lift the camera up. She needs to get inside."

My dad narrates, "This is our beloved daughter graduating from the prestigious St. James Academy with letters of acceptance to many elite colleges for the fall. She's wearing a lot of makeup, but—"

"Dad!" Out of the corner of my eye, I see Max disappear into the auditorium. The last time I stood in this parking lot at night, Claire's brother went postal and kidnapped me. This is not a good place for me.

"Now, you're going to stay with Claire after the ceremony, right? You will not be alone," my grandfather says.

"No, Grandpa. Claire's father will make sure I'm well-chaperoned, and I have my phone right here."

I calm them enough and we all take our seats. At first I don't hear Mr. Walker call my name when it's time for me to walk across the stage. All those years of preparation and I almost miss it because my mind is locked in a nightmare of epic proportions—the first grad night from the dark side that takes one girl's social ineptitude and puts it on display for all to bear witness to and ridicule.

"I got straight As!" I say to Mr. Walker as he hands me my diploma. But now I'll be remembered as the girl no one wanted to sleep with and the school made an entire celebration out of it. Correction: *celibation*.

❧ 22 ❧

Grad night begins exactly the way prom night did: with a Breathalyzer test and a pat down for any bottles on my person. The good news is that I'm not the one performing the test.

I'm frantic when I arrive to find Max and get my final moments with him before he leaves. I have to think about what I never got to possess. I was even willing to consider being a pastor's wife for Max. That should have told my parents something. It was their dream for me, and yet when I thought about Max being a pastor, being a pastor's wife was never anything but a dream. I saw myself serving alongside him and learning to speak his native tongue.

I know I have a vivid imagination, but I felt it. How do you explain that to a math brain like mine? It doesn't even make sense to me. I'm a practical girl.

The ballroom at the Fairmont Hotel is decorated in school colors with metallic balloons and streamers as if a lavish wedding is about to take place. The round tables fill the room with their gold chargers and blue linen napkins with gold napkin rings. In the middle of each table is a giant glass vase with clear crystals filling the base.

"I want to find Max."

"He'll find you, relax," Sarika says. "Men must do the pursuing, Daisy. If you learn anything from my culture, that should be it."

"He's leaving in the morning."

"Maybe you have fantasies of unrequited love. That never ends well. You should know that from all the lit classes. *Romeo and Juliet*, *Wuthering Heights*, *Les Misérables* . . ."

"I get the picture, Angie."

"Daisy, he's leaving in the morning. Why do you want to torment yourself any more than you already have? It's over. Just let it go instead of making it harder on yourself." Claire pats me on the back while Angie and Sarika nod their heads in agreement.

"That's right. He's leaving, and I want to spend what little time we have left together."

"What about us?" Angie says.

"You're going to Stanford. You're going to be half an hour away," I tell her.

"Well, Sarika's going to Harvard. She's not going to be close."

"Don't waste that perfect dress on someone who isn't going to be here," Claire says. "Seriously, this is your night to be whoever you want to be. Don't get trapped in the past. Think about your future. Talk to the other guys majoring in numbers or neuroscience, or whatever geek thing you're going to do. Max is leaving."

I realize she sounds like the voice of maturity and wisdom, but my heart is overruling that place.

"I know it," I snap, but my mind won't rest until he walks in the room and I know he's fulfilled his promise of this one real date that my father has approved of, and I have those last moments to look into his eyes. But I have this sick feeling in the pit of my stomach that maybe he won't bother to come. Maybe he'll decide it's easier to leave things as they were. With that beautiful memory of his eyes looking into mine.

The music is pumping into the room, and the smell of mushrooms and chicken fills the air. Every sensory illusion is on overload, and I want to steal away and get right with the thoughts in my head.

Chase and Amber stand in front of me, blocking my view as I bob my head, trying to see around them. "Excuse me."

Amber leans her hand back and Britney appears beside her. "We have an apology."

"We treated you bad," Britney says.

Badly, I want to tell her. *You treated me badly. Let's at least make your father feel like he got his money's worth with his hefty donations to the school.*

As I look into Amber's eyes (deep brown, only furthering the notion that her blonde hair is nothing more than a hairdresser's expertise), my own catty thoughts get to me. If Chase wanted Amber or Britney, or anyone else for that matter, who was I to care?

Claire, Sarika, and Angie surround me as though human shields to protect me from any further damage Amber might inflict, but surprisingly, I'm not bothered by her. Even if she weren't here to apologize. And even if her apology is another form of mental abuse.

"I forgive you, Amber. I'm glad you and Chase are happy, and I'm sorry if you felt I tried to come between you. No, I'm sorry if I ever did come between you."

"You didn't," she says with her spirited laugh. "As if you could."

"I forgive you, but I have to ask for your forgiveness too. I haven't always had Christian thoughts when your name came to mind, and maybe you would have been slightly nicer had I not felt that way. Maybe I gave off a bad vibe."

"Shut up."

Mr. Walker steps up to the podium to make a speech. My heart starts to pound as I know I'm next as the official host of Celibation. "Welcome, class of 2011!"

A round of shouts goes up from the crowd.

"Daisy Crispin, the official host of Celibation, will you come up here, please?" I stride to the stage and stand before the podium, and Mr. Walker shakes my hand. The throbbing music stops as Mr. Walker quiets everyone with a hand. As I look out over the crowd, I feel no fear. Only elation. *I'm here, people, and you didn't stop me!*

"Good evening." No noise comes from the microphone, and I look for a switch when the disc jockey turns it on for me. "Thank you." My words echo through the crowd, startling me with their decibel level. "Welcome, class of 2011!" I lift up my hand. "I hope you all got your trings this year, which will no doubt be the collector's item of the year! One of them has already been placed in our time capsule."

Another rush of shouts lifts from the crowd and supplies me with more energy.

"So, as most of you know, this is our Celibation!" There are a few boos. "I know, stupid name, but most excellent way to live your life if you don't want it to come back to haunt you." I look at Claire. "We've had an excellent run of four years, and if you didn't get to know me, I'm sorry for us both. I'm really a great person." I giggle, but the crowd appears uncomfortable. "The only reason most of you know me is because of what went wrong for me this year. A party that got out of hand." Raucous shouts. "An out-of-character tango at the prom, which I was forbidden to go to. You may recognize me from behind the Breathalyzer table." Like a melodrama, jeers follow. "And finally, an embarrassing prank by . . . someone who never seemed to get over me, which resulted in a car on the roof of the school and my name in infamy forever, thanks to a school play."

"Woo-hoo, Daisy!" someone shouts.

Mr. Walker taps the microphone. "Before we go on with the night, I'd like to announce that Daisy Crispin has been awarded a full-ride scholarship to Pepperdine University in Malibu." Mr. Walker hands me an ecru, linen envelope with my name scrawled across it, and I see it shake in my hand.

"No."

"Yes."

The crowd goes crazy, and I imagine if my father were here, he'd outshout them all. That's how you know true love. It always wants the best for you. Always hopes. Always perseveres. And my parents' love, though not perfect, never ever failed me.

"Oh my gosh, I'm shocked. Just dumbfounded. I planned to be at West Valley Community College this fall and live in my parents' garage."

There's a rush of laughter as though it's a joke.

"Seriously! Though I tried to do everything perfectly during my four years here, it's really the screwups we'll all remember. Thank God for his grace. Tonight I'm here to do one last thing out of character. And that"—I lift my hands—"is to announce I am going on an adventure before college. I'm going to spend the summer in Buenos Aires with my boyfriend." There are a few whistles and catcalls. "No, that's why I'm hosting Celibation. Get your minds out of the gutter, people. This is about living your life to the full. We go out into the world now with our heads held high and our armor tightly fastened. St. James Academy, class of 2011, go out and rule the world for Jesus!" I punch my fist to the sky, the envelope in my other hand, and run off the stage as though I'm a rock star.

I jump from the stairs and find myself in the midst of my girlfriends. Angie, Sarika, and Claire group-hug me, and it feels as if my entire life was for this moment.

"I've spent my whole life doing what was expected of me. This is a crossroads. If I keep it up now, I will never know what I truly want. I will only be living out other people's desires for me. I can't do it."

"Pepperdine is what you want," Claire says.

"Maybe," I say. "But maybe not. I'll find out this summer."

Max enters the room, and it's as though I have my answer. It was in front of me all along.

"Claire, do you remember your dad saying he'd pay for us to go on a trip if we went together and kept each other out of trouble?"

"Yes."

"We're going to Buenos Aires."

Claire watches Max as he crosses the room and comes toward us.

"Did he invite you? Your parents will never let you go."

"It's not like that. I'm not going to follow Max. And no, he didn't invite me. He only told me he was leaving this afternoon."

"Why, then?"

262

"Because that's why God sent me through these years of Christian school and being a complete misfit."

"So you think you'll fit in better in another country?"

"No, I won't fit in there any better than I do here, and worse yet, I won't even speak the language."

"Which is?" Claire asks.

"Spanish, but English is widely spoken."

"Your parents will never let you do this."

"If I don't get out of here, I won't ever know what I really want. My fears, all that perfection stuff—it wasn't me. It was fear of what others would think of me. I blew it. I blew it lots of times, and I'm still standing. I have to have a chance to blow it again so I can know what I'm supposed to do, not what's expected of me."

"You can't follow a guy to a foreign country. It's the opposite of everything you ever said you wanted. It's becoming your mother."

I shake my head. "No, this isn't about Max. He's just the icing on the cake. This is about doing what no one expects of us. Going to a foreign country and not shopping or living a life of leisure as we do here, but devoting ourselves to a different way of life."

Max looks at the two of us as he approaches. "Why does Daisy have that look in her eye? Daisy, what are you up to?"

"I can't tell you. But I can tell you this: school was not perfectly pointless, Max. You were right. It taught me that I will always be an outcast, and that's okay. If I'm going to be a Christian in this world, I'm not meant to fit in, so I might as well get comfortable being a misfit. That's been my problem. I fought it all these years. God must have made me good at being a misfit for a reason."

"What's she talking about?" Max asks Claire, who only shrugs.

A path of people clears, and Max is standing at the end of it. My heart leaps just a bit. I am breathless at the sight of him and want to share my joy with him. "I did it. Did you see me?" I ask him. "Not an ounce of fear because I knew what I was supposed to do."

"You were awesome, Daisy." He cradles my face in his hands, and those stunning eyes look right inside of me. "You're not serious about the summer in Buenos Aires?"

"I am. I'm using the money I earned for college to do something I'll never get another chance to do. Well, that and Claire's father said he'd pay for us to go on a trip. I'll get caught up in college, I'll start working, and life will cease to be an adventure. I don't want to live my parents' life. I don't want everything to be safe and planned. I want every day to be filled with what could be, not trying to control what is."

"I love you, Daisy Crispin."

"I do believe you implied that before." I smile and bask in the warmth such words bring. They're better than the implication.

"I believe I did, and my feelings never changed. Even if my actions and my concerns did. What we have can't be explained to others. I know that now."

"That's why it feels so magical, and I'm worried I might break the spell by opening my mouth."

"There is no spell. There is only truth, and I promise from here on out to give you and your father only the truth."

I smile.

"Daisy?"

"Yes?"

"I hope to be a part of your adventure for a long, long, long time to come." Max kisses me tenderly, and the noise of Celibation and all the crazy thoughts in my head—like that I might be kissing him wrong—disappear. He loves me, and come what may, this moment will never go away and it will never change. Even if we do.

June 4
Random fact: About 5.3 million people have social phobia in America.

I am not one of them. One reason is I faced my fears and survived them. Sure, people laughed at me, but that says more about them than it does about me. The second reason I'm not in that statistic is I'm on my way to Argentina, and if they laugh at me there? At least I won't understand the words.

All in all, I'd say I accomplished what I set out to accomplish. I'll be known as the girl who got the full-ride scholarship on grad night. The girl who was so loved that someone left a car on the roof—and let's face it, it may not be the whole truth, but why mess with urban legend when it's to one's benefit?

I'm special because I'm God's child. And he made me this way. That's what makes me special.

Life is good.

Giving up control and perfection isn't all that bad. I find

myself a lot more accepting of other people this way and, more importantly, less interested in all that I don't have. Claire once told me the secret to great acting is surrendering yourself to the character and letting the character take over. That's the way I plan to live my life now—surrendering to God's character and having some grace for myself when I mess up. It's all good.

Acknowledgments

A book is so much more than an author sitting down at the computer. Thank you, Team Revell, for putting together a package that works. First off, thanks to Lonnie Hull DuPont, the most fabulous editor, who lived up to the hype of working with her. Even if she doesn't know who Robert Pattinson is, she makes sure my readers will. Never has the red pen been so much fun. Janelle Mahlmann, thank you for your organized self. My only wish is to have one of you at home. Revell, thank you for your cute covers, your marketing, and your tireless efforts to make Daisy Crispin work.

Kristin Billerbeck is the bestselling author of several novels, including *What a Girl Wants* and *Perfectly Dateless*. A Christy Award finalist and two-time winner of the American Christian Fiction Writers' Book of the Year, Kristin has appeared on the *Today Show* and has been featured in the *New York Times*. She lives with her family in Northern California.

The countdown to prom has begun.

Daisy is determined to find a date to the prom. There's only one problem—
her parents won't let her date or even talk to a guy on the phone.
Oh, and she's totally invisible at school, she wears lame homemade
clothes, and she possesses no social skills.

Okay, so maybe there's more than one problem.

New Novel from
MELODY CARLSON

Worlds collide when a Manhattan socialite and a simple Amish girl meet and decide to switch places. Because the grass is always greener . . . Right?

New School = New Chance for That First Kiss

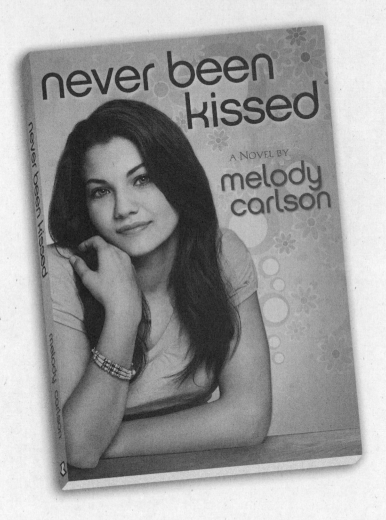

Just when it seems Elise is on top of the world, everything comes crashing down. Could one bad choice derail her future?

Skylar Hoyt is a girl who seems to have it all, but the world as she knows it is beginning to fall apart . . .

Learn more about the Reinvention of Skylar Hoyt series and meet Stephanie Morrill at www.stephaniemorrill.com.

 Revell
a division of Baker Publishing Group
www.RevellBooks.com

Available wherever books are sold.